Poetic Justice

PJ Quinn

Stairwell Books

Published by Stairwell Books
70 Barbara Drive
Norwalk
CT 06851 USA

161 Lowther Street
York, YO31 7LZ

www.stairwellbooks.co.uk
@stairwellbooks

ISBN: 978-1-939269-77-5

Printed and bound in the UK by Imprint Digital
Layout design: Alan Gillott
Cover art: Baimiang

Also by P J Quinn
Published by Stairwell Books

DI Ambrose Mystery
Foul Play
Poison Pen
Close Disharmony

By Pauline Kirk

Border 7
The Keepers (eBook)

For Anna's Carl
And in memory of Derek

With many thanks to Iain Beresford and Andrea Goodman at Collas Crill, the helpful ladies at the Priaulx Library, Guernsey, and to all at Help the Aged, Guernsey.

Prologue

Friday 11th March 1960

Her pulse raced. Stopping quickly, Meadows turned to listen. She stared into the darkness behind her. There was no one in sight.

Catching her breath to steady it, she walked on. The footsteps began again. Once again Meadows stopped. So too did the steps.

In the silence she strained to hear movement. There was nothing except the wind in the overhead wires. Urgently she shone her torch around.

The alley took a wide sweep between the houses. It was impossible to see beyond the bend. A single street lamp lit a small circle of concrete but didn't reach the curve. She flashed her torch up and down the fences either side of the alley. There was nothing but wood, and a line of scrubby weeds.

Still WPC Meadows waited. If someone had been walking innocently behind her, they'd have caught up by now. No one appeared.

Finally, telling herself she was imagining things, she continued her search. Her ears felt as if they were aching with the effort of listening: a goods train in the distance, a dog barking. Then she heard it again. Footsteps! But this time the walker was treading softly, almost inaudibly. She could be imagining the sound. Except that she knew she wasn't.

At once Meadows reached for her whistle. 'Not that anyone's likely to come,' she thought nervously. 'Not round here.' Still, the hard shape in her fingers made her feel better. "Pretend not to notice," she told herself. "Just keep going." She quickened her pace, but she didn't run. That could enrage a follower, who might well be quicker than her.

And when she came out of the alley, what then? Meadows tried to remember her training. 'Find the nearest house with a light on, and bang on the door,' she decided. 'But supposing he catches up with me?' She couldn't recall anyone mentioning that bit. No one was likely to be up at this hour anyway.

'Hit him over the head with my handbag,' Meadows thought wryly. Not for the first time she cursed being a woman. A male PC had a truncheon; a female officer was allowed a handbag and a whistle. "Fat lot of use!" she muttered to herself.

With every nerve stretched, Meadows walked out into the street, waiting for something to happen. But nothing did. The footsteps stopped. The night settled into early dawn. There was just the dog barking and the wind in the wires.

She let her breath out in relief. Perhaps the footsteps had never existed. It was dark and cold and she was tired after hours of looking for a couple of escapees from the local Approved School for Delinquent Boys. Maybe there was an echo in the passage. Or perhaps there really had been someone there, but they hadn't wanted to be seen by the Police. She must check for reports of burglaries from the houses nearby.

The tower of St George's church loomed ahead and she walked briskly past the old graveyard. In the flickering light of a street lamp the church looked threatening and bleak. Pausing to listen again, Meadows shone her torch at the graveyard and across the car park, then went around the back to the hall and tried the door. It was locked, the wire screen over the window correctly in place.

Glad to move on, Meadows approached The Brigadier pub. That too was in darkness. As usual, she tried the main entrance, then checked the back. All the doors there were safely locked. Next she looked inside the bus shelter nearby. It would be a good hiding place for a couple of young desperados. Apart from some screwed up fish and chip papers, though, it was empty. They might have rested there earlier, but they were nowhere in sight now. Then she hurried towards the phone box at the end of St George's Avenue.

The box smelled of stale sweat as Meadows entered and she wrinkled her nose. Her hands were shaking as she fumbled with the coins, and she called herself an idiot for letting a trivial incident unnerve her. All the same, she would be glad to be back at the Police Station. "Anything to report?" PC Higgins asked. "You're a bit late."

"Sorry, it was dark in the alleys." For a second Meadows paused, wondering whether to say more. She would sound a fool. No one had attacked her, or even made a threat. Reporting mysterious footsteps would only get her laughed at in the canteen. "Meadows thinks she's got a follower!" the blokes would say. She could write the script.

"No, all quiet," she replied. "No sign of the runaways from Moorlands. I've been to all the usual places. I'm just off to check the shops on the High Street, in case they've bunked up there for the night. But it looks like they had their tea in the bus shelter, so I reckon they've left Chalk Heath by now. I'll be back in half an hour."

Opening the door of the phone box, she stared across the road.

A cloudy dawn was leaking over the rooftops. In the half-light something moved. A dark shape hurriedly stepped back into the shadows.

Chapter One

Monday 14th March 1960

Higgins took the call.

"Can someone come and look at what the postman's just delivered?" a male voice demanded. "It's thoroughly nasty, threatening I'd call it."

"Who's speaking?" PC Higgins asked guardedly. Reaching for his pad and pencil, he began to take notes.

"Robin Harvey of Curiosity Corner."

"Hello, Mr Harvey," Higgins replied in surprise. The bookseller wasn't the sort to make idle complaints. "You say you've received a threatening letter?"

"No," the voice snapped. "A package. Send one of your lads round. And make it quick, it's beginning to smell."

"What is?" Higgins persisted. "The boss'll want to know. We're pretty busy."

"Tell him it looks like a death threat."

"What?" Higgins asked in surprise. He had never heard of a death threat in Chalk Heath before. And why on earth would anyone hate Robin Harvey? He seemed a decent fellow: a bit eccentric, like most people who spent a lot of time with books, but not the sort to make enemies. "I'll see what I can do", he promised. "You're at the shop now?"

"Yes. My assistant will be in soon. She can see to things while we talk."

DS Winters was just as surprised when Higgins reported to him. "Robin Harvey?" he repeated. "What's he done to get death threats?

4

Told someone a bit of old tat was a first edition? I wouldn't put that beyond him." He shook his head in bewilderment.

"No. Harvey's sharp, but he never actually lies. Besides, you wouldn't threaten him, not just for that. You'd go and complain. I'll send Meadows round." Winters paused. The death threat, if it really was one, might be genuine. "I'll be passing the shop on my way home," he added. "I'll go with her."

The clock above the Jeweller's Shop chimed ten as Winters and WPC Meadows walked down the High Street, towards the shop on the corner. Monday morning was always quiet once the children had gone into school.

There was a small group of people outside the bookshop. They seemed to be reading a notice. "The competition results," Meadows explained. "The list'll be in the paper tonight, but Mr Harvey always puts it on the shop door first."

"Ah yes," Winters agreed, although he had no idea what she was talking about.

Mr Harvey met them at the door, looking tired and worried. His horn-rimmed spectacles seemed even larger than usual. He hurried back through the shop, with Winters and Meadows barely keeping up. Curving round the corner of the street, Curiosity Corner was a warren of small rooms and compartments between bookcases. Each was labelled with a topic: 'History', 'Biography', 'The Great War' and so on.

A faint musty smell lingered everywhere: the scent of old paper, leather, damp and dust. More bookcases lined the walls and others were grouped into alcoves to maximize display space. There were so many bookcases it was almost impossible to see the stairs to Mr Harvey's private rooms above the shop.

Towards the back of the shop, tables were laden with shoeboxes full of postcards and photographs; framed pictures leant precariously against each other. A large print of a seaside scene caught Meadows' eye. It would look good above the fireplace at her new digs, she thought. The place needed brightening up.

She followed DS Winters and Mr Harvey into a small room at the back, almost filled with an old dining table and a set of mismatched chairs. More books had been stacked under the table, waiting to be priced. Papers covered the chairs. In the middle of the table was a brown paper parcel. The string had been cut but the paper was wrapped tightly back around the contents. A faint but unpleasant smell was coming from the package.

5

"Have a look," Mr Harvey said tersely. "It arrived this morning, first delivery."

Carefully, using his fountain pen rather than his fingers, Winters unwrapped the paper. Inside was a dead robin. A large needle had been stuck through its heart. Attached to the needle was a luggage tag.

The message on the luggage tag was made out of letters cut from newspaper headlines. 'Sleep well!' it read.

"Ugh!" Meadows said. Recovering herself quickly, she took out her notepad.

"Exactly," Mr Harvey retorted. "I wasn't too bothered before, but this, well, it unnerved me. What with my own name being Robin and, well, I can't help but feel..." His voice trailed off.

"You did right to call us," Winters assured him. Wrapping the packet up again tightly he put it to one side. "It's an offence to send threatening letters through the post," he added. "We'll find out who sent this. Do you have any ideas? You mentioned receiving something else earlier."

Shuddering, Mr Harvey nodded. "A pile of rubbish. A brown paper bag full of old tea leaves and milk bottle tops, egg shells, that sort of thing. Fortunately it was well wrapped or it would have leaked."

"Was there a message with it?" Winters asked.

"Another luggage label like this one. It just said 'Your books are rubbish.' I ignored it. People can be very silly. Besides, I wasn't sure whether they meant the books I sell or the ones I publish. I run a small publishing house you see. Mostly poetry but also short stories, local guides, the occasional biography."

"Bird Books," Meadows whispered to Winters.

Robin Harvey had sharp hearing. "Of course, you know all about us," he agreed. "I'm still hoping you'll enter one of our competitions."

"I didn't know you were a poet, Meadows," Winters remarked. 'A surprising occupation for a police woman,' his raised eyebrow implied.

"I don't write myself," Meadows assured him, "but one of my friends does. She got on the long list last year. We heard about it for weeks."

Mr Harvey smiled with pleasure. "We like to encourage new writers," he replied. "That's why we publish a 'long list' as well as the winners. Not many competitions do that."

"Why would anyone say your books are rubbish?" Winters continued, turning back to him. "I presume they're decent enough, or you'd have gone out of business."

6

Harvey glanced at his watch, then looked around him, as if seeking answers in the piles of papers. "I suppose I could have refused a manuscript they'd sent," he suggested. "Some of the stuff is pretty dire: pages of rhyming couplets, you know the sort of thing."

Winters didn't but he nodded sympathetically. "Are you rude about them?" he asked.

"Goodness, no! I send a polite rejection slip, wishing them luck. I aim to be kind." Harvey adjusted his glasses again. "There's another possibility. Maybe someone bought a book they thought was valuable, and then found it was a later edition. I try to be accurate, but you can't know everything." Trailing off again, he shook his head. "I threw the rubbish away and thought that would be the end of it. But now..."

"Quite," Winters agreed examining the luggage tag again. "Is this the same type of label as before?"

"I'm afraid I can't recall," Harvey apologised. "It came a couple of weeks ago. But I know the letters were cut out of newspapers in the same way." He glanced uneasily again at his watch. "I did make a note of the postmark," he continued. "It's in my desk, but my assistant hasn't arrived yet and I'm expecting a call from a potential customer. I'd rather not have to ring them back. They're in Guernsey."

"You have orders from overseas?" Winters asked in surprise.

"Oh yes. Curiosity Corner is well known in the trade."

On cue, the telephone rang shrilly in an inner office. "Do you mind having a look round for a few moments?" Mr Harvey asked. "I need to talk in private. I won't be any longer than I can help." He crossed urgently to a glass door at the back of the room, marked Private, and shut the door behind him.

Meadows looked at DS Winters, wondering what she should do. "Do as the man said," he advised. "Have a look round. You might spot something."

Taking the opportunity to look at the pictures again, Meadows went back into the shop. Yes, she liked the scene, and yes, it would look good over the fireplace in her new flat. The price tag was a disappointment though. With so little money left after she had paid her rent, she would have to save for several weeks to buy it. She needed other things first, like a couple of cushions and a warmer bed cover.

Sighing, Meadows put down the price tag. It had been very good of the Chief to help her find somewhere so quickly, but she would have to look for a cheaper place soon.

Continuing to the front door, she looked out into the street. The small crowd had gone and she lingered for a moment in the fresher air. Curious, she read the notice taped to the door. It was headed 'Bird Books Competition 1960'. In bold italic handwriting it continued: "The judges are pleased to announce the following ten entrants may submit a further three poems, one of which will be published in the Bird Books 1960 anthology. Five of these entrants will be invited to a poetry evening and prize-giving on March 24th at 7.30 p.m. at the Conservative Club (main hall), Chalk Heath. Each of these short-listed poets will be asked to read their winning poem and say a few words about what inspired it. The winner of the first prize of £50 will be announced afterwards." Below was a list of ten names, and below that a smaller note warned, "If short listed entrants are unable to attend, their place will be reallocated."

'Tough luck if you live in Penzance,' Meadows thought wryly. But fifty pounds was quite a bit of money, she knew, and having your first collection published might give you the start you'd wanted for years. Even being on the long list and published in the anthology could mean a lot. Carefully Meadows studied the list to see if she recognised any names, but this year no local poet had been successful.

Returning to DS Winters in the back room she found him glancing through a stack of manila files on the table. "I wouldn't want to plough through this lot," he remarked, picking up a file marked 'No' in bold red letters. The file underneath had 'Probably Not' written on it, while a third was captioned 'Possibles'. "Looks like they had plenty of entries this year," he added. "They all seem to be about the joys of spring. Not my sort of thing."

Meadows smiled. "The theme was 'The Countryside'," she explained. "My friend didn't bother entering. She reckoned there'd be loads of daffodils and clouds. Not her sort of thing either."

"She was probably wise," Winters commented looking up from one of the entries. "I'm no judge of poetry but this sounds pretty awful. What do you reckon?

'Each night I look out and see the trees
And think of you.
Without you, life is dull,
All is null.
I hear your voice on every breeze.'"

"At least it rhymes," Meadows remarked, smiling.

"I'm not sure what that has to do with the countryside."

"It has trees in it," Meadows pointed out. "And a breeze." Resisting a desire to giggle, she picked up another file marked 'Absolutely NOT!' in a different, bolder handwriting. "There's another good one here," she added.

'It's spring, spring, spring!
Birds are sing sing singing,
Lambs are leaping,
Clouds are winging,
Daffodils are bloom, bloom, blooming… '"

Meadows suddenly felt bad for mocking the poem. It might be dreadful but it was still someone's hard work. In the silence that followed, Mr Harvey's voice came softly from behind the glass door. Meadows caught phrases like "I'm sure you'll find them interesting," and "I don't want to send them by post," then the shopkeeper was back with them, full of apologies. "I see you've been looking at some of the entries," he commented. "Poor Wordsworth! If he only knew what he was starting. He must be turning in his grave."

Crossing to an old-fashioned bureau in the corner of the room, he began to rummage in the bottom drawer. "My note of the postmark's in here somewhere, from the last package," he muttered. "Ah! Yes, here we are!" He passed a page torn from a notebook to DS Winters. On it was written 'Bristol, 10th February'. "I don't know anyone in Bristol," Harvey added. "And I've been all through my customer lists."

Hoping for some connection Winters looked at the new package. It had been posted in Ludlow. The two places were a fair distance apart, he admitted ruefully.

Frowning, Mr Harvey paused with the piece of paper still in his hand. "I've just remembered something," he said uncertainly. "The Hon Marjorie Hodgkiss said something weird had been sent to her last week. She didn't say what and she got a bit huffy when I pressed her. You know what's she's like. But she seemed quite upset. She hasn't mentioned it since though. Presumably she threw it away, like I did the first time."

"Interesting," Winters commented. "Have you any idea why you should both…?" Even as he spoke, his expression changed to one of understanding. "Of course! She'll be judging the competition with you. The Honourable Madge judges everything round here."

Mr Harvey nodded. "There are three judges this year," he explained. "Marjorie Hodgkiss, Major Fielding and Yours Truly."

"I think we'd better have a word with them too," DS Winters said thoughtfully. "Thank you for reporting this now. It's a pity neither of you said anything earlier."

With the dead bird firmly wrapped in its brown paper bag and secured with parcel tape, Winters and Meadows walked back through the shop. "You'd better take this," Winters said. "I'm on my way home. Get it booked in as evidence."

Trying not to show her distaste, Meadows took the packet. As she did so the telephone rang again behind them. "Busy little place," Winters commented. "Can't say I've been in myself before, though. How come you know so much about it?"

"I've bought books here occasionally," Meadows explained cautiously. "Mostly as presents." She didn't want to sound too studious. "Mr Harvey likes to talk about his books. Trying to sell them I suppose. And he's always very proud of his competitions. They're getting known nationally he says."

They were just about to part in the street when Robin Harvey came rushing out to catch them. "The Major's had one too," he said breathlessly.

"One what?" Winters asked.

"A horrible package. I'm not sure what. He wasn't talking clearly. A dead rat I think."

"How unpleasant!" Meadows said, frowning.

"Precisely," Mr Harvey replied. His forced smile barely hid his fear.

Chapter Two

"Come and speak to him," Robin Harvey urged. "He's still on the phone. I told him you were here." Without waiting, he turned into the shop.

"Back we go," Winters muttered to WPC Meadows. He should have gone off duty a quarter of an hour ago. His wife wouldn't be pleased if he was late yet again.

There was a second telephone on the counter near the front door. As they entered the shop again, they could hear Mr Harvey saying, "Speak to them now. Don't ignore it. This is getting beyond a joke." He passed the phone to DS Winters. "It's a mouse, not a rat," he whispered as he did so. "Nasty all the same."

"Major John Fielding here," a voice said softly as soon as Winters took the receiver. Then the voice hesitated. "Robin shouldn't have bothered you. It's a lot of fuss about nothing."

Winters interrupted before the man could put down the phone. "We need to know what you've received, sir," he stressed. "It may be important. It's an offence to send threats through the post."

"I'd rather not talk now," the Major replied uneasily. "The phone's in the hall and well, walls have ears etc."

"Then one of us will pop up to see you," Winters offered. "Where do you live?"

"Maple View. But I'd rather you didn't come up here. I don't think the other residents would like it. If you really think the packet's important I'll bring it to you. Say 12 o'clock? That'll give me time to walk down."

The man was being deliberately vague, as if he were afraid someone might be listening. Winters decided not to press him. "If you prefer," he agreed. "Someone will see you then. It won't be me I'm afraid. I'm due to go off duty soon." About twenty minutes ago, he thought wryly.

Putting down the phone, he frowned. He would have to go back to the Station. This was too serious to pass on to a WPC, even Meadows. He'd probably be able to claim it as overtime. That would placate Fran.

Glancing towards the back of the shop, he was surprised to see Mr Harvey sitting on a sofa with WPC Meadows bending over him in concern. "You're very kind," the bookseller said to her, his voice full of apology. Looking up, he included DS Winters in his explanation. "I just felt a bit dizzy. Can't think what came over me. This silly package has upset me, I'll admit, and I didn't get much sleep last night. We were still thrashing out the short list at one this morning. Then my mind kept turning over and over. It's always hard to pare so many entries down, and this year we found it particularly difficult."

'I'll bet you did!' Winters thought. 'With the Hon Madge involved you'd have trouble agreeing the day of the week,' he added, but not out loud.

There was the sound of someone entering the shop and Robin Harvey got up quickly. "I need to go," he said.

"It's me, Miss Havering," a voice called. Then a breathless young woman hurried into the shop, face flushed and hair astray as if she had been running. "I'm so sorry Mr Harvey," she apologised, pulling off her coat and scarf. "The bus broke down and we had to walk. Then the level crossing closed and…" Seeing DS Winters and Meadows, she stopped in alarm. "Gosh! I didn't realise you'd got the Police here." She went bright red, even more confused. "Has there been a burglary?"

"This is my assistant," Mr Harvey explained. Getting up, he forced himself to appear efficient. "I was wondering what had happened to you," he remarked turning to the young woman. "We'll talk about it later. Right now I need you on the front counter. The old folk will be leaving the Darby and Joan Club soon, and some of them help themselves if you don't watch them."

"Of course. I promise I'll make up the time," Miss Havering assured him, breathlessly. She hung her coat up on a hook near the staff kitchen at the back of the shop then hurried to the front counter.

"You ok?" Winters asked Mr Harvey after the assistant had gone.

"Fine."

"You'd better make yourself a cup of tea," Meadows advised.

12

Then they left, to return to the station together. Winters took the offending packet. "The boss needs to know about this lot," he said, sighing slightly. "Probably just some idiot, but you never know."

As they passed through the shop he paused to speak to the young assistant at the counter. "Would you say your employer is well-liked in the area?" he asked.

In surprise Miss Havering looked up from a pile of envelopes. "Yes," she replied. "He can seem a bit, well, sharp, but people who know him like him. He's certainly respected, I mean, running the competition and everything. Why?" She peered earnestly from behind National Health spectacles. "Has someone been saying bad things about him?"

"He'll explain to you," Winters assured her. "Do you normally open the post?"

"It's one of my jobs. I sort it out and pass important stuff to Mr Harvey. He usually leaves me to deal with any enquiries or payments."

"But you weren't here in time this morning?"

"No. Was there something I should have done? I'm ever so sorry."

"Mr Harvey will explain," Winters repeated enigmatically. "But if you ever open something that worries you, call us at once."

"Of course." Uncertainly the woman watched as they left the shop.

Winters reported to DI Ambrose straight away. "It could just be some nutter being silly," he admitted. "Writers can be funny people." Remembering that Ambrose himself wrote, he corrected himself quickly. "Poets I mean. They feel things more I'm told. But it might be serious. I thought you ought to know."

Thoughtfully Ambrose nodded. It could all be the proverbial storm in a Chalk Heath teacup. Even so, there was a nastiness about the packets that he didn't like. Someone with a grudge was out there, someone who sounded unhinged. Their motive might have nothing to do with the poetry competition. All three judges were prominent people in the town, and might have made enemies in a different context. Despite the postmarks the sender could be someone from Chalk Heath. It would be easy enough to get an accessory to post the packages, or even ask an unsuspecting relative.

"You did right," he assured DS Winters. Then he glanced at the clock. "Aren't you supposed to be off duty now? You'd better ring your wife and tell her you've had to do a bit of overtime."

"Thank you," Winters said. "That will help. How long do you want me to stay?"

13

"Give the Hon Madge a ring and arrange to go up and see her tomorrow. Then write your report and get off home. Don't forget to fill in the overtime sheet first. Oh and tell WPC Meadows to interview the Major when he arrives."

Winters frowned, then shook his head. "Sorry sir, but I'm not sure that would work. She oughtn't to interview a neighbour. She's moved into Maple View. Didn't you know?"

"Of course. I'd forgotten," Ambrose admitted. "That's a shame. She'd have been good with him, you know. She could charm the old fellow. Leave it with me while you make your call." He smiled slightly. "I do believe you're scared of the Hon Madge," he remarked.

"Aren't we all?" Winters replied cheerfully, but he left Ambrose's office with an uneasy feeling. The DI was right. He wasn't looking forward to phoning the Honourable Marjorie Hodgkiss. He had a shrewd suspicion Ambrose hadn't fancied making the call either.

Marjorie Hodgkiss was at home, though it took her several moments to come to the phone. "Sorry to trouble you," Winters began. "This is Detective Sergeant Winters from Chalk Heath Police Station. I wondered if I might speak to you for a moment."

"What about? I'm very busy."

The reply was sharp and clear, the sort of accent Winters's father would have called 'cut glass'.

"We're investigating some unpleasant parcels that have been sent through the post," he explained. "Mr Robin Harvey suggested you might have received something similar yourself."

"I'll thank Mr Robin Harvey not to discuss my affairs without my permission," Marjorie Hodgkiss retorted.

"*Have* you received anything unpleasant, Ma'am?"

"If I had, I certainly wouldn't discuss it over the telephone."

"Then may I talk to you in person tomorrow? I can call at Garth House, or you can come down to the Station if you prefer," Winters offered.

"I will do nothing of the sort!" Miss Hodgkiss snapped.

"This is a police enquiry," Winters reminded her, trying to prevent his own voice sharpening. "You may be able to assist us."

There was a slight pause. "I take it Robin has received something more?" the woman asked.

"Yes. And so has the Major."

"And you assume that because I'm also judging the competition, I may have too?"

"It's a reasonable assumption," Winters replied. "Have you?"

"I may have."

It was like squeezing blood out of a stone. "Then can I come up and see the packet tomorrow?" Winters persisted, with growing irritation. "It may be important evidence."

"I'm certainly not keeping that disgusting thing until tomorrow," Miss Hodgkiss retorted. "And I'm not carrying it down to your station either. Tell DI Ambrose to come and see me this afternoon. He knows me. We're both Friends of the Chalk Heath Theatre. I'll talk to him, but no one beneath him. You included, Sergeant. Good afternoon."

The telephone clicked at the other end. Winters felt as if he'd just been given a detention by the chief nun at his old school. "Damn the woman!" he said under his breath. Then he knocked on DI Ambrose's door.

"She won't speak to me," he said, without introduction. "I'm not of sufficent standing. It's you or nobody." He could barely restrain a smile when he saw Ambrose's expression.

"I suppose I should be flattered," Ambrose replied. He noticed Winters' amusement. "Put your wife onto her," he suggested. "She'd be a good match for Madge. Though that could cause an international incident."

"Not funny, sir," Winters replied stiffly, but he had the grace to smile. "Fran will have my guts for garters if I don't go home soon. I promised I'd look after the little 'uns while she buys her mother's birthday present." He grinned. "Now there's someone who can really strike terror. My mother-in-law. I'd back her against the Hon Madge any day."

Though Ambrose laughed too, he sighed as Winters left. They didn't need silly twerps sending death threats. They were busy and he didn't have time to go and see the Hon Madge. He had better things to do than sit trying to look as though he was enjoying over-sweet cake and lukewarm tea. If she'd been the only one to receive unpleasant mail he wouldn't have been surprised. But Robin Harvey and Major Fielding too? That was worrying.

So was the prospect of finding someone to interview the Major in less than an hour. For the third time that day, Ambrose wished PC Sutton hadn't left. Sutton would have been perfect for the job.

Ambrose knew he couldn't blame Sutton or his wife for wanting to leave Chalk Heath and make a fresh start. The petty gossip must have got them down. But the new lad was nothing like a replacement. He might be when he'd shaken down a bit, but he was pretty clueless at present. Half the time people couldn't tell what he was saying. Usually, Ambrose himself could follow him. Having served in the Met, he'd heard plenty of rhyming slang, but it was a foreign language as far as the others were concerned. If Meadows couldn't interview the Major, Higgins would have to leave the front desk and talk to him. No one else was around.

At twelve o'clock exactly, Major Fielding arrived, carrying a packet wrapped in several layers of brown paper. Higgins took him straight into the interview room. "It's good of you to bring it, sir," he said, taking the package and opening it carefully. Hardened policeman as he was, he couldn't help a slight shake of the head. "Now why would anyone want to do this?" he asked in disgust. "Or to threaten you?"

"I'm not sure if it is a threat," the Major replied. "It's probably just a damned stupid prank. Someone's trapped a mouse; you can see the mark where the spring's caught it. Then they thought of something nasty to do with it. It would have been more impressive if it were a rat like Robin told your Sergeant. They'd have had more trouble catching that."

"Was there a message with it?" Higgins continued, beginning to take notes.

The Major opened a large brown envelope and took out a luggage tag, tied through the eye of a large needle. "I tore this off and threw it away separately," he explained. "I've had to hunt in the waste bin to find it. Sorry it's a bit smelly. They're just a few silly words. The needle was stuck through the poor critter. I do hope it was dead when the needle went in. Even so, whoever sent it ought to be put away."

Higgins read the words aloud: "'Pity I couldn't find a field mouse.' What on earth do they mean?"

"Some silly play on my name," the Major suggested. "Fielding: field mouse I suppose. They must be half a shilling short. I intend to ignore them. I only rang Robin because I was annoyed. I've calmed down now. It takes more than one idiot to rattle me for long."

"I'm sure," Higgins agreed, recognising the manner of a determined soldier. He glanced down at the notes DS Winters had left him. "Mr Harvey thought you'd received something earlier too. What was that?"

Major Fielding grimaced. "An obituary notice from a newspaper," he replied. "Some fool had cut letters out and stuck them at the bottom of the page. 'You've spurned me one too many times you're next' they said, or something like that. Couldn't even punctuate properly. To be honest, I wondered if I had an admirer I hadn't noticed." He laughed. "No accounting for tastes!" Then he paused. "It was the same sort of lettering as this packet," he added more seriously. "Sounds like we've got someone a bit unhinged out there. Presumably they're cross about the competition."

"You think it's to do with that?" Higgins asked.

"Can't think of anything else Robin and I are involved in. I mean, he's a decent chap, but we don't move in the same circles otherwise."

"I don't suppose you recall where the two packages were posted from?" Higgins asked, hopefully.

"This one was from Leicester I think, although the postmark is a little faded. The earlier one came from somewhere else in the Midlands, Birmingham, if my memory serves me correctly."

Higgins was absolutely sure the Major's memory served him perfectly.

"Thank you for being so helpful, Major," Higgins said, wrapping the mouse back up again. "We'll hang on to this and take a few photos. Then it'll have to be destroyed, unless you fancy keeping it in your fridge?"

"Haven't got one!" the Major replied, shaking his head. "And I don't suppose Mrs McEwan, my landlady, would welcome it in hers. Not that she uses the kitchen herself, of course, but you know what I mean. Get rid of the poor blighter when you're done. And when you find the daft idiot who sent it, send the men in white coats as fast as you can. It isn't safe having people like that on the loose."

Chapter Three

"Pardon?" Ambrose asked. He sighed. Even he wasn't sure what PC Alfie Green had just said. Higgins looked totally mystified.

"Would you Adam and Eve it? Them apples is wet." PC Green repeated.

"What?" Higgins almost shouted.

"Talk English." Ambrose advised the young recruit.

"Sorry, Guv, but that *is* English," PC Green protested. "It is round our way."

"You're not round your way now," Ambrose reminded him. "You're in Chalk Heath." He was about to add, 'and Chalk Heath isn't ready for Londoners, never mind rhyming slang.' Then he thought better of it. "People expect a police constable to speak..." he began, then had trouble finding the right word, "The Queen's English. They want to look up to you, not laugh at you."

Seeing the young man's hurt expression, he relented. "It's an old-fashioned place," he added. "You'll get more respect here than in the 'Smoke', but you'll be expected to earn it. Now translate for us."

PC Green flushed a deep red. "I said the stairs from the yard were slippery," he said lamely. "I nearly fell up them."

Higgins muttered something. It sounded like "We have weather here."

Ambrose chose to ignore him. "Go and write up your notes, while it's quiet," he suggested to PC Green. That should keep him out of Higgins' way.

The telephone rang. "You'd better get the dog and bone," Ambrose added, suppressing a smile.

18

Higgins grunted. Even he could work that one out. He picked up the telephone. "Talking of bones," Ambrose added, glancing towards the door. "What breed is *that?*"

WPC Meadows entered. She was dragging a large dog by a piece of rope. It looked like a cross between a Labrador and a great Dane, though the ears had a hint of Spaniel.

"A bit mix and match, I think," Meadows replied.

"No pets!" Higgins called dryly from the desk, as he put the phone down. "I've told you before."

"Is he yours?" PC Green asked, suspecting a joke but not seeing it. He found the banter between Higgins and Meadows hard to follow. He wasn't used to having women around the station, certainly not to them joining in conversations. When he was on probation in London, the WPCs kept to themselves in their own little office.

In fact, he was having difficulty getting used to his new posting generally. As the DI had said, Chalk Heath wasn't London. It wasn't anywhere particular as far as Green was concerned, just a sleepy little town, where women still wore fancy hats to church, and everyone knew everyone. He wouldn't have owned to being homesick, but he missed the bustle and colour of East London already. Though he'd only been in Chalk Heath a month, it felt like a year.

The others were examining the dog. "He was parked outside the school," Meadows explained. "The Head reckoned he'd been tied to the railings since Assembly. Kept joining in the hymns. I gather he's a good tenor."

"He can't stay here," Higgins warned. "We haven't time to take him walkies. Mind you, he could be useful on point duty."

"One growl and everyone'd cross the road," Meadows agreed. Then she was serious. "He probably belongs to one of the Gypsies. There are some caravans on Tinkers Field. Though why he was tied up at the school gates I don't know. None of the children owned up to knowing him. The pound's full and there are sheep loose on the heath. I don't think Fido would be welcome there. I could telephone Mrs Barnes and see if she'll look after him for a while?"

Ambrose nodded. "Yes, call Mrs Barnes. She always seems to find room for a stray dog," he agreed. "Then come with me up to Garth House. I need a word with the Honourable Madge. It'd be best to have some female company."

Meadows looked at him in mute appeal. 'I'd rather fly to the moon,' her expression said, but she nodded politely. "Yes, sir," she agreed.

"Where shall I put the dog till Mrs Barnes gets here? She may not be able to leave the farm straightaway."

"We've got an empty cell," Higgins suggested. "You can get a bowl of water from the tearoom." He was good with animals, especially large scruffy dogs. When he was a little boy, his father had a similar cross-breed. It turned up one morning and stayed until it died a decade later. Higgins could still remember how much he'd missed that dog.

Half an hour later, WPC Meadows joined Ambrose in the car park. She'd agreed that cycling up to Garth House was likely to undo her efforts to look presentable, but she felt nervous going on a call with the DI. Ambrose was a good boss but he was still her boss, and she did have a habit of saying the wrong thing. So she sat in awkward silence as they headed beyond Victoria Park, towards the better end of Chalk Heath.

As they passed, Meadows glanced towards her new digs with a mixture of disbelief and amusement. It didn't look her sort of place at all. With its grand portico and rows of windows, Maple View still had a faded elegance. One of the first grand villas to be built when the railway opened, it had seen better days. Even so it was determined to remain 'genteel'. A sign in the front gardens announced: 'Private Boarding House for Ladies and Gentlemen.' Beneath, in smaller letters, it warned: 'References required.'

'No wonder I feel out of place!' Meadows thought ruefully.

"Settled in yet?" Ambrose asked, as if reading her thoughts.

"It's very, er, smart," Meadows replied carefully.

"Are the neighbours ok?"

"I don't know many of them yet," Meadows admitted. "I'm out a lot of course, but the ones I've met seem all right. Mrs McEwan's very nice. She's a bit tight, like most landladies, but fair…" Breaking off in embarrassment, Meadows flushed. She was talking about their Superintendent's wife, and was thoroughly out of order.

Ambrose smiled. "I can imagine," he said honestly. Next to the Honourable Madge, Abigail McEwan was probably the most respected woman in Chalk Heath, and much better liked.

They reached Garth House. "You don't need to say anything," Ambrose advised. "Just take notes and leave me to do the talking."

Meadows was happy to agree.

As Ambrose pressed the doorbell, he felt suddenly nervous. Calling himself a fool for being intimidated, he waited. As usual it took two attempts, with a few minutes wait between, to fetch the Honorable Miss Hodgkiss to the door.

"Ah! Inspector!" she said briskly. "Do come in. I hope this won't take long. I have to be at my Towns' Women's Guild in an hour." She glanced at Meadows. "You didn't mention you were bringing the girl. No matter. I'm sure Daisy can pour another cup."

She led them down a panelled hallway, towards a lounge at the end. The air smelt of lavender polish and stained wood. 'It's even colder than Maple View,' Meadows thought. 'You'd need a cardigan on, just to go to bed.'

The lounge, however, was bright and cheerful, sun shining through french windows that looked out onto a manicured lawn. Snowdrops splashed a white fringe around an old chestnut tree. In the shelter of the house, yellow crocuses were risking coming into flower, despite the morning's frost. "What a lovely garden!" Meadows couldn't help saying. Then she remembered she was supposed to keep quiet and glanced at DI Ambrose in apology.

"Yes, isn't it?" Miss Hodgkiss said with evident pleasure. "I have a man to mow the lawns and keep the borders in order, but I do the rest myself. I think gardening's so very relaxing. Don't you?"

"I don't have a garden," Meadows admitted. "But I'm planting some window boxes."

"Oh yes, they're always good when you haven't any other space. What are you putting in?"

"Marigolds and nasturtiums."

"Good idea! They'll grow quickly and give you plenty of colour."

Ambrose smiled. The two women were developing an instant rapport, such as he'd never managed to develop with the Hon Madge, despite several years of serving on the same committees. He should have tried talking about gardening.

A young woman came in, bringing tea and biscuits on a silver tray. Narrowly avoiding upsetting the teapot, she flushed bright red as she poured them each a cup. Then giving a little bob of the knees that was almost a curtsey, she retreated.

"Poor Daisy!" the Hon Madge said, sighing. "She wants a position as a waitress, but she'll have to learn not to be so clumsy first."

"Isn't she Vicar Beresford's daughter?" Ambrose asked in surprise.

"Their youngest. He asked me if I could teach her some manners, train her up a bit. Goodness knows what they learn in schools nowadays."

Ambrose shook his head non-committally and glanced towards Meadows, who took out her notebook.

"But you haven't come to talk about waitresses or gardens," Miss Hodgkiss responded, her manner at once businesslike. "Personally I think you're wasting your time. It's a lot of fuss about nothing."

"It may not be," Ambrose pointed out. "We have to check."

"Of course it is. Someone played a silly prank, to upset me, and failed. You must have more important matters. Or are Chalk Heath's criminals on holiday?"

"At least tell us what the prank was," Ambrose persisted.

"It's not the sort of thing I want to talk about. No lady would."

Intrigued, Ambrose raised an eyebrow. "If you don't want to tell me, would you tell WPC Meadows?" he asked. "I can go into the hall."

"Nonsense! I'm not a blushing twelve-year-old. I just don't think it's important enough to bother either of you."

Ambrose sighed. He didn't want to alienate the woman, but he had to make himself clear. "I don't think you appreciate the situation," he said firmly. "We've received complaints about unpleasant mailings. If you've had one, and refuse to tell us, you could be obstructing our investigation…"

The Honourable Madge didn't let him finish. "Very well then!" she snapped. "I received a box of fungi."

Both Meadows and Ambrose stared at her in surprise. "Fungi?" Ambrose repeated. "You mean mushrooms?"

"No I don't! I mean *phallus impudicus*. I looked it up. The colloquial name is Stinkhorn. It has a horrible rotten smell, like bad meat, and looks like…" The woman paused. "I hope I don't need to spell it out."

For a second Ambrose didn't understand, then he remembered sufficient grammar school Latin to work out what *phallus* meant. He shook his head. "I get the idea," he replied. "Why would anyone send you something so unpleasant?"

"Goodness only knows. They must be sick in the head. I'll admit it was quite a nasty moment. The box was tied with red ribbon, so I thought it was a gift. Then this horrible stench greeted me. I was so surprised I dropped the box on the floor. The fungus fell out and splatted on the tiles. Fortunately I was in the kitchen and Daisy hadn't yet arrived. I wouldn't have wanted her to see it. I wiped the disgusting mess up and dumped it in the compost heap at the top of the garden. I couldn't bring myself to put it in the rubbish bin. That wouldn't have been fair on the dustmen." The woman shuddered slightly. "I hope the

22

spores don't contaminate the compost," she added. "I don't want that thing coming up among my roses."

Meadows was scribbling urgently, trying to get every word down, just as it was said.

"Was there a note with it?" Ambrose asked.

"Of course. Idiots always send a note. Mine was a bit original though, I do admit. A luggage tag instead of a typewritten sheet. They'd stuffed it inside the box. I hope their fingers smell for weeks."

"Can you remember what was written on the tag?"

"Of course! Though it wasn't written. Someone had cut letters from a newspaper, probably got the idea from a cheap novel. 'Death and decay everywhere,' it said. Quite what that has to do with me I don't know. I didn't start the war, and I don't create fungi. I leave such things to 'Higher Powers'."

Ambrose warmed to the woman. She had what his wife would have called 'spunk': character and courage. "Was the package clearly addressed to you?" he asked. "The postman couldn't have made a mistake?"

"No. The label was written perfectly clearly."

"So it was handwritten?" Ambrose asked hopefully. "Would you recognise the writing if you saw it again?"

"Easily. The capitals were quite distinctive, someone trying to do copperplate and getting the upstrokes wrong."

Ambrose opened the evidence bag he had brought with him. Carefully he took out the luggage tags and labels Robin Harvey and the Major had given him. "Was it like these?" he asked and passed them to Miss Hodgkiss.

Pursing her lips, she examined the labels and then nodded. "They're by the same hand," she announced.

"Have you any idea why someone would want to upset you?" Ambrose asked as he put the evidence away.

"I'm sure lots of people would like to upset me. I upset them. I don't suffer fools gladly and there are a lot of fools around."

"Indeed," Ambrose acknowledged. "But could this be connected with the poetry competition? I believe you're one of the judges."

Miss Hodgkiss sniffed scornfully. "It might be," she replied. "Poets can be as silly as anyone else, and some have an inflated view of their talent. In my experience though, such people usually tell themselves everyone else is wrong or jealous. They don't resort to stupid pranks. Sending a box of obscene fungus is more like a third-form boy." She paused, considering her reply more carefully. "The handwriting isn't a boy's though, and the parcel was too carefully wrapped. Besides, it had a Birmingham postmark and I don't know any schoolboys in Birmingham."

Meadows could barely keep up.

There was one more question Ambrose needed to ask. "Have you received anything unpleasant before this? In the past month?"

"No. Other than the inevitable bills."

"You're sure?"

"I don't say things lightly, Inspector."

"I'm sure you don't," Ambrose apologised. "It's just that the other two have."

"Maybe that's because they were announced as judges before I was? I thought I'd be away this month. My family has a small place in St Peter Port. We usually spend February and March there, but my sister isn't well. I mentioned to Mr Harvey that I would be in Chalk Heath after all, and he invited me to join the panel. I like to help local ventures when I can."

Glancing at the clock, Miss Hodgkiss stood up. "Now if you'll excuse me, I have to get ready for my meeting. I think you have enough to be going on with."

They were being firmly dismissed. "Thank you," Ambrose said and got up too. "If we have any more questions may I ring you?"

"I can't see what more I can tell you," Miss Hodgkiss insisted, and before either Ambrose or Meadows could say anything, they were ushered out of the house.

"No wonder we conquered an empire," Ambrose said, laughing as he opened the car door. "Women like the Honourable Madge rapped the natives with their umbrellas, and told them to sign the treaty, then pour the tea."

"She terrifies me," Meadows admitted. "Though I think she's probably nice under it all. If you're in trouble, she'd help out, I'm sure."

Ambrose humphed uncertainly, and drove back to the Station.

The rest of the afternoon was quiet. Meadows wrote up her notes, and at Ambrose's request prepared to go down to the sorting office to see if any of the staff remembered the parcels. As she passed through the front office, she found PC Green sitting at a desk with a pile of files in front of him and a disconsolate expression on his face. "You look a bit down in the dumps," she remarked.

"I'm up to me biscuits in files, and me plates are killing me," he admitted. "Everyone else seems to be doing interesting things, and I'm on me Todd, parked behind a stack of files. Plus I'm always given the rubbish that no one else fancies doing."

"You'll be asked to do more once you've got a bit of experience," Meadows advised, catching the general gist of his moan. "It was the same when I started. I just got the child minding jobs and making tea."

"But how the ding dong am I going to get experience, if no one gives me anything to do?" PC Green asked miserably.

Getting the meaning, Meadows agreed it was a fair question. She hadn't the heart to say the others regarded the newcomer as 'too wet behind the ears' to be trusted, but she felt he was owed some explanation. "You're an outsider," she said gently. "Chalk Heath doesn't take quickly to outsiders."

"I've never been in such a ten ounce," PC Green retorted. "It's totally brown bread." Seeing her bewilderment, he had the grace to laugh. "Ten ounce rump is a dump and brown bread is dead," he explained.

"There's more to the place than you think," Meadows warned him. "We have our share of bad eggs."

"Then why can't I get a bit of the action?" Green demanded.

It was difficult to explain to him without being hurtful. "You're following someone who's very much missed," she said.

"PC Sutton? I keep hearing how good he was. So why did he decide to leave?"

"He married a divorcee and people nattered about it. He wanted to start a new life I suppose," Meadows replied. She knew perfectly well why Sutton had left, having spent hours with him in The Copper Kettle talking about his decision. But she wasn't going to discuss his affairs, especially with a newcomer. "He pops over occasionally," she added. "I'll introduce you."

Looking at her watch, Meadows realised it was time she set off. "Tell you what. Why don't I ask if you can come with me to the sorting office?" she suggested. "It'd give you a bit of a feel for the town."

Ambrose was perfectly amenable to the idea, so together Meadows and Green walked along the High Street, towards the new sorting office beyond the shops. As they passed, Meadows pointed out all the features of interest: the doors you needed to try at night, the yards where a thief might hide. She had a glance for the missing runaways

25

while she was at it, but saw no sign of them. They surely must have left town by now. Green was particularly interested in Curiosity Corner, having heard the reports about strange packets being sent to the owner. Deciding to check if Mr Harvey felt better, Meadows took Green into the shop but there were several customers at the counter. All she could do was ask the assistant briefly about Mr Harvey, and introduce Sutton's replacement.

"Still got bomb damage?" Green remarked in surprise as they left the shop and passed the boarded-up building opposite. "They wouldn't leave a site like that empty in London, it'd be worth too much bread, I mean money."

"No one knows who owns it," Meadows explained.

Crossing the road, they made their way to the sorting office.

It proved a fruitless visit. No one recalled the packages. Far too many went through each day for an individual address to be noticed. No one even recalled a bad smell. "It's never too sweet in here," one postie admitted as he stuffed envelopes into slots. "People get sweaty working so fast."

So they returned to the Station with nothing to report.

It was the end of her shift, and gratefully Meadows clocked off and unlocked her bike, ready for the ride back to her digs. That was one definite drawback to Maple View. It was at the top of Park Road. After a long day walking the beat and cycling to interviews, that last slope seemed very long and steep.

Halfway up the hill, Mrs McEwan passed her, driving the other way. She slowed down and stopped on the opposite side to Meadows, winding her window down for a chat. "Sorry to have missed you, Constable," she called over. "I've just been up to check everything's all right at the house. There's some rubbish dumped beside the bins. I don't suppose you know who put it there?"

"No, I'm afraid not," Meadows replied breathlessly.

"I'll have to put a notice up reminding everyone to keep the house neat and tidy," Mrs McEwan said, sighing. "I'll call again tomorrow." With a smile, she wound the window back and continued on her way home.

It was a struggle to get momentum again after stopping half way up the hill. Meadows was tired and hot by the time she dismounted and wheeled the bike quietly round the back of the house. As she did so, she felt sure someone was watching her from one of the windows above. A curtain twitched back into place as she glanced upwards. It was the slightest of movements but it annoyed her.

Putting her bike in the shed, she walked round to the front gardens. She entered the porch, and went upstairs towards her room. As she walked down the corridor, she was surprised to see Major Fielding coming from the gentlemen's bathroom. It looked as if he'd just had a bath. "Afternoon," he said. "Or should I say evening?"

"It's almost evening," Meadows agreed and smiled.

The Major must have seen Meadows' quizzical look. "Just getting ready for dinner," he explained. "I always do my dhobi, I mean have a good wash and brush up, at four o'clock on the dot. Like clockwork," he laughed. "Got to look respectable. Although I'll be glad when they fix the door next week. One does feel rather vulnerable with just a sign on the door to protect one's modesty," he laughed again. "Then it's Gin O'Clock, followed by dinner and an evening of Bridge."

Meadows nodded. "I thought our Bridge club met just after lunchtime," she remarked.

"I'm not good enough to get into that one," the Major admitted. "They're far too keen for me: play for tripe supper as my old Nan used to say." He laughed ruefully. "They're so good the Honourable Madge comes up at least once a week. She's a much better player than I am, so I go to the church one she gave up, and have a much easier time there."

Meadows wasn't sure whether the Major enjoyed the company or the game most, but she suspected it was the former. "Have a good evening then," she replied.

"You look tired, my dear," the Major remarked as she turned away.

If anyone else had called her 'my dear' Meadows would have protested, but she liked the Major. He had been one of the few residents to make her welcome when she moved in, even carrying one of her cases up the stairs. It was a shame he'd received unpleasant mail. Meadows made no reference to it however. What she knew through her job stayed with the job. It was a rule she'd had drummed into her during her training, and that she'd followed ever since.

"It's been a heavy day," she admitted.

"Don't work too hard," Major Fielding advised. "You're only young once, however clichéd that is."

He seemed sad, Meadows thought. Not his usual cheerful military self. "Are you all right?" she asked.

"Of course. Just getting a bit maudlin in my old age." Smiling, the Major walked past her towards his room. Then he paused and looked back. "Something happened today that wasn't very nice," he admitted. "I won't bother you with it, but it's good to meet someone young and pretty, and dedicated. It reminds me that not everyone's unpleasant."

In surprise Meadows flushed. "It's nice of you to say so," she replied awkwardly.

"But don't make my mistake," Major Fielding added. "Don't devote yourself so much to your career that you have nothing else. That's what I did, and I've come to regret it. Especially today. You need family and friends, not just memories."

He glanced at her, as if that were some sort of explanation. Then he went into his room.

Chapter Four

Tuesday 15th March

Ambrose sat quietly, staring out of the window without seeing. He had other cases: a burglary, an old man dying in a house fire, a teenager missing since last month (possibly murdered or maybe just running away from her family). They were all more important than a spate of unpleasant mailings, but the packets bothered him. They were so unsavoury, so unpredictable. It could just be a silly prank but his instinct told him otherwise. It could be the work of a very unhinged individual. To such a mind, there might only be a short step between sending threatening messages and actually following through on the threats.

The threats being linked to the competition also touched Ambrose personally. Last year Robin Harvey had added a short story category to his annual competition. Ambrose had entered under his pen name of Maggie St James, and been both delighted and horrified to win a place on the short list. The rules stated clearly that winners must appear in person at the final dinner. It had never crossed his mind that he would be invited. He had only entered to give himself a deadline. Rather than have his pseudonym revealed and be the laughing stock of the Station, he urgently withdrew. At least there had been one good outcome. His story had been published in the 'Jenners Park Gazette' soon afterwards. If it hadn't been for the competition, Ambrose might never have submitted the story to the newspaper.

Which all left him with a sense of special concern. He didn't like to think of Robin Harvey being threatened. Both the Major and the Hon Madge were important people in the town too, giving their time and money to help local groups. He would pass the case to DS Winters. The lists of entrants might reveal the name of someone known to be unstable, possibly even with a record of violence.

There was a hesitant knock on the door.

"Come in!" Ambrose invited wearily.

"We've had another report of milk being half-inched, I mean pinched," PC Green announced. "I thought you'd like to know."

"What?" Ambrose growled in annoyance. "Why bother me? Get Higgins or Meadows to note it."

Green held his own, though he flushed bright red. "It might mean the two runaways are still in town," he suggested. "Could be worth another butcher's."

Pausing, Ambrose considered the young Constable. He had a point. "Where are the reports from?" he asked more civilly.

"Three properties by the park. A pint each. About what a young tea leaf, I mean thief, might have for breakfast."

Ambrose nodded, impressed. "Leave a report for DS Winters," he instructed. Then he paused, considering PC Green. They weren't involving the newcomer enough, he decided. The lad had got off on the wrong foot with his chippy Cockney manner. It had seemed disrespectful to the older men. But he was keen, and it wasn't his fault that he'd replaced a highly valued and experienced officer, the day after the farewell party.

"Give the householders a call if they're on the phone," Ambrose continued, "and go to see them if they're not. One of them might have seen something. While you're at it, check there's no one hiding in their back yard."

"Yes, sir!" Green said in delight. "Where are the botany bays, I mean runaways, from, sir?"

"Moorlands Approved School for Delinquent Boys. They're taken to the farms on working parties, and sometimes a kid does a bunk. They're usually picked up within the day. These two have managed to stay out longer. 'Mr Bigs' in the making no doubt. Still, their mothers love 'em, I'm sure." He shuddered inwardly, thinking of how badly his own son might have turned out, given the problems they'd had with him. But he and Mary had persisted until Joe started learning the guitar and found he was rather good. By the time he'd got involved with the band he'd straightened out. These boys probably hadn't had such supportive parents, if indeed they had parents at all.

PC Green hesitated. "May I say something, sir?" he asked.

"I imagine so, if it's not wasting my time."

"There's a bomb site opposite the bookshop. It could make a den to hide out in."

Ambrose considered the suggestion. "Possibly," he agreed. "Sgt Hurst is back from leave tomorrow. I'll ask him to see the place is thoroughly checked. Have a word with him tomorrow, if you want to volunteer." He was amused to realise he was talking about a case with a young rookie, just as he did with DS Winters.

Afterwards, Ambrose tried to return to the fire officer's report on his desk, but couldn't settle. It was nearly lunchtime. There would be no harm going up to Maple View to chat to Major Fielding, just for a social call, and if the Major could show him the lists of entrants, he might spot something useful.

Major Fielding was glad of a visitor, though he almost bundled Ambrose into his apartment as the neighbour's door opened. "Nosey old cow!" he said in annoyance afterwards. "Pardon my language. She checks out every visitor I have. Looking for nubile young females I suppose." He smiled wryly. "I should be so lucky."

A small kitchenette opened off the lounge. The Major insisted on putting the kettle on "for a decent cup of tea, not what you get down at the Station." As he waited, Ambrose sat beside the electric fire and glanced around him. The room was large and airy, with high corniced ceilings and an imposing bay window. It looked gracious but surely let the heat out alarmingly. Neat to the point of regimentation, the lounge had few ornaments or pictures. A photograph of a young officer on horseback dominated the hearth, but Ambrose knew the furniture came with the apartment. Maple View was proud to provide luxury furnished accommodation. The whole flat had the air of someone used to living simply and moving on at short notice.

"I wanted to see you were all right after yesterday," Ambrose explained, "and whether you've received anything more."

Returning with two cups of tea, Major Fielding shook his head. "I'm fine now, thanks. It threw me for a few hours," he admitted. "I kept wondering who disliked me enough to send such a thing."

"Did you come to any conclusion?" Ambrose asked.

The Major considered the question. As he did so, Ambrose looked again at the photograph, realising the handsome young guardsman was Fielding himself.

"No. Unless it's to do with the competition," the Major said at last.

"Do you have a list of entrants?" Ambrose asked.

31

"I've kept a copy of the long lists, but that's all."

"Do you mind if I have a look at it?"

It was not a lot of help, Ambrose had to admit, just the names of ten poets, all offered at least the chance of publication in an anthology. They would presumably be pleased to have done so well, and unlikely to threaten the judges. What he needed was a list of poets who had entered and been rejected, and presumably thought themselves unfairly treated. But, Ambrose reflected, it usually took time for resentment to build up into a desire to make threats. That meant they were looking for someone who'd entered and failed multiple times.

"Do you have the full list?" Ambrose asked, passing the paper back. "If you have the last couple of years too, that would help."

The Major shook his head. "I gave all the paperwork back to Robin Harvey," he replied. "I don't know whether he'll have kept past lists, but he might have done. He seems to keep most things." Again there was that wry smile.

Staying only long enough to drink his tea, Ambrose left. As he did so, he looked towards the neighbours' closed doors. A radio muttered behind one but otherwise the corridor was silent. He must get onto the Accommodation Office as soon as he had time, and tell them they had to find Meadows more suitable police lodgings. She must feel very out of place amongst the retired Majors and Head Mistresses.

As he walked towards the back door, Ambrose was surprised to nearly bump into Abigail McEwan. She was carrying a stack of boxes, the top one wobbling precariously. Quickly he took it from her and was rewarded by a charming smile. "No trouble I hope?" she asked.

"Just a social call," Ambrose assured her.

"Oh yes, you'll know Major Fielding from the Friends of the Theatre," Mrs McEwan surmised acutely. "Such a nice man. Always so interesting. And your young policewoman seems to have settled in very well too. We are so very fortunate with our residents."

She smiled again, her large brown eyes still beautiful, despite the fine lines that were starting to appear around them. Ambrose had always appreciated a pretty woman, though he'd only ever had one love in his life, and he'd noticed before that Abigail McEwan was good looking. On her own now, rather than standing dutifully behind her husband, Ambrose had more chance to assess her. She must have been a real head-turner when she was younger, he decided.

"Would you be a gentleman and help me carry these to the car?" she asked. "I'm afraid I've bitten off more than I can chew, as the saying goes," she added.

"I'd be pleased to help," Ambrose assured her, taking the boxes.

"I ordered these from the haberdashers," Mrs McEwan explained as she held the back door open. "They stupidly sent everything here. I've told them my change of address but they can't have noted it properly."

"I didn't realise you'd moved," Ambrose admitted.

"Just before Christmas," Mrs McEwan explained. "The builders made a delightful flat for us on the top floor, but neither of us liked living above the shop, if you see what I mean. We kept being reminded how lovely this house was when we lived here as a family. You can tell yourself something's sensible, can't you? We were rattling around once Brian left, and it's a good business venture for when my husband retires, but we don't need to live in it now. It made us sad. So we moved to one of the new detached houses they built on the Old Hall estate. It's much more suitable for us, and I can pop back here easily to see everything's all right."

They'd reached her car, a brand new Hillman, Ambrose noted. He helped her place the boxes carefully in the boot and on the back seat. Afterwards she seemed to want to stay to talk to him, rather than drive off immediately.

"I hear your son is following in his father's footsteps," he said, making conversation.

"Oh yes. We're both delighted! Brian's started his training and is absolutely loving it. It's been his choice all along. We wouldn't have pushed him into it, not for a moment. Mac was so worried it might be harder for him. You know, as the son of a Superintendent, and one who's so well known. I think we both hoped he'd choose another career. But now he's made up his mind to join the Force, and got a place, well, we couldn't be prouder." Mrs McEwan's eyes warmed with pride. "There can't be many mothers as lucky as I am," she admitted. "To have a husband and a son I can be so proud of." She glanced back at the house. "This is my little business, but I wouldn't begin to compare it to what Mac and you do."

In surprise, Ambrose smiled. "It's good to be appreciated," he acknowledged. "I hope your son does well. Give him my best wishes, when you next speak to him."

Returning to his own car, Ambrose allowed Mrs McEwan to leave first. He discovered in the mirror that he was still smiling. She really was a lovely woman: bright and chatty and with the sort of smile that made a man feel he was the most interesting person she had met all day. He recalled the gossip when he'd first arrived in Chalk Heath: the snide remarks about Inspector McEwan, as he then was, falling for a pretty little widow soon after the War ended. He could understand why they resented her. They were jealous. Beauty and business sense: they didn't often go together.

Chapter Five

Wednesday 16th March

WPC Pauline Meadows and PC Alfie Green walked purposefully around the park, "being a visible presence" as DS Winters put it. Two mothers were revolving toddlers carefully on the roundabout, but it was going cold. "Keep an eye on those two," Meadows advised, nodding in the direction of a couple of older boys huddled beside the privet hedge, smoking. "They've probably bunked off, but they could have been allowed to leave early. Dentists, school outing, whatever. They'll be full of excuses if you ask them."

"Afternoon officer," one of them called to her cheekily. He rubbed his hands, making sure she saw the cigarette. "Cold ain't it?"

"Got a lot of cheek, hasn't he?" Green commented.

Refusing to take the boy's bait, Meadows nodded towards him. She glanced at the hedge, wondering whether other children were hiding beyond it. Something, or someone, had rustled the leaves on the path, but the privet was unkempt, thick and tall, and she could neither see through or over it. Frowning, she turned back towards PC Green. It could have been a squirrel.

They walked on, towards the bottom gate. Ever since she'd taken pity on Green two days ago, the other officers had been only too happy for her to take him around with her. "Give the lad the benefit of your local knowledge," Higgins had suggested. "He seems to have taken a shine to you."

"At least you can tell what he's talking about," DS Winters agreed. "You're good at crossword puzzles."

"I have to guess at it most of the time," Meadows admitted, laughing.

Normally Meadows would rather have been on her own, but at present it was a relief to have company. She was permanently uneasy, sure someone was following her and yet never seeing anyone. She had never 'suffered with nerves' before, as her mother's friends put it, indeed she had no idea what the saying meant, except that it was usually whispered about another woman they thought wasn't all there. Meadows was beginning to wonder if that was what was wrong with her.

Now she had a chance to check her sanity. "Did you hear something a moment ago?" she asked PC Green softly. "Behind the hedge?"

To her relief Green nodded. "Faintly," he agreed. "Children, or a stray cat. Why?"

"Walk on with me, towards those rhododendrons, will you?" Meadows asked. "Then drop down so you can't be seen. There's another path beyond the bushes. See if someone is following us."

In surprise, Green nodded.

Together they walked into the thicket of rhododendrons that bordered the children's play area. When the tangle was at its densest, Meadows nodded and walked on. PC Green dropped silently behind one of the bushes.

She'd reached the bottom gate by the time he rejoined her. "Well?" Meadows asked, trying to sound businesslike.

"There's definitely someone there," Green said quietly. "They scarpered before I could get a good butcher's. I think it was a man. Could have been a woman. Hard to tell. Wearing a duffle coat with the hood up."

Meadows let out her breath with relief. "I'm not going mad then," she said, laughing slightly.

"I wouldn't imagine so," Green said with a note of respect. "Seen 'em before?"

"Not seen but heard. Several times this past week. I'm being followed." At once Meadows regretted the admission. "Don't you dare tell any of the others!" she warned. "I'll have your guts for garters if you do."

"No, Ma'am if you say not," Green agreed. He hesitated, afraid of offending her. "Pardon me for saying so, but oughtn't you to tell someone?"

"I'll have to if it goes on," Meadows admitted reluctantly. "But nothing ever happens. They don't threaten me or flash me, don't even speak. Just lurk. If I report a lurker, I'll be laughed at. The blokes'll say I'm 'going all girly'."

In understanding, Green nodded. "They do take the mick, don't they?" he agreed ruefully.

"Tell you what," Meadows suggested. "Let's see if we can scare our lurker off. I'll walk on, then double back at the end of the border; there's a way through that the kids have made. You turn round and head back the way we've come, then take another kids' path to the left. We could do a pincer movement, trap whoever it is, between us."

"Yes, Ma'am," Green said, beginning to enjoy himself.

"You don't need to call me Ma'am." Meadows smiled as she walked on.

They met amongst the rhododendrons five minutes later. "See anyone?" Meadows asked breathlessly. She'd forgotten how low the branches grew over the children's route. She had knocked her hat off twice and got twigs on her skirt.

"Sorry, no," Green said, ruefully readjusting his helmet. "I heard a lot of thrashing but I didn't clock anyone. We must have scared 'em off."

"Let's hope that does the trick," Meadows said, trying not to laugh. "You've got bits on your jacket. You'd better brush yourself down, or Higgins'll wonder what we've been up to."

The young PC went bright red, then had the grace to laugh himself.

"Remember, not a word to anyone," Meadows warned him again as they left the park. "If anyone does ask, we were just looking for the run-aways." She shook her head. "I reckon someone must have taken those two in," she added. "If they're still living rough they'll be frozen by now. A few bottles of milk won't keep the wolf from the door."

"I can't help feeling sorry for them," Green admitted.

"It's not our place to feel sorry," Meadows warned him. "Treat with compassion, but remember they won't have been sent to Moorlands for nothing. They'll have form."

"Wide boys in the making," Green admitted. "We got a lot of their sort in the East End. Right little tea leaves. Hanging round the markets half inching stuff, doing a bit of running for the bookies; busy little boys. We say they're 'behind with the rent'. I think you'd call it 'bent as a 9 bob note'."

Meadows nodded. She was finding PG Green more interesting every day. "What made you move to Chalk Heath?" she asked.

"Couldn't get full-time into the Met or the City of London after me probation ended. So I tried everywhere that had a vacancy, and a lot that didn't."

Turning towards him, Meadows considered his expression. "You were very determined, weren't you?" she acknowledged. "So was I. It wasn't easy for me to get in either. Was it worth it?"

PC Green took several seconds to reply. "It wasn't at first," he said quietly. "But I'm liking it more now."

It was a compliment to her, Meadows recognised, and she smiled in thanks.

She had one last call to make before the end of her shift. Robin Harvey had arranged to give her a list of this year's competition entries. After losing time in the park she was late. Glancing at her watch in annoyance, she hurried down the hill and onto the main street. PC Green could barely keep up with her.

Fortunately there were few customers at the counter, though several were browsing at the shelves. Miss Havering called for Mr Harvey at once.

Carrying a battered manila folder, he appeared quickly from his office behind the back room. "I'm glad you're a bit late, officer," he said, to Meadows' relief. "It took me longer to find the full competition list than I expected. Wrongly filed I'm afraid."

Miss Havering reddened and began apologising profusely. "Not your fault," he assured her. "Mine. I'd put them with the winners, instead of in a separate folder. Trying to be tidy I suppose. Never a good idea." He smiled as he passed the folder to Meadows. "I don't know what help this will be," he added.

"Have you received anything more?" Meadows asked him.

"No. I over-reacted."

"You did right to call us," Meadows insisted. "It's always best to report something that seems threatening."

As she left, she wondered why she wasn't taking her own advice.

Chapter Six

After they'd gone, Mr Harvey settled back at the desk in his office. He had a pile of invoices to go through and Miss Havering was coping well in the shop. There were orders to meet too. Most were from local customers. They could call in if he sent them a standard postcard saying he had traced their books (often simply a matter of searching the boxes in his attic). Three were from Scotland. Word had obviously got around there, perhaps from that pleasant Scots woman who visited Chalk Heath last month. One request was from the United States: an airmail letter asking if he had any photographs of Old Chalk Heath in Edwardian times. The writer had been tracing their family tree and found her ancestors owned one of the farms nearby.

Robin Harvey always enjoyed such requests and immediately began going through his stock lists. There was an old print of Chalk Heath Hall he recalled. That might show Fletcher's Farm in the background.

He was still happily going through boxes of photographs and postcards when Miss Havering tapped on the door. "It's five fifteen, Mr Harvey," she reminded him. "Shall I start cashing up? There's only one customer left, an old gentleman. I don't think he intends to buy anything."

In surprise, Robin looked up. "Of course, my dear," he said. "I hadn't noticed the time. Thursday's your night school evening isn't it?" His assistant nodded.

"How are you getting on?" he asked.

"I'm enjoying it, I can't thank you enough for paying the fee."

Mr Harvey smiled. "Enlightened self-interest," he admitted. "You learn book keeping and I don't have to wade through these." He nodded towards the spike laden with processed invoices. "Off you go. You don't want to be late."

"Do you want me to clear up the delivery first?" Miss Havering asked, looking towards the shop floor in front of the back room. It was still stacked with boxes.

"No. I'll see to them," Mr Harvey assured her. "I've got a couple of interesting orders I'd like to get onto after we shut. It'll be nice and quiet. If you start cashing up, the old gent might take the hint. As soon as he's gone, bring the cash in here and put it in the safe. I'll lock up after you."

Prompt on five thirty Miss Havering wished him goodbye. Robin Harvey was so absorbed he merely nodded and carried on with his orders. It was an hour before he remembered that he needed to lock the front door. Glancing at the boxes he decided he was too tired to start shifting them now. They could wait till morning. Finally, after locking up he went upstairs to his flat above the shop, to make himself some tea.

Even then, Robin didn't really stop work. What else was there to do on a cold March evening? Not being a church-goer, he wasn't involved in Chalk Heath's many chapel meetings and choirs. He enjoyed the readers' group at the library but that only met once a month. His work interested him far more than going to the pub or the cinema had ever done. And who would he go with if he went? A lifetime ago, it seemed, he'd been engaged to a sweet girl who worked in the same branch of Barclays as himself. After she died of tuberculosis at the end of the war, he'd lost interest in going out. The shop and Bird Books had given him the new start he needed, and nowadays they were all he wanted. He was perfectly happy settling in front of a cheerful fire in the evening, reading a couple of submissions, with his cat for company.

That night he had entertaining reading too. One manuscript was a fascinating autobiography about Colonial East Africa; just exotic enough to be exciting, but written from a British viewpoint. Another submission was a poetry collection. His heart had sunk at the prospect of reading yet more doggerel or cathartic confessions, but this collection was good, a fresh young voice. He was surprised to discover the poet was female.

It would be interesting to see her biographical details. He left his flat to find a stack of files on the landing outside. He was rummaging for the poet's original letter when he became aware of a noise downstairs.

It was soft, almost inaudible. Had he been concentrating on the poems he wouldn't have heard it. Pausing, he listened carefully. The building often creaked. Floorboards stretched in the warmth from the fire. Waterpipes hissed if he left the immersion heater on too long. Assuming this noise was just the breathing of an old house, he turned back to the files. He was pleased when he found the envelope he wanted.

Then he paused. There it was again; a faint shuffling, as if someone was moving papers very softly. His heart began to beat faster. What an idiot he'd been! He'd left the front door unlocked until well after six. A thief could easily have slipped inside and hidden behind one of the bookshelves.

Soundlessly Robin moved to the top of the stairs and listened intently. For several moments there was silence. In relief he told himself he was imagining things and turned away. Then he heard it again: that quiet, careful shuffling. It was a long way below him, but it wasn't imaginary.

Going back into the lounge to fetch a torch, Robin went out onto the landing and listened again. He must phone the police, but he'd have to decide whether the telephone in his office was nearer than the one on the shop counter. How short-sighted he'd been not to have a telephone installed in his flat, but at the time it was just too expensive.

The intruder was probably in Robin's private office, looking for money in the safe. If Robin could get down to the shop without being heard, he could lock the door to the back room (he had the key on his ring) and trap the thief. Then he could phone the police from the counter afterwards. He'd have the advantage of surprise, as long as he went down the stairs quietly enough.

He was just starting to tiptoe when there was a sudden squawk that nearly sent him plunging down the stairs in surprise. He'd trodden on the cat. "Damn you, Minnie!" he hissed, rubbing his elbow. His heart pounded with shock. It took him several moments to recover.

Realising he'd dropped the torch on his knee, he rubbed the bruise there too. Then he grabbed the cat from behind a stack of books where she had hidden in umbrage. "You gave me a proper fright," he whispered. "I thought you were a burglar." His voice shook in relief. "What an idiot!" he said to himself. That was what the noise was. Minnie! She often jumped from one pile of books on to another. It never ceased to amaze him how she managed not to knock any of the books over.

Stroking Minnie's head to calm her, Robin paused, every sense suddenly alive. There was definitely someone below. It sounded like they were opening the door to the back room. They were trying to be very quiet, but the hinge squeaked.

He placed the cat firmly back in his flat and shut the door to keep her out the way. The torch had fallen onto a pile of papers, thankfully making no sound.

With the torch in his left hand, and the right gripping the bannister, Robin tiptoed down. He turned right at the bottom of the stairs and strained his ears, pausing between two bookstacks. The door to the back room, where he'd met the police earlier, was slightly open. He was certain he'd closed it before going up to his flat. He was inching his way towards the door when he saw movement inside. The street lamp outside the shop window didn't reach this far into the shop, but he could just make out a shadowy figure going through papers on the table.

Trying to move without making a sound, Robin crept forwards but he banged his leg on a stack of books to his left. He froze, looking down at the books, worried they would topple over.

He didn't see the figure suddenly dart out of the back room towards him. When the door was flung open it caught him sharply on the side of the head, knocking him sprawling. The torch skidded across the floor as a figure leapt past him and ran towards the front door. Fruitlessly Robin shouted, "Stop! What are you doing here?" The figure whirled round briefly and then ran on.

Trying to get up, Robin tripped over one of the boxes he had meant to clear up. In the darkness he stumbled, catching his other foot on a second box and then slithering on a stack of paper. Stumbling forward in the dark, he tried to chase the intruder. His feet were sliding everywhere. He couldn't keep his balance. Crying out in fear, he grabbed at a bookcase to steady himself. But the bookcase wasn't attached to the wall. Slowly it began to topple towards him.

The books on the top shelf slid forwards. One fell onto his head, a corner of the hard binding catching him on his temple, almost stunning him. Urgently he tried to push the bookcase back, but more books were falling, hitting his arms so he couldn't hold the weight. "Help me!" he called to the running figure.

But the intruder unlocked the front door from inside, and ran into the street beyond.

"Don't leave me like this!" Robin shouted. "I can't hold it much longer. Help me!"

Then he heard the front door slam shut.

Robin's arms buckled with the weight. His head and shoulders were being bruised again and again as a landslide of books fell to the ground. Slowly, inevitably, the bookshelf keeled over, on top of him. There was the sound of splintering wood as the top shelf hit the wall behind him.

He must have lost consciousness, for how long he couldn't tell. All he knew was the crushing weight that pinned him to the ground. Feebly he tried to push the weight off but it wouldn't move. In the darkness he could barely make out the shape of one of his legs sticking out from the mound of books. He couldn't feel the other one. There was a terrible pain in his jaw. His mouth tasted of blood. Desperately he tried to move his hand to feel what had happened to his head, but he couldn't.

Even his good leg was going numb now. "Help me!" he shouted, but his voice came from far away.

There was no reply.

Chapter Seven

Thursday 17th March

"Curiosity Corner is closed!"

"Pardon?" DS Winters replied.

"I said Curiosity Corner is closed," the voice repeated. "It shouldn't be."

Winters looked at his watch. "It's only 9 o'clock," he pointed out. "In any case, what's it got to do with the Police?" He was tired. Little Caitlin had kept him awake half the night. The rash on the back of her legs looked like chicken pox, so there wasn't much chance of a good night's sleep tonight either.

"I specifically arranged to call at 8.00 a.m." the woman persisted. "No one came to the door."

At once Winters recognised the voice. "I'm sorry Ma'am," he said more politely. "I didn't catch what you said. You had an appointment but the shop's not open?"

"That's exactly what I said, Sergeant. I arranged to see Mr Harvey at 8.00 a.m. He didn't answer the bell and he hasn't opened the shop since. I went out of my way to check."

DS Winters held his breath. The Honourable Marjorie Hodgkiss represented everything he disliked. Used to commanding servants, she demanded obedience, even from the Constabulary. He had hoped the War would change Britain, but women like 'the Honourable Madge' (as she was known to everyone except herself) had slotted back into their former places, and expected everyone else to do so. Still, he couldn't afford to offend her. She was important in the town. "Perhaps Mr Harvey overslept," he suggested.

"Nonsense! Robin Harvey would never oversleep. He's not the type. Besides, there were several customers waiting."

Winters' annoyance turned to concern. Robin Harvey was a shrewd businessman. He didn't keep customers waiting.

"His assistant will be along soon," Winters suggested.

"No she won't!" the Hon Madge retorted. "Miss Havering has a dental appointment. That's why Mr Harvey suggested today, so we could talk in private. There has to be something wrong. What are you going to *do* about it?"

Winters was too slow replying. The Hon Madge sniffed in derision. "I had hoped to speak to DI Ambrose," she added. "He'd understand how important my meeting was. We're both on the Chalk Heath Theatre Committee you know."

Winters didn't need reminding. "I'm afraid the DI's on leave today," he said carefully.

"Then I'll ring him at home."

"Oh I wouldn't do that," Winters advised urgently. He couldn't imagine how the woman had got hold of Ambrose's number. He suspected she was bluffing, but if she did ring him, Winters' ears would be throbbing for days. "I'll ask someone to go round this morning," he promised.

"That's not good enough," the Hon Miss Hodgkiss insisted. "I'm certain Mr Harvey is ill. I shall hold you responsible if he gets worse."

The woman really was annoying, but Winters couldn't ignore her. As she'd pointed out, she knew the DI personally. She knew the Commissioner too. "Would you like me to go myself?" he asked.

"That would be good. There may be private correspondence lying around. Mr Harvey and I were going to discuss the competition anthology. I'm sure I can rely on you to be discreet."

"You can," Winters assured her. "Does a neighbour have a key? I don't want to break in."

"Mr Harvey leaves one on a ledge above the door. I would have used it myself, but I might have been accused of breaking and entering."

"Indeed," Winters agreed. His mouth twitched at the image of the Hon Madge in handcuffs. "I'll go round at once," he replied.

"Excellent. I'll meet you there. I came home to telephone. It won't take me long to drive back to the shop."

"I'm sure that won't be necessary," Winters began, but the phone clicked into silence.

He shook his head in annoyance. There were a couple of PCs in the canteen who should be making such a visit, not him. He was annoyed with himself for allowing the woman to bully him. His desk was covered in reports, all needing attention. If he took one of the PCs he could leave them to call a doctor, or whatever. Then he could shoot back and do his paperwork.

Glancing into the canteen Winters saw WPC Meadows finishing a bacon sandwich. She could be relied on not to gossip about competition winners. She also knew about the malicious packages.

"Meadows!" he called. "I've got a job for you!"

As soon as he had explained the situation, Meadows was concerned. "It's not like Mr Harvey," she agreed. "There's usually a light on in the corner room of his flat when I'm on earlies. Now I come to think of it, there wasn't this morning. He must be unwell, from worrying about the competition perhaps and the funny packages."

They walked briskly down the main street towards Curiosity Corner. A smart little Ford passed, then slowed down and reversed towards them. The Hon Madge leant across to the passenger seat and wound the window down. "Ah! Sergeant," she called, "Good to see you so promptly." She nodded towards Meadows in greeting. "I'll park on the corner and meet you at the door. We'll have to send the crowd away. Don't want them to see where the key's kept, do we?"

The crowd consisted of two women waiting in the porch and a man looking idly in the shop window. As Meadows approached she heard the women talking. "He could have run off with the takings," one suggested.

"From his own shop?" her companion retorted scornfully.

"You never know," the first woman replied darkly. "His assistant's not here either. Maybe they've gone off together."

"You don't half talk some rubbish, Edie," the man at the shop window called. Seeing Winters and Meadows, he paused. "Looks like trouble," he added, nodding in their direction.

"Has there been a burglary?" his wife asked hopefully.

"We're just calling for a chat with Mr Harvey," Winters assured her. "You'd better come back later."

Reluctantly the three customers went up the road, though they looked back towards the shop several times. Waiting until they were out of sight, Miss Hodgkiss felt along the top of the door lintel and passed Winters a key.

"Let us go in first," Winters said firmly. "If there's any evidence of a burglary, or another suspect package, we'll need to deal with it. I suggest you wait in your car. If we need you, WPC Meadows will let you know."

To his surprise the Hon Madge nodded. "Mustn't contaminate the evidence," she agreed.

As they entered, the shop was in darkness. The light from the windows lit up only the front portion of the shop. Meadows knew roughly where the light switch was, and running her fingers over the wall found it quickly. It made a loud click in the silence. At first there was no other sound. Then they both heard the distant mewing of a cat. It seemed to be coming from the flat upstairs.

"Not a good sign, sir," Meadows whispered. "Minnie's usually around the shop by now. She sounds distressed."

"Mr Harvey!" Winters called. There was no reply. "Are you there, Mr Harvey?" he called again, more loudly. "DS Winters here."

Still there was no reply.

Winters looked around for signs of a break-in. The door was intact. The display in the front window seemed undisturbed, and all looked normal in the counter area. The till was closed and packets were stacked beside it, ready for the assistant to take to the Post Office.

"Perhaps he's still in his flat?" Meadows suggested. "The stairs are behind one of the bookcases, towards the office. Shall I go up and check?"

Winters paused before answering. Something was bothering him. He couldn't quite define it.

All around them were bookcases, arranged so they formed alcoves. Nothing had been disturbed as far as he could see. The view of the back room was obscured by a bookcase marked 'History'. There was the same dusty smell of leather and old paper, but behind it was another smell: something unpleasant, like blood or urine. Perhaps both.

At once Winters was alert. He knew that smell from before, though mercifully not recently, not since hostilities ended. He recalled that Meadows had known Mr Harvey, had seemed to like him. "You need to prepare yourself," he warned softly. "We may have a fatality."

He heard Meadows draw in her breath sharply, but she made no other comment. Part of him wanted to send her back outside. She was a young woman and not meant to see such things. Another part told him she had joined the Force and must expect to see death. Besides, she wanted to be treated as an equal. He decided to take her with him as a witness. "I'll go first," he instructed.

As they passed through the bookcases, heading towards the back room and office, they both caught their breath in concern. In front of them was a scene of absolute chaos. Books littered the floor, scattered from a large bookcase that had fallen forwards, spilling its contents all across the floor. Wooden shelves rested on books, or protruded upwards, cracked by the impact. Some of the books had come to rest on a pile of boxes. Others lay broken-backed across the floor. A broken torch lay next to a large leather-bound Encyclopedia.

Under it all, just visible under the covers of a book, was an arm.

Meadows managed to hold her breath and say nothing. She felt very sick.

"Stay there!" Winters ordered. Stepping forward over the mound, he looked closer into the pile. Then, bending forwards, he lifted the wrist and felt for a pulse.

Looking up, he shook his head. Then he climbed carefully back. "Go and ring the Station," he said to Meadows, almost kindly. "There's a phone at the counter in the shop. Tell the Duty Sergeant we need Forensics as soon as possible, camera, the lot. And although it's his day off, you'd better ring the DI. He'll want to know as soon as possible. Then you'd better tell Miss Hodgkiss to go home. Just say there's been an accident. After that, go back to the Station and have a cup of tea. You look as though you need it. I'll stay here till Forensics arrive."

"Thank you, sir," Meadows managed to reply. "But hadn't I better wait for Miss Havering first?" Her voice sounded strange in her ears, as if she had a sore throat. "She must be late. She'll have a key."

"Fair point," Winters agreed. "I gather she has a dental appointment. We don't want her letting herself in and finding this." He turned his head slightly in the direction of the chaos behind him. "Intercept her and take her up to the Station with you. I'm afraid you'll have to break the news to her. You don't need to go into details."

"Yes sir," Meadows agreed again. Urgently she turned towards the front of the shop. The sickness was welling up in her throat. She was afraid she was going to make a fool of herself. Forcing herself to breath slowly and regularly, somehow she managed to walk firmly towards the counter. Once out of sight, though, she had to pause to steady herself. She hadn't known Robin Harvey well, but she had liked him. Such a death would have been dreadful. It was terrible to think of him trying to save himself, all alone. Tears stung her eyes. Telling herself to be professional, she blinked them away.

Holding her breath for a second, she picked up the phone from the counter.

The Desk Sergeant, Bob Hurst, was businesslike and practical. He knew exactly what needed doing.

"I'll be a while yet," Meadows explained. "The DS has asked me to speak to Miss Hodgkiss and the assistant."

"OK." Hurst replied. "I'll call the DI and let him know the situation."

As soon as she'd put the phone down, she stepped outside into the street, carefully locking the shop door behind her. The little red car was still waiting on the corner. The Hon Madge could read Meadows' tight expression as soon as she approached. Briskly she wound the window down.

"Is he dead?" she asked softly.

There was no point in lying. Meadows nodded. "Looks like it," she replied. "An accident."

Miss Hodgkiss sighed. To Meadows' surprise she seemed genuinely upset, though she remained controlled and calm. "What a pity!" was her only remark.

"I must ask you not to say anything to anyone yet," Meadows added. "We have to get a doctor here…"

"Of course!" Miss Hodgkiss interrupted her. "I won't even tell the Major, though he'll have to know soon. Goodness knows what we'll do about the Award Dinner. We'll have to sort things out between us." Winding the car window up, she started the engine.

Letting herself back into the shop, Meadows returned to the fallen bookcase, to inform DS Winters. He was no longer there. Professional curiosity and training overcame her personal feelings, and she stood alone for a moment, considering the scene. The bookcase must have fallen onto Mr Harvey, crushing him. With luck, he'd died instantly. She hoped so. She surveyed the mess in front of her, thinking how long it would take to tidy it all up.

Shuddering, she looked up and saw DS Winters coming out of the back room. Presumably he was checking whether anything had been disturbed in there or in the office behind.

Returning to the counter, she sat waiting for Miss Havering to appear. Several times, a potential customer rattled the door, despite the 'closed' sign. Then she heard the cat again, mewing in the distance. She ought to check Mr Harvey's flat. There might be some evidence there. Recalling where she had seen him appear from behind one of the alcoves, she explored until she found the stairs. They were steep and the landing half way up was half full of books stacked ready to fill spare places in the shop. Had they found Mr Harvey with a broken neck at the foot of his stairs, she wouldn't have been in the least surprised.

The main door to the flat was closed, and she could hear the cat behind it. It sounded very hungry and needed attention. Meadows realised she must be careful not to let the cat out when she entered. The last thing Forensics would need was a cat running through all the evidence.

She managed to squeeze in through the door before the cat even realised she was coming in. She found herself in a windowless kitchen. The morning sun streamed through a skylight in the ceiling, yet the electric light was still switched on. Frowning, she glanced in the lounge, taking care to touch nothing. A fire had burnt in the grate recently; the ash was still smouldering and a reading lamp still shone brightly. Beside the fire were an armchair and small table. A cup and saucer stood on the mantelpiece. Judging by the pile of papers on the table and beside the chair, Mr Harvey had been working as he sat by the fire. Everything looked cosy and secure.

Popping her head through another door, she found the bedroom. The bed was still made. It didn't look as if Mr Harvey had made it to bed last night, she thought to herself. That must be the room she could see from the outside, she mused.

Quickly she went back into the kitchen. A milk bottle was standing in a bowl of water on the draining board, presumably to stay cool. Holding the bottle with a tea towel, she poured some milk into a saucer, then put it down for the cat. The cat lunged at the milk greedily. Meadows quickly took the opportunity to leave the flat, shutting the door firmly behind her.

"Who's going to look after you?" she wondered as she went back downstairs. "At least we know you didn't trip your master up."

Fortunately, Meadows had taken the precaution of leaving the key in the lock to the shop door, so Miss Havering wouldn't be able to insert hers. Meadows had only just returned to the shop when she heard the lock being tried. Ultimately the bell rang.

Miss Havering stared at her in alarm when Meadows opened the door. "What's happened?" she demanded. "Has there been a burglary?"

"I'm afraid there's been an accident," Meadows said gently. "Come up to the Police Station with me and I'll explain."

"An accident?" the assistant repeated in alarm. "Who to? Mr Harvey?"

Mutely Meadows nodded.

Miss Havering flopped into the chair beside the counter. "I knew he'd fall down those stairs one day," she said. Putting her hands to her face, she burst into tears.

Chapter Eight

"Do us a favour and get us two cups of tea," Meadows asked PC Green.

He hesitated. 'Don't you treat me as your dogsbody, too,' his expression pleaded.

"We need one," Meadows added softly. "She does, at least." She nodded in Miss Havering's direction. "We'll be in the interview room. Could you let me know when DI Ambrose gets here?"

Green saw how pale both women were and reconsidered. "Right-oh!" he said and headed towards the teapot.

Sergeant Hurst called from the reception desk. "The DS rang a minute ago," he said, looking down at a scribbled message. "Tell Meadows to ask the assistant for all past competitors," he read aloud. "Does that mean anything to you?"

"I suppose he means the poetry competition," Meadows replied. She frowned in bewilderment. "Is that all he said?"

Once again Hurst looked at the note. "And if there's been any more packages," he went on.

"Will do," Meadows agreed. It sounded as though DS Winters was still pursuing the threats, even though one of the recipients was dead, or presumably, precisely because one of the recipients was dead.

Wishing she didn't still feel so sick, she showed the young assistant into the interview room. "Come and sit down," she invited. "I've asked for some tea. Have a good cry while you wait. You'll feel better."

Sitting uncomfortably at the table, Miss Havering leant forward onto her arms and wept softly. Meadows took out her notebook and waited in silence until PC Green appeared with two cups of very sweet tea. "Your Rosie Lee," he said, placing the cups in front of her.

"What?" Meadows demanded. "Oh I see. Tea." She shook her head at him but couldn't help smiling. The young assistant looked up and nodded thanks as Meadows put one of the cups in front of her. They both drank their tea in silence.

Finally, Meadows spoke. "I'm very sorry about Mr Harvey. I'm afraid I have to break some unpleasant news. He didn't fall down the stairs actually. One of the bookcases fell on him. It appears that he tripped and grabbed it for support."

"Oh, how horrible!" the assistant gasped and stuffed her handkerchief in her mouth. Eventually she recovered enough to ask "Which one?"

Meadows found the question strange, but shock often made people say strange things. "The one near the back room, just next to the pictures," she replied.

"That was the 'Criticism' shelf," Miss Havering said, catching her breath. "It wasn't fixed to anything. I did warn him!"

"There were some boxes on the floor," Meadows continued gently. "Mr Harvey may have stumbled on them. I'm really sorry. I appreciate how difficult this must be for you, but I need to ask you a few questions. There'll be an inquest and the Coroner will want details."

Mutely the young woman nodded, twisting the handkerchief in her hand.

"What time did you last see Mr Harvey?"

"At five thirty, when I left for my evening class."

"So you locked up behind you?" Meadows was scribbling her notes.

"No, Mr Harvey said he would lock up." A terrible thought crossed the assistant's mind. "Do you think someone came into the shop after I left?"

Meadows shrugged non-committally. "We'll look at all options," she replied. "I think my boss will want to continue investigating the threats Mr Harvey received. It'll be an open case. Do you know if he received any more?"

"No. He didn't mention any." Unable to continue, Miss Havering gulped and blew her nose. "I'm sorry."

"Take your time," Meadows reassured her. When the young woman was calmer, she tried again. "Have you any idea who might have sent the threats?" she asked.

"No. Do you think what's happened is connected with them?"

"My boss will want to explore every possibility," Meadows replied vaguely. "It looked like a dreadful accident to me, but it's not for me to say." She paused. "In case DS Winters asks, do you have the names of people who entered the competition in past years?"

Having something to concentrate on seemed to calm the young woman. "They should be listed. I think there's a folder in the filing cabinet. Would you like me to look for it?"

"If you'd be good enough," Meadows agreed, "when we're allowed back in the shop. It would make sense to check whether there were any regular entrants who might bear a grudge, known trouble-makers, that sort of thing."

She knew that was why DS Winters had given her the questions to ask. He wasn't sure Mr Harvey's death was an accident. And now she thought about it, nor was she. Something didn't feel right.

She was unsure what to say next. "Were all the other bookcases screwed to the wall?" she asked.

Miss Havering shook her head. "Some of them were arranged to make alcoves," she said. "Most of them backed onto another case or a wall, but a few were free standing."

"That doesn't sound very safe," Meadows remarked.

The assistant shuddered slightly, but she was beginning to recover her normal business-like manner. "It used to worry me," she admitted. "With not being very tall. I always had to use the steps if I needed a book from a top shelf. I was afraid of grabbing it and pulling the bookcase. I can see how..." Swallowing hard, she tried to find the right word. "How a dreadful accident could happen. Half the time Mr Harvey was in his own world. He wasn't a practical man. I used to hang the pictures for him, pack the parcels up, little jobs like that."

In acknowledgement, Meadows smiled ruefully. It all sounded perfectly straightforward: an impractical man who took risks without realising it, a pile of boxes and an insecure bookcase. So what was it that was niggling her? And clearly something was troubling DS Winters too.

Getting up, she offered Miss Havering her hand in sympathy. "I'll ask PC Green to see you safely home," she said. "When you're feeling better, I imagine one of my colleagues will want you to check nothing's missing at the shop, just to confirm there was no break-in. Would you mind giving me your address?"

"Of course not." The assistant wrote it on the notepad Meadows passed to her. "I share a room with another lodger," she explained.

"Marian's quite reliable. She'll take a message if I'm not there." She suddenly paused, as if fully realising the situation for the first time. "Mr Harvey has a brother in London," she continued. "We've met several times. I'd like to phone him myself and tell him what's happened. I'll have to ask him what to do about the shop too. It looks like my job's gone, doesn't it?" Once again her eyes filled with tears.

"See what Mr Harvey's brother says," Meadows advised. "I imagine he'll need help clearing out at least. I'll ask the Duty Sergeant if you can ring from here. You don't have a phone at your digs I suppose?"

"The landlady has one, but she doesn't let us use it."

Meadows smiled in understanding. "It's not the same as having your own place is it?" she remarked.

Then she led the way back to the reception desk. "Could Miss Havering call Mr Harvey's next of kin?" she asked Sergeant Hurst. "And then could PC Green take her home? She's had a nasty shock."

Miss Havering turned towards her. "I reminded Mr Harvey about those boxes," she said sadly. "He promised he'd unpack them later." Then she followed Sergeant Hurst into the front office.

DI Ambrose came down the stairs and called Meadows across. "I hear you've been at a fatality," he remarked softly. "Are you alright?"

"A bit shaky, but I'm fine thanks," Meadows replied, appreciating his concern.

"Anything you can add before I go down there myself?"

Meadows passed him her notes. "The assistant's just phoning the next of kin," she explained. "She's very upset, but sensible."

Glancing at the notes, Ambrose nodded. "Looks like a nasty accident," he agreed. "Go and take a bit of a break in the canteen. I'll tell the Desk Sergeant where you are."

He was half way down the corridor when Meadows realised what was bothering her. "Sir," she called.

Ambrose turned back.

"There was something funny about the light," she said.

Puzzled, Ambrose waited for her to explain. "What light?" he prompted.

"The electric light. Mr Harvey was probably using a torch. There was one near him on the floor. But the light came on fine when we entered the shop. So why did Mr Harvey need a torch?"

Ambrose nodded. "We'll have to check, won't we?" he acknowledged.

Afraid she had spoken out of turn, WPC Meadows flushed, but Ambrose merely smiled. "Sounds like a good question to me," he commented. "Now go and have a break."

The Forensics team hadn't yet arrived when Ambrose joined Winters at the shop. "Any sign of a break-in?" he asked immediately.

"No. The door doesn't show any sign of being forced and the safe's not been tampered with. It looks like a straightforward accident." Winters grimaced. "You can't see a lot of the victim though. He's buried under a pile of books." He led the way through the shop. "He's at the back, near the office."

They surveyed the chaos together. "Poor devil!" Ambrose remarked. He considered the remains of the bookcase, noting the label that was still attached to the top. "Suffocated by the weight of Criticism," he added drily.

"What?" Winters asked, then appreciated Ambrose's comment. "Wouldn't have stood a chance," he replied. "If the case had been properly secured, he'd have got a few bruises falling over the boxes, but nothing worse. As it was, he must have had books sliding from the shelves onto him. They'd have hit his head and arms. He was probably stunned well before the whole lot fell."

"But what was he doing blundering around here after the shop closed?" Ambrose asked. "And in the dark? Meadows reckons there was nothing wrong with the lights when you arrived yet he was probably using a torch. Why?"

Winters smiled grimly. "That young woman gets worrying," he said, only half joking. "We'll have to watch her or she'll be after our jobs." Then he was serious. "It's a good question," he admitted, pointing to the torch lying beside one of the boxes. "I've been asking it myself. Was there a power cut?"

"Young Green can check that," Ambrose agreed.

"When I went up to the flat, the lights were still on in the kitchen and lounge, but not the bedroom," Winters said thoughtfully. "Meadows didn't see a light there either, this morning. That suggests he came downstairs in the evening, before retiring for bed."

"Doc Halstead will give us the time of death," Ambrose agreed. "Evening makes sense, though. But why did he come down? Are you sure there's no sign of an intruder?"

"None that I can see," Winters repeated. "I've had a look in the office. It's a bit chaotic but no worse than when Meadows and I came earlier. The back windows are secure." They climbed carefully over the mound of books and shelving, and went into the back room and then the office together. "See what I mean?" Winters asked.

"Looks like he was sorting stock," Winters added, indicating the table, "bit of a messy worker. A thief could have had a good rummage and we'd be none the wiser, but the safe's still locked shut."

"It'll be worth Forensics dusting this handle," Ambrose suggested, examining the safe. It was an old-fashioned combination type and could possibly have proved too difficult for a thief to open.

The front door rattled. "That'll be them," Ambrose said.

Doc Halstead was his usual brisk self. "Morning. Bit chilly isn't it?" he remarked, as if he'd just arrived to read the meters. "Where's the Dearly Departed?"

"Through here," Winters directed. He led the way between bookcases, towards the back of the shop. "You'll have to dig, though."

They rounded the last alcove and stood in front of the fallen display.

"Lord! What a mess!" Murdoch said softly.

"I gather he was a bit of a bookworm," Doc Halstead remarked. He climbed over the mound. Then he climbed back. "I can't tell you anything at present, other than the obvious. That arm is definitely dead. I'll hang about while Charlie takes photographs. Then we'll have to unpick this lot and see what's underneath."

"Come into the back room while you wait," Ambrose suggested. He turned to Brooks. "Can you dust the door before we go in? Then do the office door and the safe inside. The deceased's dabs will be all over the place, and so will his assistant's, but there might be something fresh."

"Looks like a straightforward case," the Pathologist commented as they waited. "No one would survive that lot falling on them. It'll be multiple injuries. Unless of course there was an earlier cause."

After ten minutes or so, Murdoch tapped on the door with a gloved hand. "Photos done," he said. "Nothing much in the way of fingerprints; a lot of partials on the safe but they seem to be just one set, presumably the deceased. The office door is a pile of smudges and the front door's useless; far too many different hands have been on that. I've checked the till too. That has the same blurry prints as the safe, plus another set of smudges that'll be the assistant's I imagine. We'll need a sample of her prints for comparison. Brooks and I are about to move the top layer. I presume you'll want to watch."

Slowly, carefully, the two men moved the books and shattered shelves aside, until they reached the body. Robin Harvey was flat on his back, his legs bowed. His head was to one side, facing away from them, concealing his expression but Ambrose could imagine the terror in it. The blood-soaked floor and jacket sleeve showed how badly he had been hurt. One of the shelves had shattered as it fell and a splinter had torn through the jacket into his shoulder. Without immediate help Robin would inevitably have died. If he had called out, no one had heard him. On the corner of the block with only an empty building opposite, the shop was near none of the pubs or bus stops frequented at night. Few people would have been around to hear his calls.

Ambrose shuddered. He wouldn't have wished such a death on anyone, much less a man he had known and liked. A silence settled on the group, even Doc Halstead shaking his head. Then someone rattled the front door and the reflective moment was broken. Murdoch picked up his camera.

For several moments he worked carefully, photographing the scene from all angles. "All yours," he said to Doc Halstead when he'd finished. The Pathologist stepped forward and began his examination.

Finally, he looked up. "I'll know more after the postmortem," he said, "but I can't see any other injuries except those caused by the bookcase falling. Rigor Mortis is well established and lividity is decreasing. That puts the time of death as over twelve hours ago, but less than twenty-four. I'd estimate time of death as between seven and ten o'clock yesterday evening."

"That's consistent," Winters agreed. "We know he was still alive at five thirty, and he appears to have been in his flat for an hour or so after that, judging by the ashes in the grate."

Ambrose considered the position of the body. "Judging by his feet, I'd say he was facing away from the office when he tripped." Thoughtfully he noted the boxes lining the wall and the papers scattered over the floor near them. "What do you reckon, Winters? He came out of the office and tripped on one of the boxes, then slid on the papers and grabbed the bookcase?"

"Let's see how that works," Winters replied. Going back into the office, he came out, took two steps forward and then pretended to trip on a box. He didn't need to enact the next part of the move. He was genuinely sliding on the papers, towards Ambrose.

"Woah!" he said in alarm, catching at Charles Murdoch's shoulder to steady himself. "I'm glad you're not a rickety bookcase," he apologised afterwards.

"Well, that's pretty clear," Ambrose commented, taking care not to smile. "It looks like an accident waiting to happen. We'll appreciate your report of course," he added to Doc Halstead, "But unless you find something interesting, this looks like a case for the Coroner's Officer, not us."

The Pathologist nodded. "It's just possible he had a black-out that caused him to fall," he suggested, "or someone spiked his Ovaltine. I'll have a thorough look when he's on the slab."

The Forensics team began to pack away their kit. "Do you need anything else?" Murdoch asked. "We're pretty busy with that spate of burglaries in Old Chalk Heath."

Ambrose considered the scene for another moment, then picked up the torch lying near one of the bookcases. Frowning, he placed it in an evidence bag. "Nothing more you can help with," he said.

Chapter Nine

Monday 21st March

"Go through the files for the past eight years," Higgins said. "That's how long the competition's been going. They're arranged alphabetically, by decade. That's what DS Winters wants you to do." Higgins didn't mention that actually it was him who was meant to be reviewing the files.

PC Green sighed. "Cor lummy! It'll take me months," he protested.

"No it won't!" Higgins replied briskly. "You're only looking for matches to people who entered the competition. Didn't they teach you anything in London?"

Green was about to retort angrily but thought better of it.

Higgins led the way towards the back of the Station. "The filing cabinets are under the stairs," he continued. "We used to have a proper file cupboard, but that's full of equipment now."

There was a strong smell of paint. The corridor was being redecorated. After three decades of cigarette smoke and constant use, the original cream had become a depressing grey. "Mind where you put your feet, sirs," a young man in overalls called cheerfully. He had bright red hair that clashed with the yellow he was brushing up and down the wall. "Looks better, don't it?" he added.

"It will, when it's finished," Higgins admitted grudgingly. Anything that disrupted his normal pattern of work was unwelcome, and the decorators had been working around the Station for the past three weeks; far too long in his opinion for a small building. "We need to get through to the cabinets," he pointed out gruffly.

"No problem, sirs. Just mind where you put your feet." PC Green was dangerously near an open can of paint. "Wouldn't want your boots covered in yellow!" The man's face crinkled in amusement. He looked like a grown-up version of the kid who sits at the back of the class and makes everyone round him snigger.

With a harumph, Higgins led the way through to safety. Rows of filing cabinets lined the space under the stairs. "Here are the 1950s", he said, pulling a drawer open. Green had a brief vision of rationing and teddy boys and the Queen's Coronation all jammed into a drawer. "You can sit at the table to look through the files," Higgins was continuing. "One at a time. We don't want them muddled up." He indicated an office table and chair near the window. Both looked particularly uncomfortable.

Seeing the young PC's expression, Higgins relented. He'd spent too many hours at that table himself. "Just look at the list of competitors and see if we have a file for the same name," he advised. "If you find a match, come to the front desk and tell me the name. If it's one of the local ne'er-do-wells, I'll know the file backwards. That'll save you reading it."

"Righto!" Green agreed, though he felt anything but cheerful inside.

Left with only the smell of paint and the decorators' distant murmur, he started to work. To his surprise he found he rather enjoyed the job. The files were all neatly arranged, some annotated in Higgins' writing. PC Green began to understand why the older officer was nick-named 'Memory Man'. He had obviously spent years at the Station, since before the War in fact, and had a detailed knowledge of the local community. Victim and offender, foolish and cunning, they were all in his files, carefully noted for future reference. Though Green's task was just to look for similar names, he found himself becoming absorbed in several of the cases. He had to remind himself that he must prove he could do a routine job quickly and correctly, or he would be in trouble again.

By the time an hour had passed, he had found nothing relevant to report, though plenty of interest. Only one of the competitors had committed an offence: driving a motorcar without a licence. While Mr Timothy Billing might think the law did not apply to poetic geniuses, he didn't sound like the sort to send death threats.

Green was about to report his negative finding when DI Ambrose passed him, heading into the Station from the car park. "Having fun?" he asked.

"Sort of, yes," Green replied, speaking carefully. "The DS asked me to look for matches between your files and the competition lists. It's given me a bit of a feel for the patch, sir, so yes, I've quite enjoyed it." He began to put away the last batch of files, expecting his senior officer to walk on.

Instead, DI Ambrose stood thoughtfully, looking down at the lists Green had spread out on the table. "Did you find any?" he asked.

"Only one, sir, and he doesn't sound the loony type. Besides, he got a Highly Commended in the competition five years ago. I wouldn't have thought he'd want to cause any trouble."

"Never underestimate 'loonyness'," Ambrose advised. "It can lurk in the mildest of people. Still, you're probably right. I'd also bet we're not looking for a local, so even if they have prior convictions their name won't be in our files. I suggest you try another tack. Whoever sent those packets has been simmering for a long time. Go through the competition lists, checking for people who entered four or five times, but never got even on to the long list." He paused, thinking of his own reasons for entering last year. "They might be using the competition as an inspiration," he admitted, "but otherwise most normal people would give up after three times. To keep shelling out the entry fee they must think they're good, and the judges' final choice is wrong. That can lead to a lot of resentment."

"Yes," PC Green agreed thoughtfully. "Righto! I'll tell PC Higgins what I'm doing."

"There's another little job you might do," Ambrose added. "Pop down to Curiosity Corner and draw me a map of the main rooms and the way through, where the stairs to the victim's rooms go from, that sort of thing. The place is a rabbit warren. I can't remember what's where. Nothing fancy. Just an outline with some labels."

"Yes sir!" Green agreed.

For another hour, he went through the competition lists again. Initially he widened his net, looking for people who had entered repeatedly but not even got onto the 'maybe' list. That soon made his head spin, and he returned to DI Ambrose's narrower brief. It was like doing a gigantic crossword puzzle. Starting with the current year, he worked backwards, writing down any repeated names. Some of this year's entrants could be eliminated straight away. They were newcomers. Others had entered for a couple of years but only recently. A third group turned up intermittently, but not four times. Even so, he kept a note of their names in case they needed to be investigated later.

Finally, he whittled his list down to six people who had entered the competition four or five times without success, including this year. With a feeling of satisfaction, he presented his list to Higgins.

"Will this be ok?" he asked, suddenly nervous. He did his best to 'talk Queen's English' as DI Ambrose had advised, but it slowed him down. He felt as though he was thinking in a foreign language.

"Adrian Templar, Janice Flowers, Mrs Kenneth (Dolly) Hughes, Benjamin Carstairs, Jennie Arton and Simon Yates," Higgins read aloud. "Never heard of any of them."

"None of them are from Chalk Heath," Green explained. "Mrs Hughes is from Jenners Park. She's the nearest."

"Suspect number one I'd say," Higgins commented. "She could pop into the shop and find out about the judges. Whoever sent those packets knew their addresses. Good work."

His face going red at the unexpected praise, Green went on, "I got some gen from the judge's comments. Miss Hodgkiss put 'Can't stand rhyming couplets,' beside the Carstairs geezer, that sort of thing. The other two quite liked him. Sounds like they argy-bargied a lot this year."

"Do we have addresses?" Higgins asked, looking through Green's notes.

"Only for this year. The assistant was going to write to 'em all. Apparently that's why half of 'em enter. They get tips."

Higgins smiled drily. "I doubt if they'll like the Hon Madge's comments," he replied. "Now if *she'd* been under a bookcase, I wouldn't have raised an eyebrow."

"Do you think Mr Harvey was done away with?" Green asked in surprise.

"Not for me to say. Nor for you," Higgins warned. "It looks like an accident, but the DI's not convinced. You can tell. Watch this space."

"He seems sharp," Green remarked.

"He's one of the brightest in the Force," Higgins replied warmly. "Spots things the rest have missed. He's often asked to help other divisions. Winters is no fool either. Chalk Heath has one of the best clear-up rates in the country. It'll be a crime if we're amalgamated with Jenners Park. Being a small Force doesn't mean you're inferior. Learn all you can while you're here, lad. Goodness knows where we'll all be shunted next year."

Green was surprised at the older man's vehemence. It was clearly something he felt very strongly about. Until then, Green had assumed that if the Royal Commission recommended reducing the number of small divisions, it would be progress, a sensible move. Now he wasn't so sure. "You like the DI then?" he replied uncertainly.

"He has his peculiarities, don't they all? But he's always fair. I wouldn't be surprised if he gave you a chance when others wouldn't; you being a Londoner and him serving in the Met."

"You don't say!" Green replied in surprise. "When?"

"During the War."

Green's respect for his new boss increased massively. "He'll have had a rough time," he said reflectively. "My uncle was in the Met then. He had some horrible stories about the blitz: pulling people out of burning buildings, digging out kiddies and so on. Mum said he never told us the half of it."

"No, and you won't get the DI talking either. I've heard he had to save his own wife. The Maternity Home she was in was bombed. But you won't hear it from him. Don't underestimate us older blokes." The last remark was made with a slight smile. Higgins' mood was improving. It had been a quiet morning, and his daughter would be arriving from Sheffield later that day. He always enjoyed her visits.

PC Green felt encouraged enough to take a risk. "Would you mind me asking you something?" he replied.

"Depends what it is. If it's 'Will you buy me a beer?' forget it."

Green smiled and shook his head. "I don't drink," he said. "I saw what that did to our old Pot." He flushed. "I mean our old Pot and Pan, me Old Man, you know, my Dad. No. I was hoping you'd tell me about the chap who left before I came. Everyone's comparing me with him, only I'm just a rookie."

"He started as a rookie too," Higgins pointed out, quite kindly. The new lad was beginning to intrigue him. "And he left under a bit of a cloud."

"I asked WPC Meadows why, but she was cagey."

"She would be. They were good mates." Frowning, Higgins paused. "Well," he continued grudgingly, "you might as well hear it from me as at the 'Copper Kettle'. There was an attack at the theatre. Greg fell in love with one of the witnesses. As if that wasn't bad enough, she was married. This is a small town and there was a lot of chatter. He and Kathy are happily married now, but they got fed up with the curtains twitching. They wanted a fresh start." Shaking his head, Higgins' tone became almost avuncular. "There's a lesson for you there, lad. Don't let your heart rule your head. It doesn't do your career any good."

PC Green was about to reply that there wasn't much danger of that, when there was a commotion at the door, followed by a strong smell of body odour. "Gis us a cell for the night," a voice pleaded. "It's raining cats and dogs."

Higgins sighed. "You know we can't give you a bed, Dougie," he called.

"Then I'll chuck a brick through your window," the tramp threatened. "If I'm drunk and disorderly, you'll have to put me in a cell." Dishevelled and dirty, he could have been anything between forty and seventy. He had a pronounced Irish accent, and smelt of strong whiskey, yet there was something military in his bearing. A serviceman who'd fallen on hard times, Green guessed.

"Go and fetch the DS," Higgins whispered. "Tell him Dougie's here again."

Green hesitated, not sure what to do. "Winters is the only one who can persuade him to go quietly," Higgins explained. "Fellow countryman I suppose. I think he slips him a few coins but don't say I told you so."

Persuading Dougie to leave quietly took the best part of the next hour. When it was quiet again, PC Green left to do the drawing of Curiosity Corner, and WPC Meadows returned from her tea break. To her surprise, Higgins greeted her with, "The boss wants to see you. He's in his office."

For a moment she hesitated, assuming she'd done something wrong. Then she told herself DI Ambrose must need her to interview a woman, or perhaps look after a lost child.

"Nothing to worry about," Ambrose confirmed as she entered. "I just wanted to thank you for nursing our young rookie."

"He seemed a bit lost, that's all," Meadows said awkwardly.

"Be honest. He had a permanent cloud over him. At least he smiles occasionally now. Do you think you could cope with taking him out on an interview? If I tell him to keep his mouth shut he shouldn't alarm people too much."

"The experience would do him good," Meadows agreed cautiously. "Where do you want us to go?"

"Jenners Park. A Mrs Kenneth Hughes looks like a prime suspect for sending the packets. She's persistently failed to get onto the competition short list, despite entering every year. It would have been easy for her to come over here and find out about the judges. I'd like you to visit her with Green, and see what she says. I've cleared it with

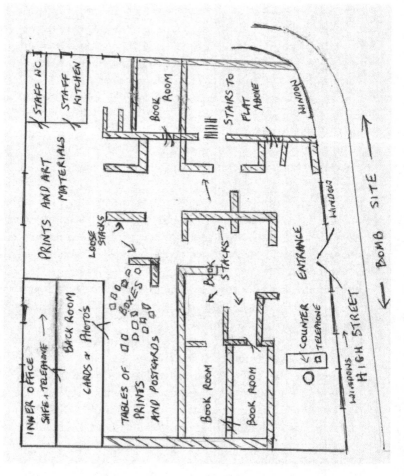

PC Green's map of the main rooms at Curiosity corner

Jenners Park. They're short staffed so they won't bother sending someone along with you."

"Is she really called Kenneth?" Meadows asked, writing down the name.

Ambrose laughed. "I presume that's her husband's name. According to her entry form, she writes as Dolly Hughes. We might be able to clear this case up quickly. Higgins is busy. Green can drive you over. I gather he's quite a good driver. Learnt when he was about twelve on his father's van."

PC Green was indeed a good driver, despite saying he was 'cream crackered' after going through so many lists and walking to Curiosity Corner. It took him a few minutes to get used to the cumbersome Hillman but Meadows soon felt more at ease with him than with PC Higgins. The older officer had a tendency to crash the gears. By now she knew the way through Jenners Park town centre and could give directions easily.

"Bit of a dump isn't it?" Green commented as they passed yet another line of semi-detached boxes lining yet another busy road.

"Don't you mean Ten Ounce Rump?" Meadows teased, remembering their earlier conversation. "I wouldn't want to live here," she agreed. "I used to long to when I was a kid. We'd come on the bus for the bright lights. We were ever so daring: trying on hats in the posh shops and giggling in the milk bar. It was much more exciting than hanging around the gas show rooms at home."

Green laughed. "Me and me ol' Chinas used to meet round the back of the market," he admitted. "It always stank of dead cabbage."

"Chinas?"

"Sorry, China Plates, me mates. If we were really going it, we'd hitch a lift to Soho and oggle the girls." He shook his head at a memory. "Until one of them invited us in."

"And?" Meadows prompted in amusement.

"We ran a mile."

Laughing, Meadows looked at the map she'd drawn before they left. "Turn right here," she said. "Then first left. We need Foxwood Crescent." They were entering a better part of Jenners Park: wider roads, and houses that had separate garages and well-kept front gardens. "Nice," Meadows commented. "I've not been down here before."

Green drove slowly down a broad suburban avenue lined with detached houses. Then he turned into a leafy crescent. The houses here were even larger and set back from the road. One had fancy gates with concrete pineapples on the posts, thought they looked more like cabbages, Green said. Another had gold balls arranged along a metal fence. The whole street gave off the scent of money and respectability. Looking for Mrs Hughes' house, Green tried to find a number, without success. Nobody seemed to want to be identified. He was reduced to turning in a driveway and going back to the only number they could see. From there they counted each house: twenty-three, twenty-five, twenty-seven and on. They needed number sixty-seven. It was a slow process.

"Pity the poor postman!" Meadows said. "I suppose you're meant to know who lives where, without asking."

Even the smaller houses looked expensive. "Can't imagine a poet living here," Green commented.

"So poets should starve in garrets?" Meadows teased. She glanced at the carefully mowed lawns and clipped hedges, all apparently regulation height. "Nah. I reckon this place is stuffed with poets. It'd drive you to write, even if you didn't already. How else would you keep sane?"

They found sixty-seven, an imposing detached residence with mock-tudor gables. "What do you reckon the noble Kenneth does?" Meadows asked. "Bank Manager or Accountant perhaps? A teacher couldn't afford this. I know I never could!"

Green parked round the corner, as Mrs Hughes had asked on the phone, begged even. She was already waiting for them at the door as they walked up the garden path. As soon as they reached the porch, she virtually bundled them inside.

"I'm sorry," she apologised as they stood awkwardly together in the hallway. "But my neighbour opposite was watching. Why did you have to come in uniform? I'll be the talk of the Bridge Club. I'll have to invent some story to satisfy them."

"You could say someone tried your door and we came to investigate," Meadows suggested.

"Yes. That would work," Mrs Hughes agreed in relief. "They're all worried about burglars. Why have you come, anyway? The officer who phoned wouldn't say. Just said you wanted to talk to me."

"May we come in?" Meadows asked. "Then we can explain."

"Oh yes," Mrs Hughes apologised. "Do come into the lounge." Fortyish, small and dumpy, and dressed in a navy pencil-pleat skirt with pink twin set and sensible navy shoes, she didn't fit Meadows' image of a mad poet. There was no chunky jewellery or 'interesting' hair; no similarity to the photographs of Edith Sitwell that Meadows had seen. This woman looked more like a receptionist at the local doctor's.

She led the way into a coldly formal front room. "Do sit down," she invited, though she herself remained standing awkwardly beside the artificial flowers that filled the empty fireplace. "I can't think what you can have to say to me. Has somebody died? The Police never call round here, unless it's bad news."

"It's not bad news," Meadows reassured her. "We just want to talk to you a few questions."

"What about?"

"You enter the Bird Books poetry competitions regularly I believe. Is that right?"

Mrs Hughes started at Meadows in amazement. "You've come all this way to talk about a poetry competition?" she asked, her voice rising.

"It isn't as trivial as it sounds," Meadows replied. "I am right in saying you enter the competition most years?"

"Yes. What if I do? There's no law against it." Mrs Hughes snorted slightly. "I know this country's going to the dogs but I didn't think poetry was illegal yet."

"Someone has been sending threatening packages to the judges of the competition," Meadows continued sternly. "We think it could be a contestant who's angry at being passed over. You haven't had any luck yourself, have you?"

Mrs Hughes stared at Meadows in disbelief. "You think I might have sent the packages?" she asked.

"Perhaps. The competition clearly matters a lot to you."

"Rubbish!" Mrs Hughes retorted, startling them both. "Sorry. I didn't mean to shout," she apologised immediately afterwards. "It's such a silly suggestion though. I don't care tuppence about the competition. I only enter because my husband likes me to. He pays my entry fee. I do it to please him."

"Why? If it doesn't matter to you?" Meadows asked, thoroughly confused. "Please explain."

Mrs Hughes sat down at last. For a moment she looked out of the window, beyond the net curtains, then she turned to them defiantly, as if prepared to meet any challenge. "My husband would like me to be a nice respectable poetess," she said and there was a bitter edge to her voice. "But I know I'm not particularly talented that way. It's prose I'm gifted for." She hesitated. "He knew what I wrote when he married me, thought it exciting. Now it wouldn't help his career. So I write under another name and don't tell him. I make quite a lot of money out of it too, though I let him think I have private means. So you see I don't need Bird Books' prize money, or their promise of publication. Fifty pounds is nothing to what I can earn."

"That's..." Meadows began. She wanted to say 'impressive,' but decided she should remain neutral. "What name do you write under?" she asked instead.

"Maddy Simone. You won't have heard of me."

Meadows was about to blurt out, 'Oh, but I have!' before she checked herself. "Do you write romances then?" she asked innocently.

"I suppose you could call them that. They're very popular. So you see I would have no reason whatsoever to send threatening letters to the judges of a provincial poetry competition. I show my husband the nice things they say about my poems. They always try to be kind and he tells his colleagues that I have a lovely hobby."

There was little point in continuing the interview. Only waiting until PC Green had finished writing up his notes, Meadows declined the offer of a cup of tea. Thanking Mrs Hughes, she led the way back to the car.

As soon as they were safely back in the car, Meadows couldn't hold her laughter any longer. "Oh that's priceless!" she hooted. Green stared at her in bewilderment.

"Maddy Simone writes the sort of book you pass round in brown paper," Meadows explained, still laughing. "I know because my kid sister had one hidden in her satchel last week. Dad went bananas. She'd got it from a boy at school. He was charging sixpence a read. He must have paid for the book several times over. Dad went flaming mad up to the school. Of course the Head said he didn't know anything about it."

PC Green began to laugh too. "You mean that frumpy little woman writes..." He couldn't find the right word.

Meadows finished the sentence for him. "Steamy novels. Yep. So steamy you could drive a train with them, only I don't think her characters are interested in trains."

"What was the book called?" Green asked.

"*Love under the Desert Moon.* Why? Are you thinking of borrowing it?" Once again Meadows laughed. "I reckon we can strike Mrs Kenneth Hughes off the suspect list."

Chapter Ten

Wednesday 23rd March

"It gets stranger," Ambrose remarked, pushing PC Green's notes across the table. "Neither the Electricity Board nor the neighbours have any memory of a power cut that night."

"Could it have been a localised fault?" DS Winters asked, frowning. "A loose connection?"

"We'll get an electrician to check properly. Our usual Sparks might like the extra work. Hurst couldn't find anything."

"If it's an intermittent fault he probably wouldn't," Winters pointed out. "I'm running out of other possibilities."

"Other than the obvious," Ambrose pointed out.

"That the victim went downstairs in the dark and didn't switch the lights on?" Winters asked. "Bit of a daft thing to do in that warren of a place. Unless he was trying not to disturb someone?"

"My thought exactly," Ambrose replied, sighing. "But there are no stray fingerprints, the door was safely locked, and the assistant's sure nothing was taken. We can get her to check again, but she had a good look the day after. By the way, what's happening about the shop? It had an 'open' sign on the door when I passed this morning."

Getting up, Winters stretched his back. He'd had another bad night with little Caitlin crying on and off for hours, and he was stiff after sitting so long on an uncomfortable chair. The smell of paint was becoming sickly too. "According to the 'Copper Kettle', the assistant's keeping it going," he explained. "Mr Harvey's brother likes the idea of running a bookshop better than being in insurance. He's given in his notice and plans to move to Chalk Heath. It's going to take him a few

72

months, so Miss Havering will hold the fort till then. Goodness knows how she'll cope, but at least she'll keep her job."

"She'll cope very well," Ambrose replied, smiling. "I got the impression she was doing the bulk of the business stuff even while Robin Harvey was alive. He mostly ran the competitions, and enjoyed himself spotting rare books at jumble sales."

"Doreen didn't know what was happening about the competition," Winters continued. "Other than that the hall's still booked for the Prize Giving."

"I presume the Hon Madge and the Major will carry on regardless," Ambrose agreed. "Talking of which, PC Higgins has traced the rest of the suspects. Two of them can be struck off." Pushing a list towards Winters, he indicated Jennifer Arton and Simon Yates. "Mrs Arton died a month after submitting her poem, of natural causes so nothing suspicious there. She *was* ninety-four. And Mr Yates is in an old people's home. He's very unlikely to have posted the packets. He's confined to a wheelchair."

"He could have asked one of the nurses to post them," Winters pointed out. "Or a relative."

"Unlikely. The Matron was certain he'd never threaten anyone. Said he's 'a lovely old stick' and all the staff are very fond of him, even if he is a bit odd, sitting writing poetry in the corner."

"It's probably more interesting than listening to the old biddies round him," Winters agreed. Trying to rub his back without being noticed, he failed, and grimaced in apology.

"These chairs are like medieval torture devices," Ambrose agreed. "And that smell of paint's getting on my nerves. Did you get a tea break this morning?"

Winters shook his head. He'd been sorting through the active cases ready for their meeting, and found several threads that needed tying up. Besides, even the canteen had 'wet paint' signs on the doors.

"Nor did I," Ambrose agreed. "At the rate we're going, we won't get a break all afternoon. I don't fancy climbing over paint tins in any case. Let's adjourn to the 'Copper Kettle'. We can finish the review over there. Hurst can cover for half an hour."

With a sigh of relief, Winters gathered up the stack of files. "Sounds like an excellent idea," he agreed. "If we ask Doreen to see no one disturbs us, no one will. They wouldn't dare."

Avoiding a step ladder, he followed Ambrose down the corridor.

It was raining outside, a fine, cold drizzle that looked like mist from inside, and lashed into their faces as soon as they stepped from the porch. In the few moments it took to hurry from from the Station and down the street, they were soaked.

A warm smell of bacon and cigarette smoke welcomed them as soon as Ambrose opened the 'Copper Kettle' door. The café was half empty, the rain keeping the usual tea and bun customers away. Shaking themselves dry, Ambrose and Winters crossed to the table near the far window and rescued their files, laying them out between them. Fortunately the papers were all still dry.

Doreen Stanley was standing beside them in seconds. "Afternoon Gentlemen," she said with her usual smile. Her long dark hair was wrapped round with a headscarf like a turban, and her apron was as crisp and clean as ever. Over her shoulder, Winters could see Les, her husband, shaking a sieve above a chip pan with one hand and spearing sausages with the other. It might be three o'oclock in the afternoon, but someone had ordered sausage and chips and a plateful of bread and butter.

"Turned out nasty, hasn't it?" Doreen remarked. "Spring can't seem to get started this year. Can I get you a cup of tea and some biscuits while you warm up?"

"Please," Ambrose asked. "We're fleeing the decorators for half an hour. Can you make sure no one disturbs us?"

"Of course. It's quiet today any way. Not good for business. Two sugars isn't it?" Smiling again, Mrs Stanley turned to see to their order.

The other customers were a good way away. If Winters and Ambrose spoke quietly, their conversation wouldn't be overheard. By now they had worked together so many times, when there were no other colleagues present they could relax. "I wish those decorators would hurry up," Ambrose admitted, hanging his jacket over a spare chair. "I suppose the place needed doing but they seem to have been around for weeks."

"Only three," Winters pointed out. "It just seems longer. I can't work out why they've been sent in the first place. What's the point in tarting the building up if we might be closed by next year?"

Ambrose frowned. "I don't think an Interim Report can close anything down," he said, more confidently than he felt. "And even when they make up their minds what to do, we're too busy to close. There'll have to be a 'nick' in Chalk Heath. You couldn't run everything from a central station in Jenners Park."

"You reckon you and I'll be left here?" Winters asked, at last voicing the worry that had been gnawing at him for a month. With a new house in Chalk Heath and Bridget and Patrick doing well at school, the prospect of a move made him nervous. It appalled his wife. Though Francesca didn't like Chalk Heath (as she said, how could she, compared to Italy?) she had begun to settle. It had been a hard ten years and she couldn't face the prospect of starting again somewhere else.

"I doubt if it'll affect us much," Ambrose assured him. "It'll be the Chief who'll feel it most. If they do amalgamate Divisions, there'll be a game of musical chairs for the top posts. He might not win. Fortunately he can't be that far off retirement."

"I can't see a pension keeping Mrs Mac in hats," Winters commented.

Ambrose laughed. "She can probably keep them both in the manner to which they're accustomed," he commented.

Their tea and biscuits had arrived and they drank reflectively. "From what Mary tells me, Mac's wife was doing nicely even before she married him," Ambrose added. "She seems to have inherited money from her first husband. Mary reckons he was a wealthy farmer. Called Fairbrush or something like that. Mac landed himself quite a catch, it seems, rather than the other way around."

To their embarrassment Mrs McEwan herself suddenly passed the window beside them. Seeing them through the glass she smiled briefly, then hurried on, her umbrella lowered against the rain. In a smart plastic raincoat and a pair of trim slacks, she looked elegant even on a grey day.

"I hope she can't lip-read," Ambrose remarked afterwards.

"I don't think we were saying anything uncomplimentary," Winters replied uncertainly. He thought for a minute. "Just about her first husband." Then he laughed. "Wherever Mac found her, she's still quite a stunner, isn't she?"

"So's your Missus."

"That's one description I can't ever see fitting my Fran," Winters admitted. "She'd have a fit if I called her The Missus. But, yes, she's still beautiful, in my eyes at least. Although I can't see her ever wearing trousers!"

It was time to get back to work. Pushing their cups safely aside they returned to the 'Active Cases' file, picking up again on the threatening packets. It wasn't actually an open murder case, but Ambrose wasn't willing to write Robin Harvey's death off as an accident just yet.

"So that's three eliminated from our list," he began. "One dead, one safely stuck in a nursing home and one writer of steamy novels who doesn't need the cash or publicity." He laughed again at Meadows' report of her interview with Mrs Hughes. "We also have a report about Mr Benjamin Carstairs." He glanced at Bob Hurst's notes from a telephone call that morning. "Pickering Station sent an officer round to talk to the fellow last night. He had his ears bent for an hour, in rhyming couplets no less. I quote PC Gray: 'It might have been a good use of time if you like long comic poems in a Lincolnshire accent, but I don't!'"

"I suspect the judges didn't either," Winters remarked. "Why a Lincolnshire accent when Carstairs lives in Yorkshire? Or is that a silly question?"

"Sounds like a sensible one to me. Maybe he came from Lincolnshire originally? Or perhaps it's easier to rhyme? Whatever his reasons, it doesn't look as though Mr Carstairs is our man, unless he has a network of accomplices all over the country. He hasn't been out of Pickering for the past month."

"He has an alibi?" Winters asked. He could feel his mouth twitching. He couldn't take this talk of malevolent poets seriously.

"Teaches violin, including Saturdays. Had pupils on all the days the parcels were posted. Got the teaching notes to prove it. "

"And Sundays?"

"Plays the organ in the local church. Didn't miss a service. Says the choirboys will vouch for him. Apparently he's very popular."

"Must be the Lincolnshire accent," Winters replied drily. "What about the other three?"

"We're waiting on full reports for them. Shouldn't be long for Adrian Templar. The Desk Sergeant at Birmingham recognised his name immediately. Called him 'the Bearded Bard.' Apparently they'd just had a run-in with him over complaints from the neighbours. He's been a naughty boy, playing Wagner full pelt at ten o'clock at night. Claims it gives him inspiration. It wasn't the first time either, though he usually prefers Beethoven I gather."

Winters laughed again. "Perhaps it was Beethoven's fault he didn't win the poetry competition. Not enough inspiration!"

Ambrose laughed too.

"On a different tack completely," Winters continued, "we can close this case." He was more serious now, indicating a bulky folder labelled 'Katherine Ibbotson'. "She's been found safe and well in London, sharing a bed-sit near Victoria with her boyfriend."

"Boyfriend?" Ambrose repeated in surprise. He knew the parents. They'd told him nothing about a boyfriend. If they had, there was no way Ambrose would have classed the case as a possible murder.

"He's a Jenners Park lad," Winters explained, "so we didn't link the two missing persons cases until last week. Both sets of parents are going up to London to bring their offspring back."

"If they don't scarper again first," Ambrose commented. "I hope someone keeps them under lock and key until then."

"They're both under age, so they'll be handed over to Social Services." Winters also knew the Ibbotson family. He couldn't bring himself to think of the worry they'd been going through, or their shame when their daughter was brought back home. They wouldn't be able to show their faces at church for months, if ever.

"Talking of runaways, any news of the two lads from Moorlands?" Ambrose asked. Though there was no file on them in Winters' pile, he liked to keep abreast of what was happening in his patch.

"Nothing. It looks as though they've moved on, though there are still reports of milk and loaves going missing from steps. Could be the paperboys of course, but the lads might be still around. Don't know where though. We've searched all the usual places and a few more besides."

They needed to go back to the Station. Gathering up the files, they called at the counter for a quick thanks to Doreen and a joke with Les, then they went out into the rain again.

As soon as they entered the Station, Sgt Hurst called to them. "Two more reports on your poets," he said, suppressing a grin.

"Give me the gist," Ambrose asked. "I'm a bit sick of poetry."

Bob Hurst looked down at the papers that had just arrived in the post. 'The Bearded Bard denies all knowledge of any packages," he began. "Says he only submits to the competition to give himself a deadline and a bit of stimulus. Called it 'His Muse', whatever that means. He got quite huffy apparently, said he doesn't need a small publisher based in the provinces, so why would he threaten the judges? He has much bigger fish to fry. Sounds like sour grapes, but it may be true. He's doing well apparently, making quite a name for himself. Has lots of invites to do readings and give talks, even gets paid for his poems. The local paper publishes him quite often."

"OK. We'll discount him," Ambrose decided.

"The second one looks more promising," Sgt Hurst continued.

"Who's that?"

"A Miss Janice Flowers. Apparently Emily Brontë dictates to her."

"What?" Winters asked in bewilderment.

"That's what she said when interviewed. She sits down and Emily Brontë dictates poems to her. She doesn't need to do anything to them. They come to her perfectly formed."

"You're having me on!" Ambrose objected.

"Afraid not, Sir. Miss Flowers was quite clear on the matter. The officer who interviewed her didn't know whether to laugh or cry. He's added a note that the woman seemed perfectly rational about everything else, except the Brontës. Apparently she adores their novels and feels she has some direct communion with the family. Sort of spiritualist stuff I suppose. Said she's a descendant, even if they're not actually related."

Ambrose was less inclined to laugh. Taking the two reports, he beckoned Winters into his office. "If you adored some writer, and felt you were their spiritual descendant, and then somebody criticised you for writing like them," he asked, "how would you feel?"

"A bit miffed. Especially if they kept criticising."

"Precisely. Where does Miss Flowers live?"

Winters scanned through the report. "Bath. It wouldn't be difficult to get to Bristol from there. Don't know about Ludlow. Maybe there's a train."

Frowning, Ambrose fetched a road atlas from the shelf and considered the relationship between Bath, Bristol and Ludlow. "She'd have to have a contact in Chalk Heath who told her the judge's addresses, maybe perfectly innocently," he mused. "I think we need to talk to Miss Flowers ourselves. I wonder if she'd come here of her own free will? That'd be a lot easier than involving Bath, or going down there to interview her."

"She might like a trip to Chalk Heath if she thought the competition was paying for it," Winters suggested. "Perhaps you could persuade the Hon Madge to invite her?"

"I'd rather ask the Major," Ambrose admitted, "But it would look better coming from a woman." He put the map book back on the shelf. "We may be getting somewhere," he added hopefully.

"Who was Emily Brontë, by the way?" Winters asked. "Was she the one who wrote *Wuthering Heights*? We did that at school, until the nuns realised it was a bit racey, all that heavy breathing on the moors."

"Well, the hills are steep round there," Ambrose agreed drily. "I'll bet your nuns had a good read in the cloisters afterwards."

Chapter Eleven

Thursday 24th March

The room was cold as Meadows entered. It was early evening and raining. While the gas fire spluttered into life, she drew the curtains across the bay window. Then she changed out of her wet uniform and hung it on the kitchen door to dry. She was tired after her shift and would have liked to go to bed for an hour or so, but she needed to cook herself a meal first. Drying her hair on a towel, she went into the kitchenette.

Her hands were stiff after the long cycle ride up hill and she dropped a teaspoon. Sighing, she bent to pick the spoon up. It had been an early start and she had worked overtime too. Sgt Hurst had asked her to interview a young woman arrested for shoplifting at the new Woolworths store. By the time she had finished processing that case, the Manager was calling for assistance after catching a lad helping himself to sweets. So instead of her shift ending, it had lasted another two hours while she gave the boy a good talking to, and then took him home, where his parents probably gave him a clip round the ear after she left.

She had some sympathy for both offenders, however. The new Woolworths was too tempting. If shops laid their goods out, to be picked up and paid for a long way away, they shouldn't be surprised if some of their customers decided not to bother queuing at the till.

Meadows filled the kettle and put it to boil on the ring. She wondered what to do about her evening meal. For the past three days she hadn't had time to shop. At her last digs in Duncan Road she would have popped out to the local chippie. Here though, it was a good half mile down to the shops and in pouring rain. Besides, she wasn't sure she was allowed to bring fish and chips back to her rooms. Mrs McEwan's rules stated clearly 'No strong cooking smells please' and 'No cooking after ten o'clock.' There was a pretty paragraph at the beginning of the rental agreement about living in harmony with other residents, but to Meadows, it felt like being at school again.

She would far rather have stayed where she was, but that was impossible. Immediately after she returned from a shift and found a 'For Sale' notice outside the house, she had begun searching for somewhere else. Every time she saw an advert for a vacant bed-sit, she rushed round as soon as she could, only to find it had been let. She was lucky. She had the Police Accommodation Department and the Chief's wife to help. Others didn't. She often thought of the couple with a baby she met on several viewings, either just leaving or arriving. She hoped they'd found something in the end.

Peering into the kitchen cupboard, Meadows examined the contents of her larder. An opened packet of macaroni was in danger of spilling on the floor, but she had no cheese to go with it. Apart from some butter in a dish, all she could see otherwise were the remains of a loaf left from breakfast, a jar of Bovril, a tin of pilchards, some blackcurrant jam her mother had made, and a packet of dried mashed potato. That was it. Then she remembered there was also a tin of peaches right at the back. She'd been saving that in case her parents came to see her new home. Now, after getting soaked and tired-out, she decided she needed a treat herself.

The opener was blunt and Meadows had to hammer it into the tin with a shoe before she could get to the pilchards. That was something else she needed to buy, she thought wearily – one of those openers with a handle you could turn. The household stall in the market should have some. Then she toasted two slices of bread under the grill and spread the pilchards on top of them. 'At least the cooker works here,' she thought with relief, not like that ancient gas stove at her last place. She'd risked her eyebrows every time she lit the jets. In fact, she had to admit that a lot of things were more modern at Maple View.

As she ate, Meadows felt better. She looked round her new flat with pleasure. It really was beginning to look very nice. The rooms were large and airy, the moulding around the ceilings suggesting the house had once been a fine gentleman's residence. The cushions she had bought at the market gave a splash of colour to the lounge, and the cover her mother had passed on to her looked good on the settee. It was a pity she was so near the Gentlemen's bathroom, especially when the Ladies' was right the other end of the corridor. Still the walls were thick and the sound of running water rarely bothered her. It was a bit irritating that the pipes in the Gents' made a drip-drip sound for a good hour after someone had a bath, but fortunately she couldn't hear it in her bedroom, only in her lounge. Miss Huddlestone's radio annoyed her sometimes, as it was beginning to do now, but generally she found it easier to sleep at Maple View during the day than at Duncan Road. There was always a lot of noise outside her window there.

By the time she'd eaten the pilchards on toast, and devoured the whole tin of peaches with a spoonful of condensed milk, Meadows had revived. She no longer felt like going to bed.

There was nothing good on the radio yet, so she decided to do an hour's studying. Picking up her police manual, she settled into the arm chair near the gas fire. She was still weak on the law regarding soliciting. Not that they had many prostitutes in Chalk Heath. She only knew of three: a couple of 'bottle-blond' women who hung around the bus depot at night, and a well-dressed woman who seemed to operate out of the Hotel. But if Chalk Heath was amalgamated with Jenners Park, Meadows might be moved. She wanted to make sure she could hold her own with the more experienced WPCs based there.

She had been sitting for half an hour, reading and trying to memorise, when there was a tap on her door. Surprised, Meadows got up to answer it. Mavis, the resident cleaner-cum-housekeeper was standing in the corridor with a paperbasket in her hand.

"I'm ever so sorry to disturb you, Ma'am," she apologised, her round face even pinker than normal. "I forgot to return your basket when I cleaned this afternoon. I took it outside to empty and left it on the top of the bin. It's got a bit wet I'm afraid. I've dried it as best as I can. Please accept my apologies."

"I hadn't noticed the basket was missing," Meadows replied truthfully.

"I do hope you're not cross," Mavis added hesitantly.

"Of course not," Meadows assured her, smiling. As Mrs McEwan said, Mavis was 'a treasure'; hard working and honest. Even if Meadows had been cross, she wouldn't have wanted to say so. "Thank you for returning it," she said instead. As she took the basket the straw did indeed feel damp. "I'll dry it off by the fire," she added helpfully.

"Thank you, Ma'am. My apologies again."

Meadows couldn't help smiling as she went back into her lounge. She wasn't used to being called 'Ma'am'. She was just settling back into her chair when there was a loud shout from the corridor. The shout turned to a scream. "Help me!" the voice called.

At once Meadows dropped her book and ran to the door. "What is it?" she called. No one was in sight.

"Someone help me!" It was Mavis' voice, echoing as if she was in the bathroom.

Pausing only to grab her key, Meadows ran out of her flat. Her heart began to pound. Judging by Mavis' voice, something terrible had happened. For a second she steadied herself. Then she pushed the bathroom door.

It swung open. Mavis was crouching on the floor. In front of her a man's body was sprawled on the floor, beside the bath.

At once Meadows was calm, moving from concerned neighbour to trained officer. Urgently she looked around. The man was lying on his back with his arms flailed out from his body, as if he had slipped on the bath mat and gone flying backwards. He was naked but for a towel over his private parts. Blood was still oozing from the back of his head, staining the white tiled floor.

It was Major Fielding.

"Help me lift him up," Mavis begged. "It's the Major. He must have slipped and cracked his head."

"Let him lie!" Meadows ordered. She couldn't help being sharp and softened her tone at once. "If he's hurt his spine, moving him's the worst thing you can do," she added. Urgently she bent down and felt for a pulse. There was nothing. She listened at his chest and could hear no breathing. Her alarm turned to horror.

"I'll phone for an ambulance," Mavis said, getting up quickly. "I can use the pay-phone downstairs."

Meadows nodded sadly. "Yes," she agreed. "We need an ambulance, but I don't think they can do much."

In disbelief the woman paused and stared at her. "You mean he's dead?" she almost whispered. "Not the Major, please say he'll be ok…" Her voice trailed off, then she burst into tears.

Again Meadows nodded. She could feel tears stinging her own eyes and blinked hard. She had liked the man. Everyone at Maple View liked him. He couldn't have been lying on the floor long. He always took his bath in the afternoon. At 4 o'clock on the dot; you could set your watch by him. It was awful to think that while she ate her meal, he was lying there, possibly still alive. Did he call out when he fell? She had heard nothing. Perhaps Miss Huddlestone's radio drowned his voice? Maybe if they had found him earlier they could have saved him?

Mavis was still weeping, but she'd straightened up. "The poor, poor man," she repeated. "He'd hate being found like this. We'd better cover him up." Looking round for another towel and finding none, she was about to fetch the Major's dressing gown from the chair by the window.

"Don't touch anything," Meadows warned instinctively.

"But we can't leave him like this for people to see," Mavis protested. She indicated the Major's body. It looked as if he had wrapped the towel round his waist as he got out of the bath. As he fell, it had come adrift. Fortunately it still covered his private parts. Whenever he went out, he always wore a neat blazer and hat and carried a carefully furled umbrella or a cane, depending on the weather. Even indoors he wore a tie and jacket. The thought of two women seeing him as he was now would have filled him with shame.

Pulling herself together, Meadows said firmly, "I'll fetch something to cover him with."

With an expression of bewilderment Mavis stared at her. Then relief lightened her face. "You're a police woman, aren't you?" she recalled. "Of course." She was still crying, but becoming calmer, letting Meadows take over.

"Stay here a moment," Meadows asked. "Stand against the door so no one can enter. I'll tap on it twice to be let in. I won't be long."

As she hurried into the corridor, she met Miss Huddlestone. Peering out of her door the old woman asked. "Has something happened? I heard shouting."

"All under control," Meadows replied vaguely and smiled. It would be better keeping the other residents out of the way. Besides, Mrs McEwan ought to be informed first.

"So long as everything's all right," Miss Huddlestone replied and reluctantly returned to her rooms, bolting her door on the inside.

Quickly unlocking her own door, Meadows stood for a few seconds, calming herself. It was her second fatality within a few weeks, and both had been men she liked. She wanted to sit down and cry. But this was no time for personal feelings. Running to her bedroom she snatched the coverlet off the bed. It was white and would stain, so she took one of the blankets instead, folding it tightly so it wouldn't look too obvious if she met someone. She was about to run back to the

84

bathroom when she had an idea. Her father had given her a camera for her last birthday. She hadn't used it much yet, just a few photos of her kid sister when they went to Butlins last September. She still had lots of shots left on the film. Jerking the sideboard drawer open, Meadows pulled out the camera and wrapped it in the blanket. Then she returned to the corridor.

To her annoyance Mr Hendrickson was walking towards the Gentlemen's bathroom, swinging his toilet bag jauntily. "Evening," he said, with a smile that Meadows found over-familiar. "Just about to do my ablutions. Then it's off to the Club for a game of billiards. Fancy joining me?" Despite his bravado, he flushed deeply. "At the Club I mean," he added hurriedly, "not in the bathroom."

Meadows ignored the invitation. "I'm afraid the Major's beaten you," she said, as cheerily as she could.

"That old duffer! He hogs the place every afternoon. I thought he'd be long gone by now." With an expression of annoyance, the young man headed back towards the attic stairs.

Mavis opened the door as soon as Meadows tapped twice. The cleaner had been crying again and her eyes were red and puffy. "The poor poor man!" she repeated as Meadows unfolded the blanket. "He was such a gentleman. Always thanked me for cleaning his rooms. He remembered me at Christmas too. Gave me a big box of Cadbury's."

"He was a very nice man," Meadows agreed. "It's dreadful to think he survived two wars, only to slip on a bathroom floor." Again, her own eyes filled with tears but she forced herself to be businesslike. "I'm just going to take a couple of photographs. There'll be an inquest; there always is after a sudden death. It'll help the Coroner if there are some photos."

While Mavis watched, Meadows fumbled with the unfamiliar camera settings, and managed to focus on the body. Then she stepped back as far as she could to take a snap of the room as a whole. "Was the door unlocked when you found him?" she asked as she did so.

"You still can't lock it," Mavis replied, shaking her head. "It broke a couple of weeks ago."

Meadows thought back. "Oh but didn't the Major say it was being fixed soon?"

Mavis shook her head. "Not yet. Mrs McEwan's ordered the locksmith but he can't come until the end of the month. The Gents have to turn the sign to show the bathroom's occupied." She opened the door a few inches and indicated a handwritten sign hanging from the door handle. "They all know to knock and listen, even if the sign says it's free."

"Wasn't the 'Occupied' sign on the door?" Meadows asked, surprised. She couldn't imagine the Major forgetting to turn the sign over when he'd gone in.

"Yes. It was,' Mavis nodded, "so at first I went away. I needed to bring some more toilet rolls, though, and came back and tried knocking. When I got no answer I thought someone had forgotten to turn the sign to 'Vacant' as they left. I couldn't hear any sounds from inside, so I went in."

"And that's when you found the Major?"

Mutely Mavis nodded. Together they laid Meadows' blanket over the body.

"I wonder if he fainted," Mavis said afterwards. "The water does get very hot."

Meadows considered the body. "It looks like the bathroom mat slipped under him as he got out," she replied.

"It shouldn't have done," Mavis insisted. "All the bath mats have non-slip backing. I sewed it on myself. Mrs McEwan asked me to do so." Bending down she lifted the corner of the mat and showed the strips. "There!" she said. She was clearly relieved that a failure on her part hadn't been to blame.

"I'll stay with the Major if you like," Meadows offered. She avoided using the word 'body' for Mavis' sake. "You go and phone the ambulance."

With an expression of intense relief, Mavis nodded and went out.

Standing against the bathroom door, Meadows waited. Someone approached the door, then paused. She held her breath until they saw the sign and went away. Mavis' voice came softly from below. She had got through to the Ambulance Service. Avoiding touching the body, Meadows leant against the doorframe as she waited. She felt rather sick but not as sick as when she first saw Robin Harvey. She wondered if she was getting used to death. Some of the men said you did. But not so quickly surely? No, she didn't feel the same because her mind wasn't really taking the situation in. It was too strange. It wasn't just that she was sharing a bathroom with a dead body. She could cope with that. It was the coincidence that bewildered her: two people she had known, both having an accident within weeks of each other. And they were both judges in the same competition. It didn't feel right.

Even that didn't explain her sense of unease, Meadows reflected. Something else was bothering her, but she couldn't think what. It was lurking at the back of her mind, but try as hard as she could to think what it might be, nothing came forward.

Finally Mavis returned. "They're on their way," she said softly. "What do we do now?"

"I'll stay here and you go downstairs to wait for them," Meadows suggested. "I'll leave the room as soon as the ambulance men come up. After that, we could both do with a cup of tea. Can you make us one?"

"Of course. I'll put the kettle on."

Meadows paused. The Coroner had to be informed of any sudden death, but normally there would be no need for her to inform DS Winters about a domestic accident. Yet her uneasiness wouldn't go away. Acting on instinct as much as thought, she asked Mavis to stand outside the bathroom door for a few minutes: Mavis steadfastly refused to stay inside any longer. Then Meadows phoned the Station.

After that, the system swung into action with a speed that left her breathless. PC Higgins arrived just as the ambulance pulled into the driveway. He went straight upstairs to secure the bathroom. To her surprise though, when Meadows went up to talk to him, he shook his head. "The boss says you're to go to your rooms and stay there," he said gruffly. When she began to object, he shook his head. "You'd better do as he says," he advised.

Hurt and mystified, Meadows went to her flat to wait until she was called. What had she done wrong? Pacing up and down her lounge, she listened to the comings and goings in the corridor outside: subdued discussions, residents' voices asking what was going on, the front door bell ringing, PC Green answering as best he could. Cars pulled up on the gravel outside the house and more sounds echoed in the hallway. One voice was Mrs McEwan's, full of concern. Soon her voice went away, as if she had been escorted out of the house. Still Meadows waited, expecting to be called to help in some way, and instead being ignored. Then, ultimately there was the sound of feet passing purposefully, carrying a heavy weight. The Major's body was being taken to the Mortuary. Most of the voices began to go away.

Suddenly there was a knock on her door. Hurriedly Meadows went to answer, ready to let whoever it was know how angry she felt. She snatched the door open but the words died in her mouth. DI Ambrose himself was standing there.

Chapter Twelve

In alarm Meadows tried to think what to say. "I'm sorry if I've brought you out for nothing, Sir," she gabbled. "I…"

"Can you come back to the Station?" Ambrose interrupted her softly. Miss Huddlestone's door was opening slowly, just enough for the old woman to see through the gap. "It'll be more private there."

"I'm sorry I wasted your time," Meadows repeated in apology. "I hope they didn't fetch you from home."

Putting his finger to his mouth, Ambrose silenced her. "You were right to call," he said quietly. "It is a very odd coincidence." He glanced towards the open door in annoyance. "We obviously can't talk here, but I need to ask you some questions. You were the second person on the scene."

"Oh Lord! I'm a witness, aren't I?" Meadows said, for the first time realising why she'd been kept away from everyone.

"Yes," Ambrose replied. "And a good one I'm sure. Come down to the 'nick' with me. I'll try not to make it too formal, but you'll have to give a statement." He smiled, softening his words. "Get your coat. It's raining again."

Her tiredness forgotten, Meadows took her coat from the door. It was almost dry. Then she followed DI Ambrose into the corridor. To her annoyance, Miss Huddlestone's door was still slightly ajar: The walls definitely had ears at Maple View.

"Don't forget to lock up," Ambrose said softly. "I suspect you might have visitors otherwise."

At first they sat in silence as PC Higgins drove them back down to the Station. Meadows only dared to speak as they passed the park. "I don't think the Major has any family," she said sadly. "What will happen about his funeral? He was a good neighbour. I hate to think of him in an empty church with just the Vicar and a couple of old ladies."

"I imagine he's made provision," Ambrose replied gently. "If he hasn't, Mrs McEwan might see to things. Do you know if he left a will?"

"No. I didn't know him that well," Meadows admitted. "He was an old soldier though, so I imagine he did."

As soon as they reached the Station, Ambrose led the way to the interview room, calling PC Vernon to come and take notes.

Meadows was indeed a good witness. Once Ambrose had eased her initial nervousness, she answered his questions quietly and carefully, recounting everything she and Mavis had found and done. She had no doubt herself that it was a terrible accident, apart from the weird coincidence with Robin Harvey's death.

Ambrose had to agree with her, though he didn't say so. The Forensics team had found nothing to suggest otherwise. It was possible Doc Halstead would find some less obvious cause during the post mortem: a medical problem leading the Major to fall perhaps or, less likely, something in his system that would have made him pass out. The Major wasn't known to be a heavy drinker however, and it would have been difficult to administer any other harmful substance. They'd already checked he had been at home all afternoon and Mavis hadn't seen him receive any visitors. No, it had to be an ordinary, sad accident. People did sometimes slip on bathroom floors, and a cast-iron bath could easily cut a man's head to the bone.

And yet... there was still that 'and yet'. The coincidence was a problem. The position of the towel bothered Ambrose too. If it was wrapped around the man's waist when he fell, it ought to be partly underneath his body. Instead, it was on top of his legs. It almost suggested someone had dropped it onto him to preserve his modesty. Yet Meadows was adamant that neither she nor Mavis had done so.

"You'll see the towel on my photos," she insisted. "I took them straight after we found the body, before the Forensics team came."

Ambrose was about to point out that she could have moved important evidence before taking the photos, but decided to trust her. Besides, he really couldn't see Meadows and Mavis the Housekeeper colluding to alter evidence.

"We'll get the film developed," he promised. "Murdoch took photos of course, but there might be something on your pictures that doesn't show up on his. Full marks for initiative, by the way."

Flushing with pleasure, Meadows smiled her thanks.

"Sorry to drag you back down here," Ambrose said finally, "but you have nosey neighbours."

Meadows smiled ruefully. "Don't I just? There's not much that slips past them, which can be an advantage or a disadvantage, depending on your point of view."

"Quite," Ambrose agreed.

"If you've finished with me can I go home now?" Meadows asked. "It's been a long day."

Ambrose nodded. "Of course. Don't forget to claim your overtime. I'm afraid there's no one free to drive you back."

"I'll be ok," Meadows assured him, though she would have loved a lift up the hill. "It's stopped raining."

"You'd better sign your statement before you leave," Ambrose reminded her as she got up.

"Oh yes." Awkwardly Meadows added her signature. "It's a bit odd being on the other side of the table," she admitted. 'Unnerving' she wanted to say but thought it better of it.

"Not pleasant," Ambrose agreed, recalling the time when he himself had been questioned in a murder case. "The past few weeks haven't been good for you, have they?"

"No," Meadows admitted. "It seems so strange, me knowing both of them. And liking them too. I feel a bit like I'm a jinx."

"It has absolutely nothing to do with you," Ambrose reassured her and opened the door.

The sense of strangeness stayed with WPC Meadows as she walked wearily back up the hill to Maple View. Perhaps that was why she had the feeling she was being followed again, though when she looked back she could see no one. By now it was six o'clock. The street lamps cast circles of light that made the darkness between them seem even darker. Twice she thought she heard a sound behind her, and twice she looked back, to see no one. Yet she was certain there was somebody there, following her. For the first time, she began to feel frightened.

PC Green was right. She ought to tell someone, she admitted. She reported ultimately to DS Winters. She ought to go to him. But she was still reluctant to do so. She had a nasty feeling he would view her fear as a sign of weakness, or just think she was imagining things. If it got round the canteen she would never live it down. Only last week Tom Vernon had been joking about how useless women were in "proper jobs", "men's jobs", that is. "They're forever crying or falling

90

in love," he'd said loudly. Since he couldn't have failed to see Meadows sitting at the table nearby, the remark was clearly directed at her. She'd had to abandon her tea and leave the canteen before she said something she would regret. Crying or falling in love? She flatly refused to do either.

Even now, Meadows was furious at the memory. Her anger spilled over, directing itself against her unseen tormentor. Stopping suddenly, she whirled round. "Show yourself, whoever you are!" she shouted. "You're a coward, hiding all the while."

No one appeared.

Chapter Thirteen

Friday 25th March

"It's too big a coincidence," Ambrose insisted.

"Coincidences do happen," Winters pointed out.

"Two out of three judges in a competition dying within weeks of each other?" Ambrose asked, shaking his head. "Both from nasty accidents? And both after receiving threatening messages?"

Winters frowned in acknowledgement. "It does look odd," he agreed. "But would someone commit murder because of a poetry competition? I know people can be competitive but that's taking it too far. Maybe if an enormous prize was involved, but not fifty quid. Besides, they'd have to be local to know the judges."

"They needn't be local themselves," Ambrose persisted. "They could get someone to do the dirty work."

"A Mafia boss who writes poetry?" Winters suggested suppressing a smile. "I'm sorry. I can't take this seriously. Is there any point in continuing the enquiry?"

"Into the deaths? Or the packages?" Ambrose asked.

"The packages. I can't see how they can be related to either death."

Ambrose got up and walked restlessly around his office. For a while he looked out of the window, onto the car park and the shops beyond. It had stopped raining and the sun was reflecting from wet roofs and tarmac. He would far rather have been on the Heath walking with Mary, or driving out for a day's picnic. Instead, he was ploughing through a pile of paperwork and trying to make sense of the oddest case he'd ever worked on, if it even was a case. "Sending threatening messages through the post is an offence," he reminded Winters stubbornly.

"Well, ok," Winters conceded. "But I think they're two separate cases. If the deaths are a case."

It was unsettling to hear Winters echoing his own doubts. "You could well be right," Ambrose agreed. "The hate mail stuff is outside my usual remit. If Mac agrees, you carry on with that enquiry. You never know, it might prove to be related. If it isn't, at least we'll stop a nutter from upsetting other people or worse. Unbalanced people sometimes go on to kill."

Once again he glanced at the written reports that had come in from the suspects' local Police. Before the Major's death, he had thought about questioning the Brontë woman; what was her name? Janice Flowers. He'd hoped the Major would invite her to Chalk Heath, and they could question her unobtrusively, without bothering another Division. That was out of the question now, and he didn't fancy asking the Hon Madge to invite Miss Flowers. They would have to go through the proper channels.

"Right you are," Winters agreed. "I'll check this lot. If it still looks like Miss Flowers is the chief suspect, I'll contact her Division and ask if we can go and interview her, or if someone's willing to bring her here."

"You'll have to ask the Chief," Ambrose pointed out. "But I don't think that'll be a problem. His mind's on other things at present. I gather his wife's very upset at what happened at Maple View." He sighed. "At least you have somewhere to start," he added ruefully. "All I have is a coincidence, a broken torch when the lights were working and a towel that shouldn't have been where it was."

Winters began to gather up the reports. "Let me have a proper read before you take them away," Ambrose asked. "I might spot something. I'll bring them round to you in half an hour."

Climbing over a paint tin and nearly tripping on a decorator's sheet, Winters left him to it. "Thank God they're almost finished," he mouthed as he left the room.

Alone in his office afterwards, Ambrose plodded through the reports. They said much the same as the earlier telephone calls, only more repetitively. The Pickering typist had a problem with the 'e' on her keyboard, which produced some interesting effects, like 'wrot' instead of 'wrote' and 'f—ls' for 'feels'. Every word with an 'e' in it had to be guessed from the context. And whoever took the notes about

Adrian Templar consistently misused the apostrophe. 'Their' and 'there' caused them problems too. Most of the time Ambrose could work the meaning out but he was stumped for a few seconds by Mr Templar refusing 'to go over their': 'their what?' he wondered at first, until he realised the word 'there' made rather more sense.

Ambrose was tempted to get out a red pen and send the report back, corrected like a school boy's homework. Still, he reminded himself, he wasn't marking the reports, just checking the facts. And the only facts of real interest were in the interview with Miss Flowers.

Thoughtfully he reread the summary.

"Miss Flowers asks for it to be noted that she has co-operated fully. She came into the Police Station voluntarily even though we wouldn't pay her bus fare. She also provided evidence of her past entries in the Bird Books competition. She knows nothing about any threatening messages or packages being sent to this year's judges."

Beneath that statement however, was a note from the officer who had interviewed her. "When pressed, Miss Flowers seemed very bitter. She said she was annoyed at comments made by this year's judges. She feels she is 'especially privileged to have an intuitive understanding of the Brontë sisters, who have guided my writing.' Beside the second quotation, a more personal comment had been added in the margin. "Miss F lost me here - I'm just repeating what she said."

Included with the report was a short poem "which Miss Flowers insisted we send. She wants to show you how good her work really is, and how unkind the judges' comments were."

Spring in the West
No senseless soul is mine,
No ignorer of the world's beauteous sphere:
I see Nature's glories shine,
And rejoice in Her bounty, throughout the year.
O spring in its fullness,
Almighty, ever-present fecundity!
Life stirs through snow and emptiness,
Till streams run with such clarity
We see our faces float through weeds,
Above stones and darting fish. Birds sing
A chorus of renewal. Forgotten seeds
Germinate in gardens,
Where snowdrops are joyfully blooming.

The lines echoed in Ambrose's mind from somewhere else. Where? He rolled a pencil round and round his fingers as he tried to remember. "That's it!" he said aloud. "Emily Brontë." He had read an article recently about new treatments for TB. The journalist had mentioned the sad lives of the Brontë sisters, how they'd died one after the other, from what was called 'consumption' in those days. While he was writing about Emily, the writer had quoted a poem. It had opened like Miss Flowers' own.

Shaking his head, Ambrose turned to the judge's comments. "*Try to be more original. This would be a good poem if you got rid of the 'poetic' language and stopped copying other poets. You have a keen eye for natural description.*" Though the comments were typed, Ambrose recognised the writer at once. It was not a good idea to let the Hon Madge write the judgement on any of the entrants. She was too sharp. Robin Harvey or the Major would have put the last, more favourable comment first, and tried to be constructive. Mr Harvey always prided himself on how kind and helpful the competition was, and how Bird Books tried to encourage talent.

Returning to the poem, Ambrose noticed some pencil marks along the side. Miss Hodgkiss had written notes as she read, and rubbed them out afterwards. Unfortunately, the pencil she had used was sharp and dark, and the words could still be read if the paper was held up to the light. "*Pure Emily Brontë*" the first comment said. "*Second-hand rubbish*" had been scrawled below that in exasperation. He couldn't make out the third comment, apart from one word: "*plagiarism*".

He could understand Miss Flowers being mortified. She had probably never intended to copy her favourite poet, but was so steeped in her poems that they came to her mind as she wrote. If she actually believed she had some kind of direct link to the Brontës, then such an accusation would be even more hurtful. But would she be angry enough to kill two of the judges? She couldn't have done so herself. No stranger had been seen either at the bookshop or Maple View, which was in a way even more frightening.

Taking the reports with him, Ambrose trod carefully over the dustsheets to Mac's office. The corridor was finished but the sheets were still down to protect the new carpet.

"Could I have a word?" he began.

"I imagine so," Mac replied and smiled. "But if it's about bringing a Miss Flowers here for questioning, I've already approved Winters' request."

95

"Good, thank you," Ambrose replied, not sure how to begin. "I'm worried about the two accidents. They're too much of a coincidence. Some details don't feel quite right either. It bothers me that the Honourable Miss Hodgkiss is the only judge left."

Misunderstanding him, Mac sighed. "Yes, she's going to have a sad job sorting the award night out on her own," he agreed. "I assumed they'd have to cancel, but the young girl at the bookshop says they want to go ahead. But why is that worrying you?"

"I'm concerned for Miss Hodgkiss' safety," Ambrose explained. "She has a habit of offending people. She might be the next to have an 'accident'." He didn't try to explain how hurtful her judge's comments had been. That could wait until they had interviewed Miss Flowers. In any case, Mac probably wouldn't understand.

"You suspect foul play?" the Chief asked in surprise. "Have you any proof? Or is it one of your famous intuitions?"

"No I don't have proof," Ambrose admitted. "But it's more than a gut feeling. There are inconsistencies in both accidents, like the light that wasn't switched on and the towel in the wrong place. You'll have seen my notes?"

Frowning, Mac nodded. "They're not much to go on," he pointed out. "Why should Marjorie be the next? This is Chalk Heath, not Chicago."

"Two men have died in odd circumstances, and within a matter of weeks," Ambrose pointed out. "That's not normal for Chalk Heath."

Thoughtfully Mac picked up his fountain pen and filled it from the bottle of ink on his desk "Even if the two men didn't die accidentally," he replied as he did so, "why should the competition be the link? It could be some business the two men were involved in. Or something from their pasts."

"But what if it *is* the competition?" Ambrose persisted. "That's the only thing that connects the three of them. Two are now dead. If anything happened to Miss Hodgkiss and we did nothing to prevent it, the press would have a field day, not to mention her family. She has some very influential connections too, like the Chief Commissioner."

As he'd hoped, the last argument bothered Mac. Getting up, he stood for a while contemplating the photograph on top of his filing cabinet, of his wife and stepson. "If it was anyone but you I'd say you were imagining things," he admitted. "But I have learnt to trust your judgement. I suppose we could put PC Green outside Miss Hodgkiss' house. It would be good training for him and not drain the budget too much. I can only afford a few days, though. If there are no developments in that time, I'll have to put him back on point duty."

"At least we'll have shown we tried," Ambrose agreed, though it was less than he had hoped.

"I'll see how Miss Hodgkiss likes the idea," Mac said, smiling ruefully. "Take a pew."

Ambrose had a feeling she wouldn't like the idea at all, but he waited quietly as the Chief phoned Garth House.

The Hon Miss Hodgkiss was at home. Though Ambrose only heard Mac's end of the conversation he could work out the replies. Miss Hodgkiss' voice echoed in a draughty hallway and some of her words were audible.

"Hello, Marjorie," Mac began cheerfully. "John McEwan here. How are you? I wondered how you were coping with the competition on your own. If you need any mailings doing Abigail's happy to help. It'd take her mind off poor Major Fielding...yes...terrible business... 'In the midst of life' as they say... Oh good... Glad you've got some support. She's a bright girl, isn't she? It wouldn't surprise me if she ends up running Curiosity Corner. I can't see Harvey's brother knowing much... An Insurance Agent they say..."

For a moment Mac lapsed into a friendly silence, listening to Miss Hodgkiss. She seemed to be talking about her sister who was mercifully recovering from a serious illness. Then the conversation returned to the recent deaths.

"Yes, it is odd the two of them dying so close," Mac agreed. "That's actually one of the reasons I've rung. We're concerned about your safety. We can't be sure there isn't a seriously maladjusted person out there planning a third accident."

There was a long pause Mac's end, and the sound of Miss Hodgkiss' voice responding in annoyed disbelief. She thought the suggestion very poor taste.

"We have to be careful," Mac insisted, when he could get a word in. "Having two judges die so close to each other does make me worry about you...I know it sounds crazy...But there could be a link between the two deaths. We have to be careful..."

Repeating the same arguments several times in different words, Mac refused to give up. "It may not be just a poetry competition to someone, especially if they're unhinged. I'd never forgive myself if I did nothing to protect you."

Grimacing towards Ambrose, Mac held the phone at a distance for a moment. As soon as there was silence the other end, he continued, "To put one of our young constables outside your house... No, not in uniform... not if you don't want... Well, who would you agree to? Which young woman? You mean WPC Meadows?"

Turning towards DI Ambrose, Mac checked that he'd heard and understood the request. "If she's the only one you'll agree to," he said to Miss Hodgkiss afterwards. "I'm sure you could rely on her to watch out for you... Yes, I'm sure she'd be discreet. She could come as your companion."

Once again there was a long pause while the Hon Madge expressed her opinion. "All right, in plain clothes," Mac agreed. "She can just accompany you to events. As you say, you're not likely to come to any harm at home. When's your first engagement?"

Urgently the Chief wrote time and place down on his pad. "She'll call for you at your home," he replied, "and accompany you there. I'll make sure she understands she is to stay in the background... As an observer..."

Finally he had the Hon Madge's agreement. "Thank you for being so co-operative," he said, though his expression implied he thought the exact opposite.

"At the risk of stating the obvious, both Robin Harvey and the Major died at home," Ambrose pointed out afterwards. "Having Meadows with her at the odd event isn't going to achieve much."

"It's all Marjorie will agree to," Mac said, shaking his head. "Though she did say Meadows might help with the gardening."

Ambrose couldn't help laughing. "I'm sure she'll be thrilled," he commented.

"Do you think Meadows can cope with the job?" Mac asked uncertainly. "I don't mean the gardening, I mean being in plain clothes, and trotting around after a woman who will probably treat her as inferior?"

"She'll find it hard," Ambrose admitted. "She's never had a plain clothes role before, and she'll think Miss Hodgkiss is a snob. But she's learning to hold her tongue. And oddly, the two women did seem to get on when they met. If I make clear it's a chance for Meadows to prove herself, she'll rise to it. She's determined to get on in the Force."

"Then that's agreed," the Chief said firmly. "For a week, no longer mind." He glanced at his notes. "Marjorie's first public engagement is tomorrow, judging a poetry competition at the Grammar School. It begins at two o'clock, in the main hall."

"I hope she's more tactful with children than she is with adults," Ambrose said ruefully. "Meadows should have finished her beat by now. I'll see if she's in and break the news to her."

"Tell her she'll get paid overtime for any extra duties," Mac promised. "That should sweeten the pill."

Treading carefully back over the decorator's sheets, Ambrose headed for the canteen. As he'd hoped, WPC Meadows was taking a break before heading out again to give a road safety class at the Junior School.

She stared at him in horror as he explained her new duties. "Oh Lor!" she said afterwards. "I shall slurp over my soup."

"I don't think soup will be involved," Ambrose assured her. "You'll just be going around with her a bit. She's up at the Grammar tomorrow, and she's Brown Owl or something on Saturday at a big Guides do. You were in the Guides weren't you?"

"Girls' Brigade," Meadows replied, smiling. "I went to Guides once. It was far too rough."

"Really?" Ambrose asked. "I'm sure the Hon Madge's Guides are much more lady-like. You'll probably be bored stiff singing campfire songs. You'll have to keep your eyes open though, in case anybody does try attacking her."

"With respect, isn't that more likely when she's at home?" Meadows asked.

Ambrose sighed. "Exactly what I said, but she won't have it. Unless you're willing to do a bit of gardening."

Taking a sip of her tea again, Meadows looked at him quizzically. "Are you serious, sir?"

"Never more so. Apparently the only reason the Hon Madge would have you around at her home is if you'd help with the garden."

"I do like gardening," Meadows replied, putting the cup down. "And if it means she has someone around more often, to keep an eye on her, I'd be willing to have a go."

Ambrose could have shaken her hand. "Good girl!" he said, and then feared he'd been patronising. "I hoped you'd say that," he went on hurriedly. "But I wouldn't have put any pressure on you."

"No sir, I know you wouldn't," Meadows replied. "What sort of thing should I wear? I'm not used to being in polite company."

"I wouldn't have said Madge was polite," Ambrose replied ruefully. "No trousers. She told the Chief she hates women in slacks. Wear a smart skirt."

"To garden in?" Meadows laughed. "I'll see if I can borrow some pink gloves and nice straw hat."

Smiling, Ambrose got up, about to return to his office. Then he realised the young WPC wanted to say something more. "What is it?" he asked.

Meadows paused, wondering if she should tell him she was being followed. She could talk to him better than to DS Winters. Then she decided against it. Given what she'd just been asked to do, it would sound like weakness or even trying to get out of the job. Besides, it didn't happen yesterday or this morning, so hopefully she'd scared the fellow off. Instead, she turned quickly to another issue that was bothering her. "I've got something at the back of my mind," she admitted. "About the Major's death. I can't think what it is, but I know it doesn't fit, like the light not being put on at Curiosity Corner."

"The towel?" Ambrose asked, pausing as he stood beside the table.

"No. That might be ok, just fallen like that. I know what one thing is, but it might be my imagination, and it's not the main thing. But I can't get the thought sorted in my head, as to what that main thing is."

"What's the minor one then?" Ambrose persisted, becoming impatient.

"The floor smelt funny. When I knelt over the Major to see if he was breathing, the floor didn't smell right. Not like the Ladies' bathroom. It could have just been the blood, but I don't think so. Maybe one of the men had used a fancy soap and it had landed on the floor earlier."

"Perhaps," Ambrose agreed, not sure where the conversation was leading. It didn't lead any further. Shrugging her shoulders, Meadows returned to her tea.

Her doubt was infectious though. For an hour afterwards Ambrose kept going over the scene of the Major's death, trying to visualise the bathroom. Finally he gave up. He needed to see the room again.

"I'm popping out for an hour," he told the desk sergeant. Deciding to walk (he always thought better when he walked), he set off to Maple View.

Chapter Fourteen

As Ambrose had hoped, Mavis Jenkins herself came to the door. Immediately she recognised him she became flustered and apologetic.

"I'm so sorry. I didn't hear the bell," she said. "I was out the back, cleaning the yard. The bin men came this morning and they always leave a mess. Have you been waiting long?"

Ambrose reassured her with a smile. "No," he replied. "Just a few moments. I've been admiring the gardens. It's good to see the daffodils coming through. Makes you feel winter's nearly over. You've got some snowdrops in flower already," he added. "They always cheer me up."

"Major Fielding bought them," Mavis replied with a sad shake of the head. "Last year. He said the gardens looked too bare, bless him. What can we do for you? Is it about the Major? I'm afraid Mrs McEwan isn't here. She'll be at home packing. She's going away for a few days."

"Oh?" Ambrose asked. It could be difficult if they had to wait for Mac's return to sanction further expenditure. "I didn't know Inspector McEwan was going away," he admitted.

"She's going on her own apparently," Mavis replied. "Taking a well-earned break in Torquay. Poor lady. She's worked so hard getting this place just right and then to have so much trouble." She sighed. "This miserable weather's getting her down too. She always feels the cold, what with coming from the Channel Islands and all, where it's always far warmer, or so I've heard…"

"I wanted to talk to you, not Mrs McEwan," Ambrose interrupted. "Can I come in?"

At once Mavis was ill at ease again. "If it's about the Major, I don't think I can add anything more."

"You don't need to," Ambrose assured her. "You've been very helpful. It'd like to see the bathroom again, that's all."

"But I've cleaned it," Mavis objected. "I scrubbed all the blood away. Your Sergeant said it would be alright. Have I done wrong?"

"Of course not. I'd just like to make a little sketch of what's where. We used to have a young PC who did drawings for us, but he's left, so I've decided to do it myself. It'll help me check if I've remembered things right."

Still mystified, Mavis led the way upstairs. "We've had to let the gentlemen use the room again," she explained. "The ladies didn't like them using theirs. It was embarrassing they said. And there was a constant queue."

They paused on the landing while Mavis rearranged a vase of flowers on the window ledge.

"I gather you like Mrs McEwan," Ambrose commented. Though he had no desire to gossip, the woman intrigued him, and it was useful to hear an outsider's view of his superior's wife.

"Oh yes. Mrs Mac's lovely to work for," Mavis replied, with obvious pleasure. "Treats you like a human being. I've known the whole family for years, used to clean for them when they lived here. I've watched Brian grow up into a fine young fellow, and it's been lovely to see how close he is to his step-father. Inspector Mac was pleased as punch when the lad got into Roedean."

"I think it's Ryton," Ambrose corrected her gently. "Ryton's a college for trainee police officers. High flyers if you like. He could end up as an Inspector too." He smiled inwardly at the image of young Brian McEwan attending a posh girls' school like Roedean. With his fine blond hair and blue eyes he would have had all the girls swooning over him. "You must have been very pleased when Mrs Mac asked you to take over here," he commented afterwards.

"Oh I was! Housekeeper! That's a step up from cleaner isn't it? And I love my rooms here. Since my Bertie died I've hated living on my own. I've always got someone around here, and everyone's so nice. Mrs Mac only accepts 'Quality Residents', you know."

They went on up the stairs and along the corridor, towards the gentlemen's bathroom. The cardboard 'Vacant/Engaged' sign still hung on the doornob. Fortunately, there was no one using the room at that moment. "The locksmith should be coming tomorrow," Mavis said as she opened the door. "This sign isn't very satisfactory. People forget to turn it over. There have been some red faces." She paused at the open door. "Shall I leave you to it?"

"If you would. Where will you be? I'd like to have a quick word afterwards."

"I'll wait in my rooms, last door on the left before the back door." Uncertainly Mavis left him standing alone in the bathroom.

Ambrose took a couple of folded sheets of paper from his jacket pocket, and leaning against the closed lavatory lid, made a sketch of the room. He could add the position of the Major's body from the Forensic team's or WPC Meadows' photographs, whichever was clearest. Both films should be processed and waiting for him when he got back to the Station. Then he sat on the edge of the big metal bath and tried to visualise slipping as he got out. He moved the bath mat into several different positions. The non-slip tapes on the back were effective each time. He simply couldn't make the mat slip across the tiles. Turning it over, he frowned. He was unable to explain how Major Fleming could have slipped so badly that he caught his head on the edge of the bath. Even if he'd had soap on his feet, the bath mat should have stayed firmly in place.

"Unless, of course," he mused, "it's a different bath mat now?" Mavis might still have the original mat. With no suspicion of foul play at the time, he doubted if it had been bagged and brought back to the 'nick' as evidence.

As he bent down to replace the mat Ambrose recalled WPC's Meadows' concern about the floor. Getting down onto his knees, he sniffed at the tiles. They smelt like any other bathroom tiles to him, that slightly acrid combination of disinfectant and carbolic cleaning fluid. But something had worried Meadows, and could be significant. Whatever it was, though, he couldn't find it now.

With his sketch folded in his pocket, Ambrose went down to Mavis' rooms. She appeared at the door at once. "Is there anything more you'd like to see, Inspector?" she asked warily.

"Do you have the original bath mat, the one the Major fell on?" Ambrose asked.

"I'm afraid not," Mavis apologised. "It was horrible. We used it to mop up the floor, so it was soaked in the poor man's blood. Your lot had taken loads of photographs so we thought it would be all right. Should we have kept it?"

"It might have been helpful," Ambrose admitted. "But I can understand you wanting to be rid of it. What did you do with it?"

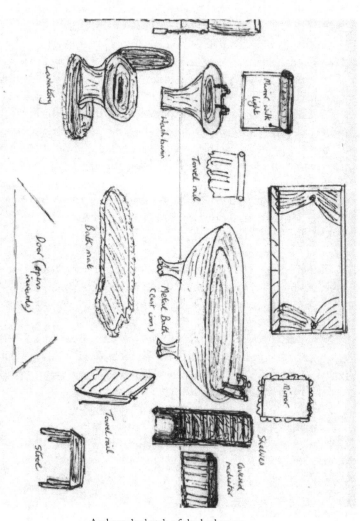

Ambrose's sketch of the bathroom

"Put it in the Aga." Mavis saw Ambrose's bewilderment and explained, "The water's heated by a coke-fired Aga. The fire gets ever so hot. When you burn something in it you don't get the smell you do from a bonfire. We didn't want to upset the other residents."

"Who's 'we'?" Ambrose asked.

"Me and Mrs McEwan. I mean, Mrs McEwan and I," Mavis corrected herself. "We cleaned the bathroom together after your men had gone. We couldn't leave it like it was."

"Of course not," Ambrose agreed. "One last question: could I have a look at the cleaning fluids you use?"

"If you really want to," Mavis was becoming irritated by his persistence but was trying not to show it. "They're all in the housekeeper's room. I'm sure you won't find anything of interest there though." Her tone implied, 'not that a mere man would find interesting anyway.'

She led the way to the housekeeper's room under the stairs. Ambrose was surprised to see the door wasn't locked. "The residents need to be able to get a cloth if they spill something in their rooms," Mavis explained. "And why should we lock the door anyway? Who's going to steal floor polish?"

The room was cramped so Mavis sat on the three-legged stool in the corner, watching as Ambrose considered the array of mops and dusters and gallon tins of different cleaners. He began to feel a little silly. What relevance could such mundane items have? "Which do you use for the bathroom floors?" he asked, putting on his official voice.

Getting up, Mavis indicated a couple of sponge mops and a flagon of cleaner. Cautiously Ambrose unscrewed the lid and sniffed the contents. The carbolic made his eyes water. There was certainly nothing sweet about that smell. "Do you mind if I smell a couple of the others?" he asked afterwards.

"Help yourself," Mavis said, barely hiding her amusement.

"Furniture polish, window cleaner, brass cleaner..." Ambrose identified each one in turn, checking the label afterwards. He wouldn't have described any of them as sweet. At the fourth he paused. Yes, if you had a keen sense of smell, you might describe that as being like fancy soap. He looked at the label: 'Wood cleaner'. "What do you use this for?" he asked.

"Cleaning the wooden floors around the carpets," Mavis replied. "It brings them up ever so nice."

"You don't use it for bathroom floors?"

"Goodness, no. They're not made of wood."

Frowning, Ambrose replaced the cap. An idea was beginning to form in his mind. It would be useful to talk to Meadows again.

Thanking Mavis for her trouble, he wished her good afternoon and walked back down the hill, towards the Police Station. All the way past the park the idea niggled. Anyone could have accessed that Housekeeper's room. But if he was right, they would have to be very cool and very patient. But why? What could be the motive? There were nearly twenty residents at Maple View. It was going to take a long time to interview them all again.

To his annoyance when he returned, WPC Meadows had already left. "Gone up to Garth House," Higgins explained. "Apparently she's needed to do some gardening there. The Hon Madge rang." His tone was drily factual, but his expression suggested disbelief.

"Ah," Ambrose replied non-committally.

"Wearing a nice print dress she was, and a fancy straw hat. Looked quite a picture."

"Did she now?" Ambrose commented. Higgins clearly wanted to say something more, but was being careful not to do so. "And?" Ambrose prompted.

"Well, there's been quite a bit of talk in the canteen," Higgins admitted guardedly.

"About what, exactly?"

"About a WPC being sent on plain clothes duties. You can imagine the tattle from one or two, mentioning no names of course."

"I can indeed," Ambrose replied, equally drily. "Well 'no names' are just going to have to get used to it. WPC Meadows has been briefed to do more than gardening, and for some reason the Honourable Marjorie Hodgkiss prefers her to a male officer. Can't think why, but there it is."

"No accounting for tastes," Higgins replied with a barely concealed sneer.

"Spit it out, man!" Ambrose said, becoming irritated. "What's the problem?"

"Well..." Hesitating for a second, Higgins launched into an explanation, his own tone sharper than usual. "It's causing some ill feeling, that's all. Can't say I'm chuffed myself. She's a bit young isn't she? I mean, several blokes would love the chance to do some plain clothes work, and they've been passed over for a WPC who's half their age."

Ambrose sighed. "If it helps, tell the canteen that Meadows will be escorting the Hon Madge to the Annual Poetry Competition at the Grammar tomorrow and then to a Girl Guides jamboree," he suggested. "I might be able to arrange for one of them to go as well, if they're still so keen to go under cover."

Higgins had the grace to laugh. "I don't think you'll get many takers," he admitted. "The Hon Madge, school kids, poetry and Girl Guides! That sounds like a penance to me."

Chapter Fifteen

Friday 1st April

Being back at her old school felt odd. Pauline Meadows glanced at the rows of seats and remembered the 'numb bum of her youth' even before she sat down. She looked at the boards on the far wall. Since her last Speech Day, new names had been added to the list of Head Girls and Head Boys, and a Kenneth Newman had been added to the Headmasters' roll.

So 'Nodder' Tidesdale had finally left. He'd seemed ancient even when Meadows was in the First Form, but she reflected, he couldn't have been that old when she was a pupil there. Looking back, they had been horribly unfair. With the cruelty of children they had made fun of his tremor. None of them had understood what it meant to be in captivity during the War, building the Burma Railway. She wondered what the new Head was like. Clearly he had new ideas. They didn't have a Poetry Day in her time.

Apart from the Headmaster, little else seemed to have changed. Even the smell was the same: that musty scent of hymn books and polish, distant school dinners and well-worn blazers. The old black-out curtains had been replaced with blinds, and the scenery folded at the back of the stage was for a different school play, but otherwise she could have been a girl again, giggling with her mates. Except that nowadays there seemed to be less to giggle about. She wondered how many of the school children had dared to do April Fool's Day jokes that morning.

As she watched the staff file onto the stage, Meadows pondered how many other teachers had gone since she'd left six years ago, or was it seven? 'They still wear gowns!' she thought with a smile. The rest of the country was modernising but Chalk Heath Grammar still pretended it was a Public School. Her amusement was softened by affection. The staff had done her proud, supporting her when she decided to stay on at her Grandmother's to continue with her O Levels, rather than move with her family to Staines. "What do you want to do exams for, anyway?" her mother had asked, genuinely puzzled. "You'll only get married and waste it all." Miss Kay had understood. She and Mr Henry had given her extra lessons, to help her cope with the upset of it all. They encouraged her to aim high too. "Why shouldn't a woman be in the Police?" Mr Henry asked. "If that's what you want to do, go for it!"

Wistfully Meadows recalled Miss Kay's English lessons. She had probably enjoyed those afternoons more than any before or since. Even now she smiled at the image of Johnnie Taylor playing Juliet. Anxiously she looked along the line of teachers. Yes, Miss Kay was there, older but still looking as though she enjoyed life. Meadows was glad. The woman had given her sound advice. "Keep trying to get in," she had urged. "While you wait, get a job where you'll meet lots of people. You'll be a much better policewoman if you do." She'd been right too.

With a start, Meadows reminded herself that she was meant to be watching Miss Hodgkiss.

The Hon Madge was sitting directly in front of her, chatting to Councillor Crossman. Other than allowing Meadows to accompany her in the car from Garth House, she had paid no attention whatsoever to her presence. She had insisted Meadows get out of the car before they turned into the school gates. No one would have known they were together. That was wise of course. If she was being followed and at risk of harm, then better no one knew that Madge had a bodyguard. But Meadows suspected Miss Hodgkiss had other reasons. She was quite happy to have someone help her in the garden, particularly as the wind was still sharp and the soil heavy. She would even deign to offer a cup of coffee in the kitchen (after Meadows had removed her shoes and jacket in the back porch). But her manner made very clear that to expect any semblance of equality or friendship was ridiculous. She had no desire to be seen in public with anyone so clearly beneath her.

At first Meadows had found the woman annoying, if not downright rude, but she'd told herself that she should just get on with the job. In its way, though the opposite end of the spectrum, escorting the Hon Madge was no different to taking Maisie Miller home after one of her binges. Neither woman appealed to her much, but she wasn't expected to become friends, just to see that they stayed safe. Quite what, or who, could harm Miss Hodgkiss in a school hall with nearly four hundred pupils and a hundred or so parents and dignitaries present, Meadows couldn't imagine. The few moments while the woman walked from the car park alone were probably far more dangerous. But there was nothing Meadows could do about that. The Hon Madge was adamant.

With a final flourish, the organ music came to an end and the organist got down from his stool. Wrapping his gown around him, he joined the other members of staff. So 'Taffy' Williams was still there too. His Chemistry lessons had been double helpings of mumbled formulae, punctuated by amusing smells and bangs. But he could still play the organ well, even if it had developed a wheeze since she'd last heard it played, Meadows thought.

Rising to his feet and beaming at the hall generally, Mr Newman introduced the afternoon's proceedings. "My Lord Mayor, Councillors, Ladies and Gentlemen," he began, "members of staff, pupils, and of course our esteemed judge, Miss Marjorie Hodgkiss, I am delighted to welcome you to our first ever Poetry Day. We will be hearing some of the prize winning poems later, read by the poets themselves. First I want to compliment every class on the quality of their work this morning. You've all tried very hard; even you boys!" He glanced down at the third and fourth formers below him and there was a ripple of laughter among the parents.

Still looking around benignly, Mr Newman continued: "First we are going to hear some splendid examples of poetry through the ages, read by our Head Boy and Girl, and some of the Prefects. Thanks to Miss Kay, we have a widely read and up-to-date sixth form."

There was a general clearing of throats and shuffling as the readers appeared on stage. One after the other they stepped forward. Most read well, remembering to hold their heads up and 'sound as if you believe it' as Miss Kay used to insist. Only three of the poems were virtually inaudible. Fortunately they weren't long. Then the Hon Miss Hodgkiss got up to present her judge's report.

To Meadows' surprise, she was generous with her praise. "I wish some of the adult poets I have the misfortune to judge had the same freshness and natural ability," she admitted. "Don't lose it as you grow older. Don't think that you have to be 'poetic' and start writing 'thees' and 'thous'. You don't talk like that in real life, do you? I'm afraid even some of you sixth formers fell into that trap. Why do you have to be miserable just because you've turned sixteen?"

There was much laughter from the parents, even while some of the pupils probably squirmed at the criticism. She was a good speaker, Meadows had to admit, and a lot of what she said was probably true.

Then the winners in each class read their poems, shyly and quietly in some cases, bellowed in others. They were all pretty good, Meadows thought with increasing pleasure. As the Hon Madge said, they were not the sort of maudlin teenage angst she had expected, and clearly daffodils had been banned. One girl in the fifth form was particularly impressive. 'There's real talent there,' Meadows thought. 'You can see that from Miss Kay's face.'

All in all, the school assembly passed more quickly and pleasantly than Meadows had feared. Only once did her mind drift, when Mr Symonds, the other English teacher, publicised the forthcoming school play, *Pilate's Wife's Dream*, written and directed by himself of course. As he talked about the joys of a school production, Meadows found she was dwelling again on the death of Major Fielding. It had upset her deeply, more than she wanted to admit. It wasn't just the death of a man she liked. It was something more, something that irritated within the general sadness. What was it? Becoming increasingly cross with herself, Meadows tried to bring the niggle into focus.

With a start, she realised the event was coming to an end. Mr Newman was thanking the Hon Madge for "devoting a whole day of her invaluable time". Meadows had to admire the ease with which the Hon Madge responded, and the evident respect with which she was treated. Whether she liked the woman or not, the Hon Madge was probably the most capable and intelligent person in Chalk Heath, apart from DI Ambrose perhaps. An absurd thought came to her mind. 'If anyone's capable of getting away with murder…'

Horrified, Meadows considered the idea. The woman had known both men. She'd also known where the key to Curiosity Corner was hidden and visited Maple View regularly for the Bridge Club. She could have found her way round both places. 'Supposing she had…' Urgently Meadows stopped herself. She was thinking absolute nonsense, half asleep no doubt. Getting up, she wished her neighbours a good afternoon.

Meadows' grudging respect for the Hon Madge grew as the assignment continued, as did her irritation. Clearing out the kitchen cupboards was not her idea of an appropriate job for Her Majesty's Constabulary, but if it was the only way she could persuade Miss Hodgkiss to let her stay for the rest of the afternoon, then she was prepared to do it. Being in plain clothes was not the glamorous change from routine she'd imagined. She would never admit that to her colleagues though. If they suspected she had been little more than an unpaid dogsbody, she would never hear the last of it.

So, when she returned to the Station to fill in her timesheet, Meadows smiled, and gave a good impression of someone having an interesting time. "I'm at a Guides Fun Day at St George's tomorrow," she explained cheerfully. "The Hon Madge has visitors afterwards so I'll see her home, then call here. Hopefully I'll make it by six."

"Where've you been today?" PC Higgins asked as he took Meadows' timesheet.

"At the Grammar and then Garth House."

"You do get around," he commented drily. "Did she give you a cuppa?"

"In bone china."

"Any biscuits?" one of the decorators called. They'd been around so long they were almost part of the team.

"McVitie's finest," Meadows assured him.

"What it is to nob with the upper classes," the red-haired painter replied, grinning. "I prefer Bourbons myself."

Before she left, Meadows reported to DI Ambrose. Cautiously she tapped on his door. He was evidently on the phone, so she waited. When she could no longer hear his voice, she tapped again.

"Ah, our undercover agent," Ambrose said, smiling as she entered. "How's it going?"

"Fine," Meadows assured him. "Basically Miss Hodgkiss is going about her normal business. I escorted her to the Grammar School today, and stayed at her house as long as she would let me. I've not seen any evidence of threats towards her, but I'm keeping my eyes open."

"You need to," Ambrose agreed. "Don't get bored or complacent. You may be wasting your time, or you might be the one person around to protect her. How are you getting on? I imagine she can be, shall we say, demanding?"

"I'll admit I found her irritating at first," Meadows replied carefully, "But I'm beginning to respect her, almost to feel sorry for her."

Ambrose raised an eyebrow in surprise. "Why?" he asked.

"Well, I didn't mean to snoop, but she left me on my own in the kitchen after we got back. I noticed a couple of photos. I think she may have lost someone and be coping by being busy and efficient. And she is from a different class to most of us round here, so she can't mix with people. She must be quite lonely."

Putting down his pen, Ambrose considered the idea. "Who were the photos of?" he asked. "It might be relevant."

"A young blond man in a blazer. 'To my lovely Marjorie,' was written at the bottom. The other was of Miss Hodgkiss as a girl with the same young man. They were standing by some boats with their arms round each other. I reckon he was killed in the war."

"That might explain a lot," Ambrose said thoughtfully. "Interesting. I've never noticed any photos myself."

"I don't suppose you've been in the kitchen," Meadows replied. "I imagine she'd forgotten they were there when she sent me."

Ambrose nodded. "See what else you can notice," he asked, "but make sure Miss Hodgkiss doesn't see, or she'll refuse to have you. Good luck with tomorrow."

Meadows felt she needed it.

Chapter Sixteen

Saturday 2nd April

The following morning Meadows met the Honourable Miss Hodgkiss at the gates to Garth House, and accompanied her in the car to St George's Parish Hall. This time Miss Hodgkiss agreed to walk from the car with Meadows. It was windy but not so cold. "Typical March weather," Miss Hodgkiss commented as she struggled to hold the car door, "except that this is meant to be April."

"I quite like the wind," Meadows admitted. "It clears the fug away. But it's heavy going when you're on a bike."

"You must be very fit," the Hon Madge replied approvingly. "I've passed you going up Victoria Road and admired your tenacity."

To Meadows' surprise, as they walked towards the church they chatted quite easily. It seemed as if Miss Hodgkiss was beginning to enjoy having a companion, though she would never admit it. As they walked round the side of the church towards the hall at the back, Meadows sighed inwardly with relief. A Guides' Fun Day had to be more interesting than the inside of a cupboard at Garth House.

Meadows' presence was explained by the Hon Madge without a flicker of embarrassment. "This is a young acquaintance of mine," she said airily. "Some of you may know her, WPC Meadows. She's interested in becoming a Guide Leader. I said she could come along and see what we get up to." Meadows had no choice but to agree. So she joined in the proceedings, hoping no one would pursue her later to become a leader. It would be difficult for her to find the time. Fortunately the other adults hardly gave her a second glance. They were too busy keeping a hundred girls between the age of eleven and fourteen amused. Most were in any case from out of town. The Fun Day catered for several troops of Girl Guides from Chalk Heath and the surrounding area.

As the day passed, Meadows decided she definitely didn't have the time, or the inclination, to be a Guide Leader. Though she'd been prepared for noise, she had been a girl herself, after all, she had underestimated how much noise a hundred excited girls could make. A hundred pairs of feet running backwards and forwards on a wooden floor sounded like an approaching hurricane. Even at lunch time the girls milled around and skipped and wanted the nearest 'Miss' to help them do whatever they weren't meant to be doing. The Hon Madge was presented with a plate of hot sausages prepared for her by one of the Patrol Leaders, but Meadows had to cook her own on a camp stove in the Vicarage garden, along with everyone else. The wind was uncooperative, blowing out matches and making gas sputter, but there was plenty of laughter to compensate.

In the afternoon the Hon Madge presented a thousand or so badges, or so it seemed, and was then allowed to sit at a trestle table and drink tea while the games resumed. Meadows was granted no such privileges. She was a fit young adult who could be dragooned into playing. If she tried to snatch her breath, she was dragged from her seat. By the time she'd played 'British Bulldog' three times, with half the room determined to bring her down in a heap, she had an ache in her back and a bruised knee. There was no respite. Two sessions of 'Chain Tag' followed, with Meadows chosen as 'Pig in the Middle' immediately afterwards and then as the 'bone' in 'The Farmer Wants a Wife'. When time for campfire was called and she could flop onto the floor, her hair was stuck to her forehead with sweat. She felt as though she had been on a week-long training course.

At last, the afternoon quietened into songs and stories, as everyone, including the Hon Madge, sat cross-legged on the floor and rested. Meadows knew some of the words to 'Ging Gang Goolie' and just about kept up with the actions, helped by a capable twelve-year old either side. Again, it was not the sort of thing she'd imagined doing as a plain clothes officer, but it was exhilarating.

At four o'clock, the Fun Day came to an end. Parents' voices could already be heard in the porch. The Hon Madge prepared to leave straight away. Tidying up and seeing that all the girls were safely escorted home were jobs for other people. She strode ahead, towards her car, Meadows almost running to keep up.

With a clearer sky, the light was better that afternoon. Though the wind made the hall door slam, there was a hint of spring. Daffodils were budding along the path around the church, and a clump of snowdrops still bloomed in the shelter of a tree. "What a lovely evening!" Meadows smiled.

Then she heard a shout from the car park.

"Look out!!"

Urgently Meadows looked around her. At once she heard the sound. Something was sliding down the church roof, above her. It sounded big. With a gasp she ran forwards, pushing the Hon Madge hard in the back. "Run!" she shouted.

The Hon Madge tried to turn round, shouting "What the…!" but Meadows had pushed her so hard the momentum made her stagger forwards. Trying to save herself, she started to stumble. Half running, half falling, she went flat on her face on the path, with Meadows tripping on top of her.

The sliding sound became a crash. Slates and chunks of mortar fell behind them, crashing into bushes and impaling in the soil between them. The ground seemed to shudder. Meadows could feel the rush of air as pieces narrowly missed her. Urgently she protected her head with her hands. Something hit her elbow. In pain she cried out. Her ears were full of the sound of falling debris.

Then everything went quiet.

Opening her eyes, she realised she was lying almost on top of Miss Hodgkiss, who was struggling to push her away. People were shouting from the hall porch. "Are you all right?" voices called.

For a moment Meadows felt as if the breath had been knocked out of her. She couldn't speak. Rolling away from Miss Hodgkiss, she tried to sit up. At once she gasped in pain. Urgently she lifted her head until she could look towards the car park. Someone had shouted a warning. She stared through the dusk. She could see no one, just parked cars.

Dropping back onto the path, she tried to get up. Her right arm wouldn't take her weight. Reason told her to stay where she was, but the path was cold and hard and she was desperate to see what had happened. A cluster of ancient tombstones stood near the path. Crawling towards them, she grabbed at the nearest with her good arm, and hauled herself into a sitting position.

The effort made her heart race. As soon as it had calmed, she examined her arm tentatively. She could flex her thumb and fingers but she couldn't move her arm at all. Her thick winter coat had protected

116

her from whatever hit her, and there was no sign of blood, but her shoulder didn't feel at all right. Risking another stab of pain, she tried moving her injured arm again. For a second she felt faint. Keeping very still, she waited until the mist cleared from her eyes.

The first of the parents had reached them and was staring in horror at the debris. "Are you all right?" she repeated.

The Hon Madge managed to speak first. "I think so," she said shakily.

Meadows took a deep breath. Carefully she pushed her sleeves back into place and rested her injured arm against her other hand. Despite the pain, her mind was clearing. She could see a large ridge tile wedged in the earth just behind where she and Miss Hodgkiss had fallen. It must have slid down the church roof, dislodging slates as it fell, then crashed to the ground. A piece of broken slate had hit her arm as she pushed Miss Hodgkiss to safety. She had been lucky. If the tile had hit ether of them they would have been killed.

Several of the Guide leaders had run out of the hall, and were joining the parents fussing around Miss Hodgkiss. None of the paid Meadows any attention other than a quick, "You OK?"

"I'm *fine*," the Hon Madge announced. "Just a bruised knee. See to the Officer." She looked in horror at the debris around and behind them.

Immediately one of the Guiders was bending over Meadows, helping her into a more comfortable position. "Call an ambulance!" she shouted enthusiastically towards the hall. It wasn't often they had a real life first-aid case.

"I don't need an ambulance," Meadows protested. "Doctor Simmons will do."

Another Patrol Leader arrived with a blanket and insisted on wrapping it around her. "You might have shock," she said. Her tone suggested she hoped Meadows would oblige.

Embarrassed by the attention, Meadows pushed the blanket aside. "Just get me to the hall," she begged. "It'll be warmer there."

At once the Hon Madge was helping her to her feet "You saved my life," she said. "I'm very grateful. I shall see your superiors know about this."

"It wasn't just me," Meadows replied. "Someone shouted a warning."

Miss Hodgkiss looked puzzled. "I didn't hear anything," she admitted. "One minute I was walking. The next you were sending me flying. But my hearing isn't as good as it used to be. Whatever happened, I am very, very grateful. I'll come with you in the ambulance."

"I don't need to go to hospital," Meadows insisted.

"But you must my dear. You need an X-ray at least." The Hon Madge looked again at the fallen slates. "I warned the Vicar this building was unsafe," she said crossly. "He said there was no money to repair it. Now the church will have to find the funds, or close. We can't have bits falling off as people walk by."

"Falling?" Meadows wondered. Could someone have got up onto the roof and pushed the ridge tile over, just as the Hon Madge passed? Surely that was impossible. But who had shouted the warning? She was certain she'd heard a man's voice. Was it the same man who was following her? If it was, why was he at the church hall that afternoon? Had he known the Hon Madge would be attacked, and wanted to make sure she wasn't hurt as well? Did she have an unknown Guardian Angel?

One of the leaders met them at the hall door. The Vicar had been sent for, but he was at the Shalimar Hotel, the other side of the Heath. He'd been doing his bit at one of the old people's groups they hosted. He was terribly upset at the news and sent his profoundest apologies. If the Officer was kept in the hospital, he would visit her tomorrow morning.

'I sincerely hope I'm not!' Meadows thought. She hated hospitals. Besides, the Reverend James H Beresford was nice enough, but he had a habit of insisting on long-winded prayers, whether you needed a prayer or not. He also kept forgetting people's names, which made it hard for him to pray for someone, unless he'd written their name down beforehand.

The bell of an ambulance sounded through the streets, getting nearer. While everyone waited Meadows was entertained royally in the church hall. Propped on a chair with a pile of prayer kneelers at her feet, and wrapped in a car blanket, she was definitely the star attraction of the afternoon. Those girls who had not yet gone home would have an exciting story to tell their parents, much better than a run-of-the-mill Fun Day.

"I'll come with you to the hospital," Miss Hodgkiss repeated. "We need to see you're not kept waiting around."

Sighing, Meadows resigned herself to being taken to hospital. With a dozen or more keen first-aiders fussing around her, she wasn't going to be allowed to go home quietly. "Can someone let the Station know?" she asked. "They'll wonder why I haven't come in to sign my timesheet."

"I'll talk to them," the Hon Madge said, frowning.

At once Meadows realised she'd jeopardised their cover story. "I didn't sign it before I left this morning," she lied quickly. "I promised to call back after I'd finished here."

The frown disappeared. "Of course, my dear," the Hon Madge said lightly. "Don't you worry about a thing."

Chapter Seventeen

Monday 4th April

News of WPC Meadows' injury spread quickly around the Station. "Dislocated shoulder, all back in place now, but likely to be off a couple of days at least," Higgins explained.

PC Green was deeply impressed and worried. The prospect of a couple of days without Meadows' encouragement left him feeling awkward and out of place amongst the more experienced male officers. He hoped she wouldn't be off work any longer. When someone suggested they send her some chocolates and a card, he offered at once to go out and buy them.

Even PC Vernon grudgingly conceded that having a female officer around had been useful. "Bit of a heroine I gather," he admitted. "Saved the Hon Madge. Not sure that was such a great achievement, though," he added with a wry smile. "But it'll go down well with the boss."

DS Winters was tempted to agree but frowned appropriately. He had no liking for the Hon Miss Hodgkiss but he wouldn't have wanted her to be crushed by a pile of fallen slates. "So it should," he replied firmly. "But for Meadows' quick thinking, we'd have the Press baying at our door, not to mention a whole pile of 'aristos' wanting to know why we didn't protect an Honourable."

Going back into his office, he sighed. He felt responsible for Meadows' being hurt. He'd agreed to her protecting Miss Hodgkiss, even though he thought it wasn't a suitable job for a woman, and doubted the need for protection in the first place. "Thank goodness neither of them were killed!" he said to himself several times. Though

Meadows' injuries weren't serious and the Hon Madge was full of thanks, it might have been very different. He shuddered at the idea.

Even so, Meadows being injured was inconvenient. The Hon Madge was going to London. They couldn't protect her there, but hopefully the threat was linked to Chalk Heath anyway. Miss Hodgkiss had willingly agreed to let Meadows accompany her again after she returned, but would Meadows be well enough by then? If she wasn't, they'd have to try to persuade Madge to accept PC Green. He doubted they'd have much success.

There was also a more immediate problem. The Superintendent in Miss Flowers' Division had given permission for her to be brought to Chalk Heath for questioning, providing she agreed to come voluntarily, which to everyone's surprise she did. She would be arriving that afternoon. Ordinarily WPC Meadows would have been present at the interview. With so little notice, it was going to be difficult to arrange another woman officer to come. Jenners Park had already said they couldn't help. He could go ahead with the interview, with Green or Vernon as witnesses, but he hesitated. Miss Flowers sounded volatile, if not actually unstable. She ought to have female company. Getting her to agree to come at a later date could be difficult. Besides, with such a long drive, the car bringing Miss Flowers had probably already set off.

There was also this new incident to consider. Before he interviewed Miss Flowers, he ought to know whether the damage at the church could be linked to the deaths of Robin Harvey and Major Fielding. If it could, it became less likely that an outsider was involved. Miss Flowers would only be under suspicion for sending the malicious packets. That would affect the way he questioned her. But for Meadows' quick action, the third judge of the poetry competition could have been lying in the morgue.

As soon as PC Green returned from the shop, Winters called him into his office. "You're probably the most agile of us," he admitted. "I want you and Vernon to go St George's. See if there's a way up onto roof, and whether anyone could have thrown that roof tile. I've arranged for the Vicar to meet you in the car park."

Green was pleased to be involved more. Vernon was less enthusiastic. It was always dreary and cold at St George's. "Keep your eyes open for the two runaways," Winters instructed, by way of additional persuasion. "I've a hunch somebody's sheltering them. They may have mates on the estate."

The Reverend Beresford was sitting in his car when Vernon and Green arrived, keeping out of the wind. Greeting them, he led the way to the church. An area of garden and path had been roped off and a large sign warned 'Danger. Unsafe Building.' In the morning light the damage to the garden was frightening. Broken twigs and flattened daffodils lay everywhere. Several bushes had been battered, their branches snapped. Slates still stood upright where they had knifed into the soil. A large ridge tile lay on the path, its edges chipped. "Don't go too near," the Vicar warned. "There may be more loose up there."

"Cor Blimey!" PC Green said, pausing to stare at the devastation. "Would you Adam and Eve it?"

The Vicar looked at him uncertainly. "Dreadful business!" he agreed. "I keep telling the Diocese this place needs urgent work, but it isn't high on their list."

"I suppose there's a lot of bomb damage to repair still," PC Vernon agreed. "Jenners Park was hit quite badly, wasn't it?" When he wanted, he could be disarmingly pleasant.

"They were indeed," the Reverend Beresford agreed. "They have to have priority. This is just a village church that doesn't have a village any more, and its congregation is dwindling I'm afraid. If they go anywhere, people on the estate walk to St Edward's, the new church, or to the Sally (sorry, I mean Salvation) Army. They do a good job round here." He smiled ruefully.

PC Green followed him as he led the way towards the porch. Vernon lingered outside, walking round the side of the building to examine the pieces of broken slate.

The Vicar unlocked the church door. It creaked as it swung open. Removing some litter from the porch, he led the way into the duller light inside. "St George's has rather outlived its usefulness," he admitted, "though the hall is much in demand. The congregation struggles on out of respect for history, as much as anything. The nave is Norman. It would be a crime to let so old a building fall down."

The inside of the church smelt to PC Green of musty hymn books and wet coats. It reminded him of school assemblies. He blinked in the gloom. "Is there a way up to the roof?" he asked, doing his best to speak the Queen's English.

"Steps up to the bell tower. From there you can get onto the roof through a hatch. I hope you have a good head for heights. Fortunately it's not too wet today."

PC Vernon joined them. "The ridge tile's too damaged to tell if anyone prized it off," he announced.

"Goodness! Is that what you suspect?" the Reverend Beresford asked, appalled. "That someone did this deliberately? Surely not. They'd have had to have a key to this door." He nodded in the direction of the porch.

"Who does have one?" Vernon asked. "Apart from you? And the Verger, I suppose?"

"Only a few people: the flower arrangers and some of the Scout and Guide leaders." The Vicar paused thoughtfully, then added, "I suppose the lady who cleans has one. The Sunday School leader will have too, and Miss Maplin who polishes the brasses."

"That sounds like quite a few to me," Vernon commented.

"But I can't see any of them crawling on the roof," the Vicar protested.

"It would let you off the hook if someone did do it deliberately," Vernon pointed out.

The Reverend Beresford nodded. "But I really do doubt it," he insisted. "The roof was relaid at the beginning of this century, but nothing much has been done on it since. The slates are fixed with nails and they can work loose. The wind starts swinging them around until the nail hole gets bigger. Ultimately the slate comes away. We've had a few down recently." He shook his head. "This is the first time a ridge tile's come off, though. They're fixed with cement."

He opened the door to the tower. A flight of narrow stone steps led upwards. A little light filtered in through a slit of a window, but it was hard to tell where the steps led.

"Bit of a tight squeeze isn't it?" Vernon commented. He turned towards PC Green. "You're the thin one," he remarked, grinning. "You pop up and tell us what you can see."

"The hatch is right above you," the Vicar assured him. "Just push it with your head and it'll open. There's no lock. It's a good view from there, although I admit I haven't been up for a while." He patted his rather large belly as he spoke.

'Climbing church towers wasn't in the Manual,' Green thought wryly, but he said nothing. Vernon passed him his torch. "See if there's any stray Girl Guides up there," he joked.

The stairs were easy enough. Green was fit and lanky, well able to squeeze into small places. He wasn't happy at the unevenness of the steps, but an old rope attached to the wall gave him some support, though he took care not to pull on it too hard in case it came off. At the top he found himself in a dusty bell tower. The bells looked as though they hadn't been rung for years and there was a pigeon's nest on the beam above them. The whole place smelt of damp wood and rusting metal. A line of light showed him where the trapdoor was set into the roof. Pushing at it with his head, he lifted it away. To reach outside, he had to climb on an old wooden step ladder that had been left against the wall, presumably for that purpose.

The roof of the tower was covered in lead and appeared quite sound. Tentatively, Green pulled himself off the ladder. The wind had dropped since yesterday, but up there it still howled. It blew Green's hair into his eyes and tugged at his jacket. He was glad he'd left his helmet with PC Vernon, or it would be half way to Jenners Park by now. As the Vicar had said, he did indeed have a good view, over the whole St George's estate in the one direction, and the allotments the other. To the north he could see St Wilfred's Catholic Church and the Railway Station, the theatre and the shops along the High Street. To the east the Heath spread out before him. If he leant forward he could just make out Old Chalk Heath Village, and the spire of the ruined church there.

He had climbed up to look at the roof, Green reminded himself. A maintenance ladder was fixed along one side of the ridge, and there was another at the far end, giving access to the gutters around the outer edges. About a foot away from the tower, a gap like a broken tooth marked where the missing ridge-tile had once stood. Slates were broken or missing in a widening line below it. As the top ones had fallen, they had dislodged more and more below them. One slate was still in the gutter, pointing like a jagged knife towards the sky.

Carefully PC Green reached through the lower part of the castellated wall around the tower roof. Without stretching too much, he could touch the gap where the ridge tile had stood. It would have been possible for someone to dislodge the tile without risking stepping on to the maintenance ladder. They would have needed a steady hand and a cool head, however.

Standing up, he looked down at the churchyard and the allotments. He could see no sign of a tent or a bivouac. The runaways were not hiding there in full view. Twenty or more sheds were scattered around the allotments. They could be living in any one of those, though he would have thought the allotment holders would have spotted them by now. Still, it would be worth asking if the sheds had been checked.

Then he looked towards the west. On the ground, it was hard to see between the privet hedges, but from there he had a clear view of the gardens across the estate. A lot of them had sheds. They too would make a good hiding place, but Sergeant Hurst had arranged for leaflets to be distributed, telling householders to lock all out-buildings. The boys would have been found unless, as the DS suggested, someone was sheltering them. Apart from the remains of an old three-piece-suite on someone's back lawn and a car on blocks, he could see nothing else of note. Then he saw a narrow service road running behind a row of the larger houses. It led to a block of lock-up garages, invisible from the road. They might not have been checked. He would mention them to PC Vernon.

Beginning to feel very cold, he went back to the hatch. "Blimey it's taters up here," he called down. Then he hurriedly translated, "it's freezing with all this wind. Pass the camera, while me hands still work."

He took several photographs for DS Winters before climbing back into the tower. The camera and torch were a nuisance, even in his pockets, and he nearly slipped on one of the steps. Urgently he grabbed at the rope. Fortunately the bolt holding it to the wall held his weight.

Afterwards he explained to PC Vernon and the Vicar what he had seen. "Someone could have deliberately dislodged the tile," he concluded. "And they'd have been able to see Miss Hodgkiss coming."

The Vicar shook his head in denial. "I'm sure there's no one in Chalk Heath who would do such a thing," he said firmly. Then his conviction wavered. "It is an odd coincidence though. I'm afraid the Honourable Miss Hodgkiss isn't very popular in the town. She means well and does a lot of good, but she tends to ride roughshod over people. I'm sure she'll have made enemies." He shuddered. "I thank the Lord, and your young WPC, that she wasn't hurt."

They returned to the Station soon afterwards.

DS Winters frowned uneasily as he listened to Vernon and Green's report. He would have preferred a clearer answer than "It could have been deliberate, but was probably a coincidence." He didn't like coincidences. They usually turned out to have hidden links. Still, coincidences did happen and he didn't have sufficient grounds to assume that Miss Flowers was involved in the deaths of Robin Harvey and the Major. Equally, he couldn't discount her, just because there was no way she was climbing on the church roof during the Guide

125

Day. He would have to wait and see what the woman was like. More than ever, he wished WPC Meadows was available. She could often tell when another woman was lying.

"No sign of the runaways," Vernon added. "Though Green's got a few suggestions."

"Write them down," Winters instructed, turning towards PC Green. Then he paused.

"What do you reckon?" he asked Vernon. "What's your gut instinct? Was it an accident?"

Vernon grimaced. "Dunno Guv," he said honestly. "Green went up on the roof. I didn't. The lad did OK, by the way. I wouldn't have wanted to go up there. The stairs looked iffy to me."

PC Green flushed at the praise, and from such an unexpected source. Until then he hadn't particularly liked Tom Vernon, and thought the feeling was mutual. "You'd have to be a cool customer to go up the stairs, climb out and wait for someone to pass below," he agreed, choosing his words carefully. "But you could do it."

"The Hon Madge is adamant it was a coincidence," Winters pointed out.

"The Vicar isn't," Vernon replied. "I bet he's felt like throwing a ridge-tile at her more than once."

Smiling, Winters nodded. "Go and brush your uniform," he advised PC Green. "You're covered in cobwebs. There's a brush on the window ledge in the lavs. Use it." He shook his head as the young Constable flushed again. "Take a quick break, both of you," he added. "Go and get a cup of tea. You both look perished."

Afterwards, Winters sat staring ahead reflectively. He felt even less certain now about interviewing Janice Flowers. Reluctantly he rang Maple View.

Mrs McKewan herself answered the phone. "I'll see if Miss Meadows is at home," she offered. "She's quite a heroine I gather. Everyone here's very proud of her."

As he waited, Winters wondered whether Pauline Meadows appreciated everyone at Maple View being proud of her. From what he'd heard, it was hardly her sort of place. By now she'd probably had enough of being congratulated on the way to the bathroom.

"Hello, Sarge," Meadows' voice greeted him at last. She sounded relieved to have a phone call.

"How are you feeling?" Winters began tentatively.

"Fine in myself, thanks. My arm's a nuisance, it's all strapped up, but the hospital's given me some pain-killers so it's not too bad. I'm sure it'll be fine again soon."

"Are you well enough to come to the Police Station for an hour or so?" Winters asked. "I could do with you sitting in on an interview."

"I'd be happy to," Meadows replied, "But I'm afraid I can't ride my bike at the moment."

"I'll send a car up for you," Winters offered quickly. "The interview shouldn't take long. We have a Miss Janice Flowers coming for questioning about the malicious packages. I've a feeling she'll either prove to be completely innocent, or confess immediately. She seems a bit odd. That's why I'd like to have you with us."

"I'll get changed at once," Meadows agreed, with pleasure. "I'm bored out of my skull here, and I won't notice my arm so much if I'm busy." She hesitated. "Give me half an hour, though. Sorry. I'm a bit slow at the moment and I'll have to put my jacket on over my sling."

"No need to apologise," Winters assured her.

He was surprised at how relieved he felt. He hadn't looked forward to interviewing Miss Flowers, even with PC Vernon present. Slightly dotty women scared him. He never knew whether they were going to burst into tears.

Chapter Eighteen

Miss Flowers arrived five minutes after Meadows. PC Green fetched them both a cup of tea, and then attended to the driver who had brought the suspect from Bath. Not for the first time, Green felt like the office tea boy but he didn't mind at all fetching a cuppa for Meadows.

Winters glanced into the waiting area curiously. He had expected a much older woman, mousy and drab, the sort of bitter, frustrated spinster he associated with poison pen letters. To his surprise, Miss Flowers was very attractive. She was probably only in her thirties and wearing a pretty lace blouse and long black skirt, nipped in at the waist. Her face was beautiful, in a pale, fragile way, framed by dark hair twisted into an elegant chignon hiarstyle. With her neat black boots peeping under her skirt, she looked like pictures of Victorian ladies he had seen. When he noticed the crocheted shawl draped over the back of her chair, he decided the effect was deliberate. Someone must have told her she had the face of a Victorian heroine, so she dressed to suit.

When Meadows and Miss Flowers had drunk their tea, he invited both of them into the interview room. He began his questioning informally, hoping to keep Miss Flowers co-operative. "It's very good of you to come such a long way," he began. "I hope you had a comfortable journey."

The woman shrugged elegantly. "It was an outing," she said.

"I hope we haven't put you to a great deal of inconvenience," Winters continued.

"But you have," Miss Flowers replied. "I had to ask a neighbour to sit with my mother." She spoke as elegantly as she looked, slowly and softly, almost dreamily.

"You look after your mother?" Winters asked.

"Yes. She's almost bed-ridden. I couldn't leave her on her own for a whole day."

"Of course not," Winters agreed. He nodded towards Meadows, inviting her to join in the conversation. For a second Meadows couldn't think of anything to say. Her shoulder was hurting, making it difficult to concentrate. Something was distracting her too, niggling at the back of her mind. She couldn't think what that something was, except that it was connected with the weather. As she came down from Maple View in the car, it had begun to rain. Water was dripping outside the interview room window now, splashing onto metal. It kept reminding her of something, something at Maple View.

Forcing herself back to the woman in front of her, she remarked, "It must be very difficult for you, caring for your mother every day. How long have you looked after her?"

"Five years. Since she had her last stroke."

"That's a long time," Winters agreed. "How did you explain coming here to your neighbour?"

"I told her my sister was very ill."

Winters thought of his own sister looking after their mother back in Donegal, and nodded sympathetically. She didn't get many outings. The offer of a day trip would have been hard for her to refuse. No wonder Miss Flowers had agreed to come. "Where does your sister live?" he continued.

"I don't have a sister. She died last year. That's why I don't get any help with my mother." Miss Flowers sighed. "I do have a cousin," she went on, "but I thought a sister would be more convincing. I didn't want to tell my neighbour I was coming to a Police Station."

"Of course not," Winters agreed. "People do tittle-tattle, don't they?" He wasn't sure how to proceed without alarming the woman and making her more guarded. Glancing at WPC Meadows he nodded slightly, suggesting she take another turn.

"I imagine writing poetry is a big help," Meadows suggested, "keeping you sane while you're stuck indoors."

"Oh it does!" Miss Flowers replied, smiling for the first time.

"When do you write?" Meadows asked. "One of my friends is a poet. She writes a lot early in the morning, before the rest of the family gets up."

"In the evening," Miss Flowers said, turning fully towards Meadows, as if to a friend. "Mum likes to listen to the radio, but she often falls asleep in her chair. Then I go into the kitchen and have a blissful hour or two to myself. I can read when she's awake, but I can't write."

"You read a lot by the Brontës, don't you?" Winters joined in.

"Oh yes. I can read their novels over and over again. And of course I have a special relationship with Emily."

Winters wasn't sure how to reply to that statement, and merely nodded. There was an awkward pause. A gutter above the window was evidently blocked. He could hear water dripping from it onto the drain cover below. The decorators were supposed to have sorted the problems outside. He would have to mention the blockage to Higgins. He usually dealt with such things.

Miss Flowers nodded towards Meadows' sling. "What did you do to your arm?" she asked. "Was it in the line of duty?"

"A bit of roof fell on me," Meadows replied vaguely.

"I thought it might be something exciting."

"It was at the time, a little *too* exciting," Meadows replied wryly.

"I used to want to be a police lady," Miss Flowers said unexpectedly. "Or an air hostess, something interesting, but my mother wanted me to stay at home."

"So did mine," Meadows said, smiling slightly.

"Why did you want to talk to me?" Miss Flowers asked her. "The policeman who rang said it was to do with the competition."

"That's right," Winters agreed vaguely. "I gather you enter every year?"

"My cousin sends me the entry form."

"Your cousin lives in Chalk Heath?" Winters asked. He took care not to betray his sudden interest. "Whereabouts?"

"Near the Park. I don't see her often. Do you think your driver would let me call there afterwards?"

"He might," Winters replied. He needed to think about this new development, and how to re-angle the questioning. Once again he glanced in Meadows' direction. She could give him a moment's pause.

"I'm fascinated by your special relationship with Emily Brontë," Meadows said, honestly. "How does that work?"

"She guides me when I'm writing. Sometimes she gives me whole lines. I hear her sisters sometimes, but Emily's my friend. We often chat when I'm alone in my bedroom."

Meadows managed not to show surprise. "It must be very lonely, just you and your mother," she suggested. "I can see you'd need a friend. I used to have an imaginary friend when I was little."

130

"Emily isn't imaginary!" Miss Flowers retorted. "People aren't gone after they die. They're still there in spirit! Emily realised I'm as lonely as she was, and came to help me."

For a moment neither Winters nor Meadows could think of another question. The woman's reply was too strange, and worrying. Winters decided to see what would happen if he startled her. "Did you send the packages?" he asked abruptly.

"I don't know what you're talking about," Miss Flowers retorted, but a bright patch of colour was spreading up her cheeks.

"I think you do," Winters insisted, more gently. "You were angry with the competition judges. They didn't value your poems enough, or understand they were really written by Emily. So you sent threatening notes to them, wrapped with whatever you thought would give them a fright."

"No I didn't!" Miss Flowers insisted but the flush was deepening across her cheeks.

"Did Emily ask you to?" Winters persisted.

"No! She would never do such a thing," Miss Flowers said vehemently. "I want to go home. You brought me here under false pretences. I didn't know you were going to question me about silly packages." She stood up abruptly.

Meadows had an idea. "Emily wouldn't ask you to send them," she agreed. "But her brother Branwell might have done."

Miss Flowers hesitated, her hand on the back of her chair.

"Did he?" Winters asked.

"Perhaps."

Miss Flowers' reply was so soft that Winters wasn't sure he had heard correctly. "It's the sort of thing Branwell would do," he bluffed, "and he's very persuasive. *Did* he tell you to send them?"

Sitting wearily back in her chair, Miss Flowers nodded. "I never could say no to him," she admitted.

Winters caught his breath. He had a confession, but not in the way he'd expected. Until the woman was properly cautioned it wouldn't be allowable as evidence. He wasn't even sure Miss Flowers was fit for trial. To his horror, she began to cry. He never could cope with a woman's tears, as his wife knew. In alarm he looked towards WPC Meadows.

Meadows was less affected, recognising the technique. When she was a teenager she had tried it on her father several times, and got her own way as a result. She could tell a try-on now. "Did Branwell tell you to kill Mr Harvey and Major Fielding?" she asked sharply.

"Kill them? No of course not!" Miss Flowers stopped crying and stared at her in horror. "He wouldn't kill anyone! He just asked me to worry them a bit."

"Worry?" Winters repeated sharply. "You were threatening them. We can charge you with making death threats."

"No! Branwell just told me to give them a taste of how it feels to look for the post, expecting something nice and then finding a horrid rejection slip inside. Not even just a rejection; horrible snide comments from someone who doesn't know what they're talking about!" Miss Flowers was becoming genuinely upset. Then she stopped in alarm. "Has something happened to Mr Harvey?" she asked.

"He's dead."

"He can't be!" Once again Miss Flowers started to cry.

Winters shook his head in bewilderment. "You deny killing Mr Harvey?" he asked firmly.

"Of course I do! I sent the packets because Branwell told me to, but I had nothing to do with Mr Harvey dying. How could I? I live in Bath. This is the first time I've left my mother for nearly a year, and last time was to go to the dentist's."

"So how did you send them out from different towns?" Winters demanded. "You can travel if you want to."

"No I can't! Ask my neighbours or the Doctor. I never leave my mother. The last time I did she fell and broke her wrist."

"So how *did* you post them?"

"I asked my neighbour's husband. He's a Commercial Traveller. I don't know where he posted them from." Miss Flowers was going very red, anger making her voice quiver.

"And Major Fielding?" Winters persisted, though he knew the answer. "Do you also deny killing him?"

"Is he dead too?" Taking out her handkerchief, Miss Flowers began to wail into it, rocking back and forth. "I didn't. I didn't," she kept repeating.

Winters decided to stop the interview. "I think we all need a break," he said. "WPC Meadows, would you take Miss Flowers into one of the other rooms where she can be quiet? Stay with her. I'll ask Green to bring another cup of tea."

DI Ambrose wasn't in that day, so he went to see Mac.

Briefly he explained the situation. "What do we do?" he asked finally. "I don't think the woman's sane. There's no evidence she killed either Robin Harvey or the Major, and I doubt if a jury would convict her of deliberate malice towards them, if it even got to a court."

"Leave it to her own Super to decide," Mac advised. "Get Higgins to interview her again under caution, so there can be no question of you exerting any duress. If she confesses again, I'll forward her statement to Bath, with the request that they take it from there. If she's as disturbed as you think and they decide she's a danger to others, or herself, they'll go for sectioning, rather than a criminal charge. They may just ask for psychiatric reports and give her a warning. It's up to them." He shook his head. "Poor woman!"

Relieved at not having to make the decision himself, Winters went back to the interview room. As he glanced through the window he could see Miss Flowers had calmed down. She was talking to WPC Meadows almost cheerfully.

He called Meadows outside, to explain Mac's decision. "Higgins will interview her now and see if she confesses again. Then we'll send her back to Bath."

"She needs a meal first," Meadows pointed out. "I could ask the Copper Kettle to send something over. She says she can pay."

"Good thought," Winters agreed. "You're looking worn out yourself. I'll get Green to drive you back home."

"Thanks." Hesitantly Meadows turned to leave. Then she turned back. "I've remembered something that's been niggling me, Sir," she said. "About the Major."

Winters was anxious to speak to Higgins and start the formal interview, but he waited. "What?" he asked.

"My rooms are near the Gents' bathroom. Whenever one of them has a bath, I hear the tap dripping for about an hour afterwards. I didn't hear it when the Major was found."

"Sorry, I don't see the relevance," Winters admitted.

"I don't think the Major had been using the bath recently," Meadows explained. "He might have had a bath, but not in the hour before Mavis and I found him."

Winters frowned. He couldn't see why a tap not dripping could be so important. Maybe it didn't drip every time. But Meadows was clearly concerned, and he'd learnt that her judgement could be as sharp as any man's. She had the gut feeling or instinct, whatever you liked to call it, that made a good copper. "Talk to DI Ambrose about it tomorrow," he suggested. "See if he thinks it's important."

Chapter Nineteen

Tuesday 5th April

Ambrose stared ahead thoughtfully. It could be nothing. Just a dripping tap. Sometimes it dripped. Sometimes it didn't. That was all there was to it: just a trivial detail with no special meaning.

But WPC Meadows was sharp. If she felt a detail was important, it might be. Was it possible the Major hadn't run the bath water within the hour of his death? The bath was empty when they found him, so the temperature of the water was no guide. He was still wet but he wasn't soaked. He could have been there some time. And what if he had lain there a while before being found? That didn't necessarily mean it was foul play.

Frowning, Ambrose drank from the cup of tea Meadows had brought him, and considered the possibility. Did Major Fielding lie on the bathroom floor for an hour, dying? Doc Halstead had given the cause of death as blood loss, following an injury to the head. The Major might not have died if someone had found him in time. No wonder Meadows was upset. Her rooms were near the bathroom. She could have saved him if she'd realised he was hurt. She was being too hard on herself of course. With an 'occupied' sign on the door, a Gentlemen's bathroom wasn't a place a young woman could just barge into. Besides, if she hadn't heard the Major cry out, there was no way Pauline Meadows could have known he needed help.

But why didn't any of the male residents realise the Major was taking too long? Were they so used to him being ages in the bathroom, they didn't notice? And why had the Major fallen in the first place? The bath mat had non-slip tabs on the back according to the

Housekeeper, and the post mortem hadn't shown any sign of high blood pressure, heart problem, or drugs that might have caused him to black-out. For his age, he was a very healthy specimen Doc Halstead had declared ruefully. Perhaps the bath water was too hot or the room too steamy. Either could have made him faint.

Another, more intriguing possibility occurred to Ambrose. Did someone know the Major had fallen and leave him there to die? That might explain the odd position of the towel. Could they even have caused his fall? Supposing they had, and Meadows was right about the tap, they must have done so more than an hour before he was found. But how? And, more importantly, why?

The more he thought about the suggestion, the more worrying it became. If Robin Harvey's and the Major's deaths were linked, someone in Chalk Heath was very clever, and very dangerous. They were so clever they could kill twice and make both deaths appear accidental. They could also leave no clue as to their identity or motive, at least so far as Ambrose could see. It would have been much simpler if the suspicious parcels had been sent by a local person, and not by a sad little woman from hundreds of miles away. With Miss Flowers' formal confession and her strong alibi, a promising line of enquiry had come to an end. She clearly hadn't murdered either man. He needed to go to Maple View again and see if he and Winters had missed something.

The telephone rang, breaking into his thoughts. "Call for you, from Miss Havering," PC Higgins said.

Sighing, Ambrose replied, "What about?"

"She says something's gone from the shop."

"Put her on," Ambrose said at once, sitting bolt upright.

"I'm so sorry to bother you," Miss Havering began. "But I think something may have been stolen after all. Mr Harvey's brother asked me to do an inventory before he takes over. I've been going through the photos. I think an envelope is missing."

"Just one envelope?" Ambrose repeated in surprise. Urgently he grabbed a pencil and notepad.

"Yes." Miss Havering's voice echoed, as if she were phoning from the desk at the front of the shop, rather than the office. "A lady from Jenners Park died a few months back, a Mrs Adelaide Vaudin I believe. Her husband was clearing her belongings and sold Mr Harvey a box of photos and old postcards. He told me a lady he knew in Guernsey would be interested in them. She's a researcher at the Priaulx Library. I typed the letter to her myself so I remember it clearly. She replied saying she particularly wanted to see the photos of German soldiers. They're the ones that are missing. When you asked me to check after Mr Harvey died, I saw the box and assumed everything was inside. I'm so sorry."

"Can you recall what the photos were of?" Ambrose asked. The pencil was going blunt and he scrabbled in his drawer for another. "You say some had German soldiers on?"

"Two, with their girlfriends. They had their arms round the girls. One of the girls was looking a little," she paused, "well, *large*," she finished.

"Large?" Ambrose queried.

There was another slight pause.

"Well, to stop beating about the bush, one of the girls looked like she might have been expecting."

"Ah," Ambrose said, understanding the implications. "I see. Do you remember anything else?"

"Yes. There were inscriptions on the back, something like 'You, me, Rudolf and Albrecht', and 'Having a lovely day together'. There might have been one on the third photo but I don't remember. The envelope had '1942' written on it."

"How do you know they were taken on Guernsey?" Ambrose asked, puzzled.

"Mr Harvey recognised the scenery. He used to go there on holiday."

"And you're sure about the men's names?"

"Yes," Miss Havering insisted. "I thought it odd that Germans should be photographed so casually in 1942. I read up a bit about the Occupation afterwards. At first, it was quite relaxed, almost friendly, at least until people started being deported. The girls who fraternised got a bit of a bad name, though."

"I can imagine," Ambrose replied drily. "Do you remember anything else?"

Miss Havering paused, as if trying to visualise the photographs. "There was a sign saying 'Ferbrache Farm' on one," she said at length. She spelled the name for Ambrose. "The two couples were walking in front of it. I think there was a building behind them. Another picture showed a beach, as if they were out for the day together. They weren't posed photos; sort of candid shots, if you see what I mean. I can understand the Guernsey lady being so interested. My book said there's still a lot of secrecy about the Occupation."

"Could Mr Harvey have taken them out of the box?" Ambrose checked.

"No. I've searched his desk and his rooms," Miss Havering replied. "They're not lying around and he didn't ask me to post them."

Ambrose was becoming increasingly intrigued. "Might he have posted them himself?" he asked.

"I don't think so. He was always careful with customers' material, more than he was with his own things." Miss Havering's voice thickened with grief at the loss of a man she had liked more than she'd realised. "He preferred to deliver packets personally," she went on. "I heard him on the phone discussing whether he should go to Guernsey, or the lady from the library should come to us. Even if he'd decided they couldn't meet, he'd have sent the envelope special delivery and kept the receipt. I can't find a receipt either."

The assistant paused. When she spoke again she sounded worried. "I think Mr Harvey heard someone in the shop and came down," she admitted. "That's why he blundered into the bookcase. I don't imagine a thief was looking for old photos, more likely the safe or the till. They probably tipped the box up and grabbed the stuff off the floor. Maybe they didn't even mean to run off with the envelope. I mean, who'd want old photos? But if they were after the money, they might come back. I'm beginning to feel a bit frightened here on my own."

'They might indeed come back,' Ambrose thought grimly but he instead he said reassuringly, "I'm sure you're safe during the day, but I'll ask our officers to keep an eye on you. Make sure you lock up when you leave, and take the key with you. Don't leave it in the usual place. Then if the thief does return at night, they won't be able to get in easily. I'll get whoever's on that beat to call regularly."

"Thank you." Once again Miss Havering paused. "It was an accident, wasn't it?" she asked uncertainly. "I mean, the thief couldn't have pushed the bookcase onto Mr Harvey, could they? That'd be awful." She sounded near to tears.

"We've recorded it as an accident," Ambrose assured her. "We'll investigate all possibilities though. Would you mind if I borrow the box and look through the photos myself? We can see if there are any fingerprints on it too. It's worth a try."

"Thank you," Miss Havering repeated, though she hardly sounded reassured. "I'm so sorry I didn't spot the photos were missing."

"Why should you?" Ambrose commented. "Just one envelope in a box? You've done well to remember it now."

Afterwards, he returned to his tea. It was cold by now, and bright orange; undrinkable. He might dissolve his spoon in it, he thought wryly. Reading his notes, he made a few words clearer and underlined others, then sat in thought again. The name Vaudin was vaguely familiar. He hadn't come across it professionally he was sure. Then he recalled being introduced to a middle-aged woman in a red dress. It was at a reception at the Jenners Park Theatre. She was one of their donors. Mary had remarked how pale and thin the red dress made her look, though perhaps she was ill. That would be consistent with a woman dying recently. He hadn't realised she was from Guernsey, but there was no reason he should, just by looking at her. After all, the Channel Islands were part of the British Isles, despite being closer to France.

'Could she have been the 'You' or 'Me' in the photo?' Ambrose wondered. From the way the inscriptions were worded it sounded as though someone had sent 'You' the envelope, someone who was 'Me'. If Mrs Vaudin had still been alive, he could have asked her, but it was her death that had led to the photos surfacing. Her husband might know, but he doubted it. He had probably never looked at the photos, or he wouldn't have taken them into Curiosity Corner for sale. Even now, families would be touchy about a relative who might have fraternised with the enemy.

Another thought suddenly struck him. Could Mrs Vaudin have had the photographs for less innocent reasons? A spot of blackmail perhaps? He'd have to get someone to look into Mrs Vaudin's finances, preferable on the quiet.

Picking up his cup and saucer, he took them back to the canteen, then knocked on Winters' door.

DS Winters looked up in surprise. "Fancy a cuppa at the Copper Kettle?" Ambrose asked. "My last one was stone cold, and I need to bounce some ideas off you."

"Anything to avoid writing reports," Winters agreed cheerfully.

Calling at the front desk to say where they were going, Ambrose was surprised to have a scribbled note passed to him. "Bath not charging, sectioning, pending psychiatric reports." For a moment he thought of the wrong sort of bath and was thoroughly bewildered. He looked at Higgins quizzically.

139

"The Chief's had to go to one of his drinkie-poo meetings," PC Higgins replied. "Some dignitary visiting our patch. He left that for you."

"Ah, Miss Flowers," Ambrose replied, understanding. "So they're not treating it as a criminal matter. Poor woman! What's going to happen about the mother?"

"Dunno about any mother. Didn't say."

It was milder that afternoon, so without stopping to fetch their coats, Ambrose and Winters went down the street towards the Copper Kettle, talking softly as they walked.

"So that's another we can tick off," Ambrose remarked, but he felt little pleasure. "I suppose the mother'll have to go into a Home."

Winters nodded. "I've seen that happen so often," he commented. "The daughter wears herself out to look after Mum or Dad, and then breaks. Both end up ill or dying. I'm worried about that happening to my sister, but she says it's her duty." He laughed cynically. "That good old Irish sense of duty! I'd outlaw it, if I could."

Ambrose nodded. "We Methodists can rival you on that one," he admitted. "An 'over-developed work ethic' Mary calls it. She reads a lot of books that try to analyse human behaviour. Personally, I don't think any expert can explain the weird things people get up to," he smiled ruefully.

"Shame about Miss Flowers," Ambrose continued. "But you can't go round making veiled death threats, even if you feel like it."

A postman was delivering along the street and they paused to let him come out of one shop and into another. "There's been a development in the Harvey case," Ambrose said afterwards. He outlined Miss Havering's phone call. "An envelope of old photos doesn't sound much of a motive," he admitted, "but it looks like Harvey heard someone downstairs."

"That would explain the torch, and the lights being off," Winters agreed. "But if someone else was in the shop why didn't they help when the bookcase fell? They must have heard the noise. Or maybe our intruder didn't realise what had happened? Just thought something had fallen over? If you're trying to avoid being caught, you don't stop to look."

"Possibly," Ambrose agreed, holding the door open as two women came out of the café.

Merely chatting about the weather and next Saturday's match, they crossed to the counter and ordered their usual "cuppa and a bun each please Doreen". Then they settled at a table well away from other customers. "Doc Halstead said death wasn't instantaneous," Winters continued. "So Harvey probably called for help. Didn't the intruder hear? Or did they think it was just a noise outside?" He shook his head, answering his own question. "Nah, they must have known."

"If they did, and ignored him, that's tantamount to murder," Ambrose replied grimly. "Manslaughter at least. Though I'm not sure just leaving someone who's hurt untended qualifies as either. It ought to."

Doreen came across with their tea and buns, and stood for her usual chat about 'things not being like what they used to'. Then with a joke about Harold MacMillan she'd heard on the radio, left them to it.

They concentrated on their tea and buns for a moment. As Ambrose remarked, it was certainly a great deal better than the apology served at the 'nick'.

"I reckon now we know there was a theft, we can treat Robin Harvey's death as murder," Ambrose decided, "at least until proved wrong. Do you agree?"

"Yep. And a particularly callous one."

"And the Major?" Ambrose asked. "Did someone, the same person perhaps, just leave him to die?"

"Bit of a coincidence isn't it?" Winters agreed, leaning back on his chair. He grimaced as the full possibilities occurred to him. "Or did they *cause* the bookcase to fall? And the Major to slip and crack his head?"

"My question exactly," Ambrose agreed. He concentrated for a moment on eating. Today's bun was particularly good, freshly made by Doreen herself. He felt relieved that at last he could see some way through the fug that had surrounded Robin Harvey's death. It was always reassuring to hear Winters coming to the same conclusions as himself. "Do you reckon our thief was really after a few photos?" he asked. "Or were they interrupted before they got what they wanted? And what could they have stolen from the Major's bathroom?"

Winters considered the questions quietly, rolling himself a cigarette while he thought. "Maybe the Major knew about the photos," he suggested. "Or had some others? They wouldn't have been in the bathroom though. Are we sure his body wasn't moved there?"

"Aahh." Ambrose responded thoughtfully. "There's an idea. Okay. Suspects?"

141

Winters let out his breath in mock despair. "Goodness knows. Everyone in Chalk Heath. Everyone who had access to the shop and Maple View at least." He began to smile, then corrected himself. "I can think of one person who fits that bill."

"The Hon Madge." Ambrose said the name for him. He too smiled, though inwardly. "We have to admit it's a possibility. Now we've separated the malicious packets from the deaths, she doesn't look so unlikely. Do you reckon she had a fling with a German soldier?" He paused, taking the idea more seriously. "Meadows saw a photo of a young man in her kitchen. Ask her to see if Miss Havering can describe the two soldiers, and if so, whether either of them is like the chap at the Hon Madge's. We know her family have a house in Guernsey, so it's a possibility."

Winters savoured his cigarette thoughtfully. "I thought you'd given up," Ambrose pointed out.

"I have, well, almost. Just the odd one when the wife's not looking. It helps me think." Sighing, he stubbed the cigarette out. "Okay," he agreed. "You're right. I hadn't better." Frowning, he played with the saltcellar instead, needing something to occupy his hands. "Do you really think the Hon Madge could kill someone?" he asked.

"Perhaps. If she could see no alternative. She always strikes me as the sort who will do things others only think of, and she had the opportunity: knew where the key to the shop was and the lay-out; goes regularly to Maple View to play Bridge." He shook his head. "But I can't see her leaving someone who'd been hurt, just to die. "

"Nor can I," Winters agreed. "But you can think you know someone, and not know the one thing about them that really matters. For example, is she originally British or was she born in Guernsey? And where exactly was she during the War?"

For some time after Ambrose had settled back in his office he sat staring ahead of him. He knew almost nothing about Guernsey, except that it was one of the Channel Islands. Yet this case might revolve around something that had happened there. He needed to do some research but he didn't have the time. He could ask PC Green, or one of the others, to find things out for him, but they didn't have spare time either. "Mary could do it," he thought. "And be more reliable; certainly more perceptive." The past year, his respect for her intelligence had grown, though he'd always known she was bright. That was one of her qualities that had attracted him in the first place. Nowadays she'd probably have gone to University, but war, and marriage to him he admitted, had spoilt what slim chance she'd had of doing that.

Thoughtfully, he picked up the telephone. It rang several times before his wife answered.

"What is it, Love?" Mary asked, sounding slightly breathless. "I hope you haven't got to work late. I need the car. It's my WRVS night. I shall have to cancel if you don't get the car back here in time."

Ambrose heard the sigh in her voice and felt guilty. He'd had to let her down several times recently. "No," he assured her. "That's not why I'm ringing. Have you got anything planned for this afternoon?"

"Only clearing out the cupboards. I'm happy to put that on hold."

Ambrose smiled. "Would you do a bit of research for me in the Reference Library?"

"Of course. What about?"

"Guernsey during the War. The Occupation particularly." Ambrose left his request deliberately vague. "I could ask one of the team but we're busy."

Mary asked no questions. She never did, just helped as he asked. She had been a hidden partner in several cases lately, and had been utterly discreet. Ambrose knew he could trust her.

"I'll see if I can find some books," she replied. "Shall I make some notes for you?"

"If you would. See if there's anything about local girls fraternising with the enemy."

"Right you are," Mary said cheerfully. "I can call on Aunty Joan on the way back. She used to go on holiday to Guernsey before the War, so she might have some thoughts too. I don't have to leave till six. I've already cooked a pie for you and Joe."

"Thanks. Where are you tonight?" Ambrose asked.

"Pushing the book trolley round the hospital. And chatting to patients of course. I should be back by ten. Sorry I was so long getting to the phone. I was upside down in a cupboard."

"Thanks, Love," Ambrose said quietly. "The cupboards look fine to me already, by the way."

Chapter Twenty

Wednesday 6th April

"I've brought your milk Miss Meadows," Mavis said softly.

In surprise, Meadows opened the door. "That is kind of you," she said, looking at the bottle and wondering if she could carry it safely.

"I'll put it in the kitchen for you if you like," Mavis offered.

"Thank you. You are kind," Meadows repeated. "I'm sorry to make you come upstairs. I'd have got it later."

"I bring all the bottles in nowadays," Mavis explained, walking towards the kitchenette. "It's not safe to leave them on the step. They disappear." She paused. "And if I leave them outside our rooms they, shall we say, get mixed up?"

"Oh?" Meadows prompted. "You mean they disappear here too?"

Mavis sighed in answer. "Make sure your door's always locked if you're out," she advised. "I'm afraid age can do some funny things. It's very sad."

Putting the bottle on the draining board, she glanced towards the door to check that it was closed. Meadows waited, sensing that the woman wanted to say something more important. Finally Mavis found the courage. "Would you pass a message to Inspector Ambrose for me?" she asked.

"Of course. Is it about the Major?"

"Yes. It may be nothing. But the Inspector did ask me to tell him if I thought of anything…." She trailed off into uncertainty.

Meadows smiled. "I'm sure he'd like to know," she replied.

"Well, it's just that one of my cans of polish vanished. Then it came back."

It took Meadows a second to realise the significance of what the housekeeper had said. "Which one?" she asked.

"The wood polish. After the Major died I had to open a new can, though I thought I'd got some left. I decided I'd used it up and forgotten. A couple of days ago, I found the missing tin. It was at the back of the dusters, as if I'd put it in the wrong place. But I'm sure I didn't. I'm very careful. I have systems and I stick to them. I couldn't get through all my work if I had to hunt for things." Mavis paused, frowning. "I wasn't sure whether to bother Mr Ambrose. One of the residents could have helped themselves and put it back. It could just be poor Mr Roberts wandering. But after the Inspector spent time smelling all my polishes the other day, well I thought he might want to know," her voice faded again. "Sorry to bother you when you're not well," she added, "but I thought I could talk to you, rather than go down the Police Station."

"You did absolutely right," Meadows insisted. "Tell me, if you put wood polish on tiles, would it make them slippery?"

"Oh yes, awfully." Mavis' voice faltered. She, too, realised the implication of what she'd said.

"I'll go down and tell Inspector Ambrose in person," Meadows promised. "I don't want to trust the phone here."

"Thank you. I was awake all last night thinking about it. I feel better now I've told you."

After Mavis had left, Meadows considered what to do. She would have to walk down to the Station: she couldn't ride her bike. Her head had begun to ache though, and she needed a rest first. Sitting on the sofa, she settled against the cushions.

"Delivery for you, Miss Meadows," a voice called from outside the door.

Opening her eyes Meadows started. She had fallen asleep. In annoyance, she struggled to get up. The painkillers were making her drowsy. She would have to stop taking them as soon as possible. She hated feeling she was at half power. "I'll be with you in a minute," she called, hastily running her fingers through her hair and straightening her skirt.

Miss Huddlestone was standing at the door with a bouquet of flowers in her hand and a smirk on her lips. "A florists' boy delivered this," she announced. "It's for you. I was just chatting to the postman. I'd seen Mavis go out so I brought it up."

In amazement Meadows stared at her. "For me?" she repeated stupidly.

"Well it says 'For WPC Pauline Meadows' on the label. From your colleagues perhaps?"

"Probably," Meadows replied, gathering her senses quickly. "Thank you very much for bringing it up." She reached out to take the flowers.

"They must think a lot of you," Miss Huddlestone said, still with that odd smirk, and still holding the bouquet.

"They're very kind," Meadows assured her. She could see a gift card stuck in the wrapping at an odd angle. Miss Huddlestone had no doubt had a good look at it before she knocked on the door. "I shall have to ring and thank them."

Miss Huddlestone was not giving up so easily. "It's nice to know you're appreciated," she said, smiling. "I don't think anyone's ever sent me flowers. Not by special delivery. You must be very important to someone." One of her eyelids twitched slightly, as if she was trying to give a knowing wink, but was out of practice.

It took another five minutes of conversation to persuade the woman to hand the bouquet over, and then only after Meadows had repeated several times that she was feeling better and would soon be back at work. With a parting remark about the weather and how nice it was to see the daffodils ("so sad to think of the poor Major who had bought them"), Miss Huddlestone relinquished the bouquet and let Meadows close her door.

"What the?" Meadows said aloud as soon as she was alone. "Who'd send me flowers?" As she hurried into the kitchenette, she ran through the list of possibilities. Her parents? She hadn't told them about her injury, knowing it would worry them. Her kid sister? Marion might have been concerned when she didn't receive her weekly letter, but she couldn't afford flowers, even if she had thought of sending them. The Station? They'd already sent a card and chocolates. Friends? She had few outside the Force. There wasn't time to keep up with old school mates, and working unsocial hours made it difficult for her to meet new people. She ran out of possibilities.

Cursing her immobilised arm, Meadows scrabbled in the kitchen drawer with her other hand for the scissors. With an effort, she cut the wrapping until she could read the gift tag.

'Police work is too dangerous for a pretty lady,' it said.

146

That was all. No 'to' or 'from', no greetings or good wishes, just that one enigmatic statement. There was no handwriting to help her identify the sender. The message had been typed onto the card.

In annoyance Meadows flung the bouquet down. The words sounded faintly threatening. The gift had to be from the man who was following her. Miss Huddlestone had interpreted it as being from an admirer, hence the smirk. But she didn't know the truth.

For several moments Meadows sat on the kitchen chair, feeling thoroughly unnerved. It was as if her home had been invaded. Whoever had sent those flowers knew that she'd had an accident, where she lived, and that she would be at home. They also knew her Christian name. What else did they know about her?

Breathing slowly, Meadows calmed herself down. The message need not be a threat, any more than her follower had to be hostile. He had warned her of the falling roof tile, and possibly saved her life. This message could be genuine concern: someone who thought working for the police was dangerous (which it could be) and cared about her safety. So did that mean he was actually an admirer?

Though her first reaction was to dismiss the suggestion as absurd, Meadows forced herself to consider it. She'd been told that she was pretty several times, though she'd never believed it. Years of being warned of vanity by her mother had convinced her she was no more than ordinary, not ugly thankfully, but nothing special. She'd learnt that most men didn't like a woman who was clever, or sporty, or in a position of power. She probably appeared to be all three, though she never felt it. A WPC was someone to be extra wary of too, in case they shopped you for something you said or did. All the same, perhaps the man who had sent the flowers (and surely it was a man) meant a compliment, not a threat?

Picking the bouquet up again, Meadows contemplated putting them in the waste bin downstairs, then realised Miss Huddlestone would see her, and be even more fascinated. Besides, they were lovely: an arrangement of spring daffodils and freesia, backed by some interesting looking leaves and mimosa. It would be a shame to destroy them. She recalled seeing a vase listed on the inventory when she moved in. Putting the bouquet in the sink to keep fresh, she began to look at the back of the cupboards. Finally she found an expensive looking glass vase, managed to fill it with water, and arranged her unwanted gift in it.

Then she wondered what to do about the sender. Once again she examined the card. There was no name on the back, but there was a little floral image a shop might use as its trademark. Crossing to the window, Meadows looked down the hill. She could walk into town after she had delivered Mavis' message, and check if any of the florists recognised the trademark, or remembered the flowers.

To her surprise, as she stood at the bay window, she saw Alfie Green dismounting from his bike near the pavement. Opening the gate, he began wheeling the bike up the garden path. Grabbing her key, Meadows hurriedly locked her door and ran as quietly as she could downstairs to intercept him before he could ring the bell. She was out of breath when she bundled him through the hall into the residents' lounge.

"Hey, hold yer 'orses; it's not that urgent," PC Green responded in surprise. "I've got a message from the Sarge, that's all."

"Nosey neighbour," she hissed as she closed the door. Then she smiled. "She'll think you're my admirer."

Green flushed. "What?" he asked.

"I've received an anonymous bunch of flowers," Meadows explained, taking him towards the window. Anyone listening at the door would have difficulty hearing them from over there. "It has to be from the chap who's following me. The wretched neighbour's gone all romantic over it."

Alfie Green smiled. "But you don't think it's romantic?" he asked.

"Course I don't. How many florists' shops do you know in town?"

"I've never really looked," Green admitted. "Two. Maybe three. Gillian's on the main street, and one by the theatre. I forget the name. Maybe 'Katie's Flowers'? I've seen another but dunno where."

"On the corner near the Old Hall Estate," Meadows remembered. "You can't think of any more?"

"No. But he could have gone to Jenners Park."

Meadows sighed. "That's a thought," she agreed. "Probably not, though. My neighbour said a delivery boy came, so he was probably on a bike. Thanks. I'll do a bit of snooping."

Green raised an eyebrow. "What'll you do if you find it's someone you know?" he asked.

"I've no idea," Meadows admitted. "Put salt in his tea perhaps. That'll scare him off." She recalled why PC Green had come. "Sorry to bother you with all this. What's the message?"

Opening his pocket book, PC Green read out carefully, "'Ask WPC Meadows to call at Curiosity Corner, as soon as she's well enough. See if the assistant remembers what the Germans in the photos looked like. Could one of them be the man she saw in the photo at the Honourable Madge's?' The DS wrote you a note too in case I didn't find you in." Fumbling in his jacket pocket, Green found an envelope and passed it to her.

"Phew!" Meadows commented in surprise. "That would set the cat among the pigeons. I can call there now: I was coming down to the Station with a message for the DI. Then I'll go flower hunting. I'll have to walk though. I'll need a cuppa by the time I'm finished."

"It's a long way back up," Green remarked. "And you don't look all that well, pardon me for saying. Shall I ask if someone can drive you home?"

"You're a star!" Meadows replied. "That'd be a big help. Tell you what. Let me get my coat, and my notebook. I can't write much at the moment. If I dictate to you what I want to tell the DI, would you deliver it? That'd save me calling at the Station first. Hang on a mo."

Running back upstairs, Meadows unlocked the door to her flat. Finding her notebook, she put it in her coat pocket and leaving at once, relocked her door. A tell-tale click further along the corridor made her smile. Miss Huddlestone was having an interesting morning. Pretending she hadn't heard, she hurried back to the residents' lounge. PC Green was waiting for her there, looking uncomfortably out of the window. "Okay. What do you want me to write?" he asked, taking the notebook from her and getting out his own pencil.

Carefully she dictated to him what Mavis had told her, as nearly as possible word for word. Then, with difficulty she signed the page. Folding the paper in two, she asked Green to address it to DI Ambrose. Then they walked out of the lounge together. Miss Huddlestone was probably watching from the landing window as they left the house.

"I'd hate living there," Alfie Green commented as he picked up his bike. "You've got twitching curtains. How do you cope?"

"I don't cope," Meadows admitted freely. "I need to move out as soon as I can, but I never get the time to look for somewhere else. Not that I can afford any way." She sighed. "I can't really afford this."

"I'd like to get out of Police Lodgings," Green agreed, "but I can't see how either. My landlady's a right royal Scrooge. Serves a knob of butter the size of an 'alf-crown and that's your lot. I'll swear she dries the tea leaves and uses them again."

"She's pretty typical," Meadows advised. "She probably only gets a few bob for you, and she won't be doing it out of the kindness of her heart."

Chatting comfortably, they walked down the hill together, Green wheeling his bike beside her. Then he mounted the bike and turned towards the park gates. "Off to catch the Botany Bays: that's runaways to you," he grinned. "Don't worry, I won't say a Dicky Bird about your admirer," he joked as they parted.

"Don't forget to give the DI my note," Meadows called back to him.

The assistant at Gillian's Flowers didn't recognise the card when Meadows showed it to her. "Not one of ours," she said, handing it back. "Afraid I can't help you." She looked at WPC Meadows curiously, recognising her and wondering why she wasn't in uniform. "Is it important?"

"Might be. Can't say more," Meadows replied vaguely. "Thank you anyway."

Leaving the shop bell tingling behind her, she went out, towards the theatre. The girl at 'Katie's Florists' knew Meadows too, and also looked at her curiously as she took the card. "Doing a bit of plain clothes work today?" she asked.

"I do sometimes," Meadows replied, smiling. "Is this one of your cards?"

"No. Ours are all like this." Helpfully the assistant passed a stack of silver-edged gift cards, all with pretty images on the front, but none on the back.

"Very nice," Meadows commented, studiously not noticing the girl's enquiring expression.

It made sense for her to call at Curiosity Corner afterwards, before she set off for the Old Hall Estate. The shop was only a hundred or so yards further along the main road and she needed to keep walking to a minimum today. As she approached, however, she frowned in disappointment. A large van was parked outside. Two men in overalls were carrying a bookcase from the shop and into the back of the van. Pausing to let them pass, Meadows opened the shop door and looked around for Miss Havering.

The assistant was not at the till, nor among the bookcases at the front of the shop. Books were stacked in boxes all round the counter, and even on the counter itself. Meadows tried ringing the bell for service.

A breathless Miss Havering came running down from Mr Harvey's flat. The bookcase that had masked the stairs had been moved and Meadows saw her at once. "So sorry to keep you waiting," the young woman called apologetically. "What can I do for you?" Seeing it was WPC Meadows, she became even more embarrassed. "Please forgive the mess," she added.

"Are you closing down?" Meadows asked sadly. "We'll miss having a proper bookshop."

"Goodness no!" Miss Havering assured her, smiling. "Just refurbishing. Mr Harvey's brother gave me permission to replace some of the old bookcases. I've ordered some nice second-hand ones with proper backs. They have screw holes too, so you can attach them to the wall. Much safer."

"Very sensible," Meadows agreed. "It looks like a big job."

"I don't think I realised how big," Miss Havering admitted. "And the dust! I was having a wash upstairs when you came in. I thought it would be safe for me to pop up while the men were around." She sighed and looked around at the boxes. "Much as I liked Mr Harvey, I have to say he wasn't very organised. His mind was too full of his publishing." She sighed again, then brightened. "So what can I do for you? If you're wanting a particular book I'm afraid it could take me a while to find it, even though I labelled all the boxes."

"Detective Sergeant Winters asked me to call," Meadows began carefully. "He wondered if you could describe the two men on the photos that are missing. It's possible someone may be able to identify them. Did they have fair or dark hair, for instance?"

Miss Havering screwed up her nose as she tried to recall the photos in detail. "Fair," she said firmly, "Especially the taller one; he was very blond. What I'd have called typically German."

"Age?"

"Early thirties I'd say." Miss Havering paused, staring ahead of her. "The younger looking one was tall and thin, but strong. His friend was shorter and stockier, with slightly darker hair, maybe light brown. It's hard to tell in a black and white photo. But it was the young one, the tall one, who had the most stripes," she added. "Or whatever it was the Germans used to show someone was an officer."

"You remember all that?" Meadows replied in surprise. "What about the women? Were they tall or short?"

Once again Miss Havering concentrated. "The *larger* one, you know the expecting one, she was taller than the other one," she decided. Meadows hadn't known one of the women was pregnant but she kept her surprise to herself.

"Great," Meadows replied, not sure whether it was safe to believe such detailed descriptions. "You sound pretty confident. I'm surprised when you only saw the photos briefly."

"I have a very good memory for pictures and faces," Miss Havering said matter-of-factly. "Mr Harvey called it a 'visual memory'. If I close my eyes I can often see pages, and remember them almost word for word. It's very helpful in exams."

"I'll bet!" Meadows agreed. "If you close your eyes now can you see anything more about the men? Or the two women?"

For a moment, they had to pause as a man in overalls came into the shop and asked, "What next, Miss?"

"That case over there," Miss Havering instructed, nodding in the direction of an empty bookcase blocking the way to the back office.

"Oi, Larry, one more!" the man called from the open door. Then he and his mate picked up the bookcase to take it outside. It was heavier than they expected and there was a good deal of puffing and swearing.

Miss Havering turned back to WPC Meadows. "Hopefully we'll get a few pounds back on the old ones," she said softly. "They're not in bad condition, just not very safe in a shop."

Meadows noticed the 'we' and smiled inwardly.

As soon as the men had removed the bookcase, Miss Havering thought hard. "The girls looked happy," she remarked. "And in love."

"Can you describe them?" Meadows asked.

Once again the assistant closed her eyes. Then she opened them again and shook her head. "I can't see them much," she admitted. "Just girls. They were both darker than the men. I assumed they were local but they mightn't have been. Sorry." She shrugged her shoulders. "I'm afraid the men interested me more. I mean, German soldiers being photographed on a beach and near a farm. It didn't seem right somehow. I assumed the girls were fraternising and didn't think much of them. But I might have been wrong. I'm afraid I haven't been much help."

"You've been a lot of help," Meadows reassured her.

"Would you like a cup of tea?" Miss Havering asked. "You look tired and I can get to the office now."

Meadows accepted gratefully. "Could I have a sheet of paper and write down what you told me while you make the tea?" she asked. "I'd rather not trust my memory and it's going to take me a while to write it all with my bad arm."

"Yes, I heard you'd had a nasty accident," the assistant agreed. Seeing Meadows' discomfort, she laughed. "It's all over town," she warned. "Everyone's saying how you saved the Honourable Miss Hodgkiss' life."

"Oh Lor'!" Meadows said in embarrassment, though she managed to laugh.

She spent a pleasant half hour at the shop afterwards, chatting to Miss Havering and drinking tea while she checked the brief notes she managed to write for the DS. Hopefully she would be able to speak to him in person in case he couldn't read her scrawl. Having a painful shoulder didn't improve her handwriting. Then, thanking Miss Havering again, she set off towards the Old Hall estate.

Chapter Twenty-One

'Flowers and Things' was nearly a mile away and Meadows' shoulder was hurting by the time she got there. She should have put her sling on before she left Maple View. That would have attracted even more curiosity however, she admitted, so it was perhaps a good job she hadn't. She began to hope fervently that her walk wasn't for nothing. The shop might be shut. She should have rung in advance.

At last she came to the little parade of shops recently built on the edge of the new estate. 'Flowers and Things' proved to be exactly that; an odd assortment of flowers in buckets and miscellaneous gifts. 'Anything that'll sell round here,' Meadows thought with sympathy. Fortunately, the shop was open. As she opened the door, a strong smell of potpourri mixed with the scent from hyacinths in plastic clogs. A woman in mauve overalls greeted her.

Meadows wasn't known round here and could afford to be a bit more specific. "I received some flowers this morning," she explained, "The gift card somehow got mixed up with the wrapping and thrown away. I wondered if you could remember them so I can thank the sender."

"I always remember our orders," the woman replied. She didn't add, "We don't send a lot out," but Meadows suspected that was the case. "Can you describe the flowers?"

"Daffodils, freesia and mimosa, with a green backing. They look lovely and I must say thank you."

"Oh yes, I remember!" the woman said and reached for her order book. "The girl from the college dealt with it while I was out. The customer was most insistent we included some freesia she said." Opening her book, she frowned. "The silly girl forgot to take the

154

sender's address," she said in annoyance. "Really, these college kids are so useless! You wonder what they've been taught at school." Turning towards the back of the shop she called loudly. "Nora!"

A girl of sixteen, but who looked younger, emerged with a frightened and apologetic face. "Yes, Miss Reed?" she asked. 'What have I done now?' her expression implored.

"I've told you before. You must take customers' names and addresses in case there's a problem with their cheque." Turning towards Meadows, she added, "You'd be surprised how many bounce."

"The gentleman paid cash, Miss," Nora said faintly.

"Well you should still have got his details. There might have been a complaint about the flowers."

The girl bit at one of her fingers, pulling at some dry skin. "He wouldn't leave his name," she managed to say. "Said it was to be a surprise."

"They do sometimes," Miss Reed conceded, softening her tone somewhat. "Usually on Valentine's Day though."

"Can you describe him?" Meadows asked.

The girl nodded. "Bright ginger hair," she said.

"Ginger?" Meadows repeated in surprise. "How old was he?"

"About thirty I'd say." Responding to Meadows' kinder manner, Nora thought hard. "Not fat," she added. "Quite thin really. Polite, but firm. He simply wouldn't give his details and I asked a couple of times. He just said you'd know who it was."

"Of course," Meadows replied, as if she understood. "How sweet of him! Sorry to have bothered you both. The flowers were lovely, and arranged very well. I really liked the way you'd tied the bow," she added, smiling at the girl. Delighted, the girl smiled back.

Leaving the shop Meadows walked briskly back down the road. As soon as she was out of sight, however, she stopped to gather her breath and her thoughts. Bright ginger hair? She could think of only one man who fitted that description. But that didn't make sense. Why would he send her flowers? It couldn't be him. Surely? Could it?

Meadows' head pounded and she felt faintly sick. She would have liked to go straight home and think more clearly on her own. But she had to go back to the Station and report to DS Winters. That was going to be very difficult. She would be bound to go bright red when he spoke to her, or worse still, lose her temper. What on earth did the man mean? He was married, with kids. And her boss too! Did he really fancy her, or had he been following her to check whether she was walking her beat properly? That sounded more likely. Of all the mean things to do. Her face went hot with anger.

"Oh, come off it!" Meadows said to herself firmly. She was leaping to conclusions. She had no evidence, other than a young woman's description, and one who didn't appear to have an especially good memory. If a conclusion didn't make sense, it probably wasn't the right conclusion. Try as hard as she could to talk some sense into herself, though, she still felt hot and angry as she walked back towards the main road.

To her intense relief, neither DS Winters nor DI Ambrose was available when she arrived at the Station. "Out on a case," PC Vernon explained. "Woman found dead up on the St George's allotments. Probably just a domestic. I thought you were on sick leave."

Meadows wanted to reply that it wasn't 'just a domestic' to the woman who had died, but managed to keep silent. "The DS asked me to check something," she said instead. "I'll leave a note for him. Is Alfie Green in?"

"Should be back any moment. I sent him down to Pendles' to get some sarnies." He looked up as the front door opened. "Talk of the devil! Or should I say 'talk of the Peril'"?

PC Green looked nonplussed as he walked in. Then he twigged. "Nah, you mean talk of the Henry Neville or the Old Harry! But good of you to give it a try, me ol' China!"

If Vernon was confused, he didn't let on.

"Only had egg and cress left," Green apologised as he placed three paper bags of sandwiches on the front counter. He saw WPC Meadows and smiled ruefully. 'Errand boy again!' his expression conveyed but he took care not to let PC Vernon see. "Got you a lift back up the hill," he said to her aloud. "One of the Specials is heading up that way."

Meadows smiled her thanks. "Can I have a word?" she whispered as PC Vernon turned towards the tearoom.

"What about?" Green asked softly.

"I've found out who sent the flowers. It sounds like the DS."

Green stared at her in amazement. "Nah!" he said in disbelief. "Why'd you think that?"

"The girl at "Flowers and Things' said the sender had bright ginger hair."

For a moment, Alfie Green was silent, though he shook his head. "I don't believe it," he said finally. "Is that all you've got to go on? Ginger hair?"

Meadows shrugged, beginning to feel silly. "The girl at the shop said the sender had bright ginger hair and was quite thin, and about thirty." Even as she said the last words, she saw the discrepancy herself. "That's too young, but I can't think of anyone else with that coloured hair."

"I can," Green said, beginning to smile.

"Who?" Meadows demanded.

"Think about it," Green advised. "Did she mention an Irish accent?"

"No," Meadows admitted, feeling even sillier. Clearly her brain wasn't functioning quite right. It must be the painkillers. She couldn't think who else had ginger hair, but Alfie Green clearly could.

"Leave it with me," he suggested. "Let me see if I can scare him off."

For once Meadows found herself having to accept the young rookie's advice, rather than give him lessons. It felt odd to have their usual roles reversed.

"Ok," she agreed. "But I'd like to ring his neck myself."

Green shook his head. "I don't think neck ringing'll be needed," he said. "If I were you, I'd ignore it. Just go home and have a good sleep."

Ambrose returned less than ten minutes after Meadows had left the Station. He felt drained after a particularly unpleasant murder and wasn't in the mood to talk. Shutting himself in his office for a cup of tea and half an hour's quiet, he ignored Meadows' message. He'd seen it on his desk but decided to leave it for tomorrow. As he was returning his cup to the tearoom however, PC Green passed him. "Did you see the note from WPC Meadows, Sir?" the young PC asked. "She asked me to tell you it was about Major Fielding."

Ambrose was tired and inclined to be brisk. "Can't it wait?" he demanded.

"I think it might interest you," Green persisted.

"What do you know about it?" Ambrose demanded.

"Sorry sir. I didn't mean to be rude," Green apologized. "But WPC Meadows dictated it to me, being as she couldn't write too well. She said it might be a break-through, and you'd want to know."

"Very well," Ambrose agreed. "I'll look at it before I leave."

He almost forgot the note even then, only recalling it as he was putting on his coat. Pausing, he unfolded the page. As he read, a slow smile spread across his mouth. He was indeed interested. "So that's how it was done," he said aloud. At once his tiredness left him. Quickly he dropped his coat onto the chair and went to see if Winters was still in his office.

DS Winters was labouring over a report, "To deaden my mind a bit," he admitted. "I didn't feel like doing anything constructive after we got back. I was going to see if I could catch you before you left, though. Meadows left me a note."

"You got one too?" Ambrose asked. "About the polish?"

Winters looked at him in bewilderment. "Polish?" he repeated. "No. I asked her to call at Curiosity Corner, as you suggested, to see if the assistant could recall what the Germans in the photos looked like."

"What did she say?"

Winters passed the note over.

"Blimey! Her writing's worse than ever!" Ambrose commented. Then he remembered. "Written with difficulty I suppose. You'll have to translate. You know her handwriting better than me."

"Miss Havering v. gd. memory," Winters read. "Both men 'typically German'. One v. blond, early thirties, higher rank. Second: slightly older, stockier, slightly darker hair. Both girls happy; one pregnant. Assumed local. Blond officer, poss. same as Madge's photo. Hard to say. Need to find missing photos and compare."

"Yes. Indeed," Ambrose agreed. "Now you read my note. It's even better." He smiled. "Bit like a parlour game, isn't it?"

"Aahh," Winters said afterwards. He too was suddenly wide awake and more cheerful. "So that's why the floor was slippery. Presumably the bath mat was switched to one that had no strips on the bottom. I don't suppose it's around anymore."

"Doc Halstead may have found some fibres from it. You never know," Ambrose suggested. "It'll be worth having another look at his report. Meadows' photos show a brown bath mat. If the fibres are any other colour we're onto something."

"Bit of a long shot," Winters pointed out, "but we might be lucky." He pushed the file he'd been updating to one side. "I reckon we can work on that hypothesis even if there's no proof," he added. "Which gives us possible means but I'm less clear if we have a probable motive yet." He remembered something and rummaged quickly among the papers on his desk. "Nothing yet from Mrs Vaudin's bank," he complained. "I'll have to chivvy them on a bit."

"Tomorrow," Ambrose advised. "Let's call it a day for now."

Chapter Twenty-Two

His brain wouldn't call it a day though, even after Ambrose got home.

Joe was out at a band practice and Mary had prepared a special evening meal. For once they could spend a quiet evening together but all through the meal Ambrose's mind was churning away, suggesting questions, coming up with possible answers. His wife knew better than to ask him why he was so quiet, but he could feel her concern. Finally, when he poured himself an unusual second beer and moved near the fire in the lounge, she remarked gently, "Bad day, Love?"

Sighing as he sat on the sofa, Ambrose nodded. The St George's case would be headlines in the Chalk Heath newspapers tomorrow. He'd seen Larry from the *Gazette* sniffing round even before the body was taken to the mortuary. How he'd got wind of it Ambrose could only guess. Probably tipped off by the landlord at The Brigadier, or a local resident hoping for a quid or two. There could be no harm in sharing a little with Mary. "A girl was found dead near the St George's estate," he replied sadly. "On the allotments. Some children found her on their way to school."

"Poor kids," Mary said sympathetically.

"Not a nice thing to find," Ambrose agreed. He shuddered slightly. "She was only about seventeen. Beautiful too. Makes me glad we haven't got a daughter."

"Sam Winters has," Mary pointed out. "More than one in fact. Was he with you?"

"Yes. I could see he was thinking of them. He never says much though."

"You're home now," Mary advised. "Leave it behind." She walked round behind him and rubbed the back of his neck with a gentle soothing motion.

"It isn't just that," Ambrose admitted, moving his head about in pleasure. "We've probably got a real scorcher coming up, someone who's very important and isn't going to like being accused of things. I'm not sure what to do about it. Or even if I'm right." Turning round, he glanced at Mary's face and knew that she was guessing the name. She made no comment, however.

For a few moments they were silent, comfortable together beside the fire. "Did you manage to find any books on Guernsey?" he asked, as if it were a new topic.

"Only a couple. There isn't a lot about the Occupation. I get the impression it's a sore subject. No one wants to write about it yet."

With a quick kiss on the back of his head, Mary went back into the dining area to clear the table. "Even our Government seems to have brushed it under the carpet," she called as she carried plates into the kitchen. "One book said everyone was very brave, which I'm sure most were, and opposed the Occupation from the start. I'm not so sure about that. I mean, an unarmed country and lots and lots of soldiers? There was one report saying there were almost as many soldiers as residents. How could you openly oppose the Germans if there's one of them for every one of you? You'd have had to keep your head down. At the best, they'd have had to do it on the quiet, you know, like the French Resistance."

Mary carried on. "There was a bit about people trying to confuse the Germans as they marched around. Apparently there were no road signs so the German put stone arrows on the ground to show which way they'd come, but as soon as they were out of sight, locals would turn the stone arrows around. One old chap wrote that they'd managed to lose a whole cohort of Germans for over four hours, but it got the locals into trouble."

"Was there anything about girls fraternising with the enemy?" Ambrose asked, beginning to relax. His wife's good sense always put things in perspective.

"Nothing much," Mary replied, walking back in holding some handwritten notes. "Just that a few did and weren't popular. They called them 'Jerry Bags'. At first I thought that would only be in Jersey but it's the term used in Guernsey too. The books didn't mention any tarring and feathering like in France. I got chatting to one of the

161

orderlies at the hospital last night, though. I was on book trolley duty, and he was waiting for someone to come out of the operating theatre. I knew he'd been with the army when the islands were liberated. He'd mentioned it before. What he told me was more enlightening. Hang on a mo."

She returned to the dining area. Dropping a knife as she cleared the table, Mary paused. "These knives aren't properly balanced," she complained. "The handles are too heavy. I'd love a decent set." Then she carried the dirty crockery into the kitchen.

"I'll wash up," Ambrose called to her. He waited until she came back into the lounge. "Go on," he invited. "You were telling me about your ex-army chap."

"Iain said everyone was nearly starving by the time the islands were liberated, and glad to see them, whichever side they were on. The Red Cross sent a shipload of food parcels, but only in the last few months and they were for the residents. The Germans didn't steal them, so they ended up the hungriest. That surprised me. Iain reckoned most of the soldiers were pretty decent all round, young men like our lot, just doing as they were told. It was the officers and the SS that were the rotters, and even some of the officers were okay, at least at the start. They were from good families, well educated, and they treated the local big wigs with respect." Sighing, Mary shrugged her shoulders. "Apparently Hitler wanted to show how nice being occupied could be," she added. "He was hoping we'd hear good reports, and welcome him here. Goodness knows how we were meant to do that, when he'd cut all communications with the Islands. Silly man!"

Ambrose smiled. "Can you understand a girl falling for one of the German officers?" he asked.

Mary nodded ruefully. "If she was young and got carried away. Think how many GI babies we had, even in Chalk Heath."

"The Yanks weren't invaders," Ambrose pointed out. "At least not officially."

"Nor were the Germans in a sense," Mary replied. "They didn't use much force when they arrived in the Channel Islands; they didn't need to. The islands weren't defended. We'd declared them demilitarised and pulled out, and then forgot to tell the Germans. It depends when your young woman fell in love. It sounds like the States (that's the Channel Islands government) were quite welcoming to the Occupying Forces at first, although they were probably just being sensible. It mightn't have seemed so wrong to be friendly then, especially if it got your family extra food. It wasn't as if we were around to defend them."

"Fair point," Ambrose conceded.

"What's this all about?" Mary asked. "Can't you tell me a bit? Then I'd know what to ask Iain when I see him next week."

"There's a photo of a couple of German soldiers with what are probably local women, one possibly pregnant," Ambrose replied vaguely. "But the woman I'm thinking of doesn't have a child now. Any suggestions?"

Sitting down on the couch beside him, Mary considered his question. Ambrose waited, knowing not to hurry her. "The baby might have been adopted," she suggested.

"That's an idea!" Ambrose agreed. "If the girl wasn't married, her family could have made her give the kiddy up. Especially if it was half German."

"I think some of the children were sent to Germany," Mary recalled. "Especially the boys. Presumably there were lots of girls, but not many young men left, like here." She sighed. "It doesn't make much difference which side you're on, does it? Ordinary families are always the ones that suffer."

Nodding, Ambrose stared into the fire reflectively. "Or maybe the child just died," he added thoughtfully. "A little one needs food, and you say people were nearly starving by the end." He sighed in sympathy. "Both make sense. The trouble is, it's all so remote. I can't visualise it. I always do much better when I can put myself into a situation. I don't know anything about Guernsey except what you've told me."

For some time, they sat together in silence watching the flames flickering in the grate. "Tell you what!" Mary said suddenly. "You've got some leave due, haven't you? Could you get away for a few days? Sam Winters could cope with your new case, couldn't he?"

"I suppose so," Ambrose admitted. "I don't think it'll last long. We're bringing a suspect in for questioning tomorrow. Why?"

"Let's go to Guernsey then. Give you a feel for the place, and let you ask around a bit."

"We can't afford it," Ambrose objected, shaking his head.

"Yes we can," Mary assured him. "I've been promising Aunt Joan for months I'd take her on a little holiday. She hasn't been anywhere since her fall. I know she stayed on a farm in Guernsey before the War and got quite close to the family. I remember her telling me how

163

relieved she was when they wrote after the Liberation. I don't think she's visited them for over ten years. I'm sure she'd pay the fare over, at least for her and me. If they invited her to stay on their farm, you and I could stay in a Bed and Breakfast nearby, or they might even invite us all to stay."

"Mm," Ambrose replied doubtfully.

"Oh, go on!" Mary urged. "You need a rest. And you would be working still." Her eyes began to shine with pleasure at the thought. "We can take her wheelchair, and Aunty will have a wonderful time. I'll push her around while you ask questions. We won't get in the way."

Giving in, Ambrose squeezed her hand in gratitude. "You're a genius!" he told her. "You have a chat to your Aunt, and I'll see Mac about taking a few days off." Then he paused. "It'd have to be very short notice, though. I can't leave the case waiting too long. If Joan's friends can help us find accommodation quickly and you can book the ferry, then it's possible. But only then." He paused. "Where does the ferry go from?" he asked.

"Weymouth I think," Mary replied. "There's a train from Paddington. I remember Aunty telling me about her last trip across. I imagine it's still the same." She didn't mention her Aunt had encountered foul weather and that everyone on board had been very sick. "We might even get a few hours together," she added instead. "Aunty will be quite happy sitting in her chair looking at the view."

Then she paused. "But what about Joe?" she remembered. "He can't take time off school, not with his exams so soon." Her happiness faded. "And it wouldn't be fair to leave him on his own so long. He'd turn into a baked bean."

Ambrose leant back against his chair sadly. "No," he conceded. Then he came to a decision. "He can stay with one of his mates," he said firmly. "We've had them here often enough."

"You'd trust him to work?" Mary asked in surprise. "Not mess about?"

"He's getting quite sensible. He wants to do well, and stay on into the Sixth. I reckon we can trust him."

Getting up, Mary kissed him impulsively on the cheek. "It does me good to hear you say that," she said. "I sometimes thought I never would." Then she went into the hall. "I'll phone Aunty now," she called. She was positively beaming.

If it had been any other member of the family, Ambrose would have protested. The thought of spending several days with Mary's Mother would have had him ringing the Station for an urgent case. But Aunt Joan had clearly inherited a different set of genes to her sister. Feisty and independent, she was still good company despite a badly mended broken hip that ached continually. She'd made shells in the First World War and taken in evacuees during the Second. Along the way, she'd taught in an East End School, outlived her husband, and lost a daughter to a random doodlebug. Mary was her replacement daughter. Fortunately, that suited Mary. She had far more in common with her Aunt than with her own mother. It was fortunate also for Ambrose, who felt entirely the same way about Mary's mother.

Aunt Joan always took several moments to get to the phone. As Mary waited, Ambrose could feel her longing for the phone to be answered. He too hoped for an answer, not so much for himself, but because his wife had so clearly set her heart on the plan. She had a habit of doing that: coming to a sudden conclusion then acting so quickly that he had little time to argue, not that he often wanted to do so. Her ideas were usually good. Sometimes, however, things didn't work out as she'd hoped and she was very disappointed. He didn't like to see her hurt.

At last he heard his wife's voice. He found he was nervous, trying to hear what she said, and whether she was receiving a positive reply. He hoped so. She would have a great time with her Aunt, watching the people on the train and doing crosswords with her. And he might get to the bottom of a case that was eluding his grasp. So long as things could be arranged quickly, otherwise he would have to say no, or at least defer the trip.

It was a long call full of laughter, and one-sided comments like "Really?" "Never!" "Did she?" as calls to Aunt Joan often were. He caught the gist of Mary's request, however, and her delight when her Aunt agreed.

"All sorted!" Mary said as she came back into the lounge. "Aunty loves the idea and she'll phone her friends straight away. She'll ask their advice about our accommodation. I'll book the ferry as soon as I hear from her." She laughed. "I shall need some new slacks, you know. And a new suitcase..." Her voice trailed off in thought.

Kissing him on the forehead, she headed for the kitchen. "Oi," she called from there. "I thought you said you'd wash up!"

Chapter Twenty-Three

Thursday April 7th

It was good to have the Station to themselves again. Without men working everywhere and dust sheets and tins to trip over, the place felt unnaturally quiet, almost spacious. Everything was bright and clean, "at least for a few weeks" as Ambrose remarked drily. There was a strong smell of paint, and doors and windows were tacky, but normal life was starting again.

Mac worried about having a couple of windows still propped open at the back. The two civilian typists had been told to watch them at all times. "We'd look daft if the local lads pinched the tea things," he warned. When one of the women remarked that the windows were only small skylights, and surely no one could climb through those, Higgins shook his head. "You'd be surprised how small a space a local m'laddo can get through," he remarked. "They don't seem to have a bone in their bodies, except their heads, and those were shrunk when they were born."

The area under the stairs (laughingly known as the filing room) stank of carpet cleaner used by the bucket load after one of the workmen upset his flask. Green was grateful to be allowed to work in the typists' room, even if it was freezing with the windows open. "I'm afraid I can't find anything," he told DI Ambrose apologetically. "I've had a Butchers' at John Vaudin's bank account. His Missus didn't have one."

"Not with his bank, that is," Ambrose cautioned.

Green was a step ahead, however. "I've called the other banks in Jenners Park, too," he added. "They don't recognise the name. She could have used an alias but it'd be difficult. The Manager'd want to see her credentials. He'd probably know her, too. I mean, she sounds the sort people'd know."

Mentally Ambrose awarded the young PC a couple of stars. "You'd have thought so," he agreed. "OK. Good work. Call it a day, and do something more interesting." He smiled. "Like making a cuppa." He saw the lad's expression and smiled again. "For yourself I mean."

As soon as he was on his own, Ambrose frowned. So, blackmail wasn't involved; at least there were no financial payments. Mrs Vaudin might have kept the photographs to maintain a hold over someone, or it could have been a kind of reciprocal blackmail: "I won't tell your secret, if you don't tell mine." Perhaps 'Me' had her own set of the photos, so there was a kind of balance of fear. 'Like Russia and the U.S.,' he thought grimly.

They knew little about Mrs Vaudin, Ambrose admitted, other than her address in Jenners Park, and that she had died last October leaving a husband but no children. He'd assumed she was the girl who wasn't expecting, but as Mary suggested last night, the baby might have been adopted, or just died. Mrs Vaudin could have kept the birth secret from a husband who was now a respectable Jenners Park resident. It might even be the husband who had stolen the photos. If he'd only just learnt that some incriminating pictures were in the box he gave to Robin Harvey, he could have returned to retrieve them. It wouldn't be difficult to drive across from Jenners Park. Not knowing the layout of the shop, he might not have realised a bookcase could fall with such disastrous results, or was too ashamed or frightened to admit an accident had happened while he was there.

But he couldn't be involved in the Major's death, Ambrose reflected, frowning. Whoever killed him had to know their way around Maple View. They needed to be local: unless his death really was another accident?

'Unlikely but possible,' Ambrose thought ruefully. 'And what about the tile that nearly killed the Hon Madge?' No one could have come from Jenners Park, climbed onto St George's roof and waited for her to pass beneath, without arousing suspicion. How would they have known the way up the tower in any case? Unless that was an accident too?

He began to feel annoyed. To paraphrase an old army saying, two accidents were possible; three were enemy action. He needed to know more about Mr and Mrs Vaudin. Until he did, he would go round in circles. He would have to delegate the investigation however, or leave it till later. The more urgent task was to go up to the Incident Room at St George's Church Hall and see how Winters was getting on with the new murder.

Even then Ambrose paused. Having the same area turn up in two different cases bothered him. Was that yet another coincidence, or was there a connection between the attack on Miss Hodgkiss and the girl from the St George's estate? Goodness only knew.

Thoroughly irritated, Ambrose strode down the corridor to the tearoom. As he'd hoped, PC Green was still finishing his cup of tea. "I've got another job for you," Ambrose said briskly. "Find out everything you can about the Vaudins. It's an unusual surname so you shouldn't have much difficulty. I think Mrs Vaudin may have been born in the Channel Islands. See if I'm right." He smiled, softening his tone. "Use your loaf. When did she come to Jenners Park? When did they marry? That sort of thing. Somerset House should have records. I think Meadows is coming back in. If she does, ask her to help. It'll be a quiet job without using her shoulder too much and she's dealt with Births, Deaths and Marriages before."

"Yes, sir!" Green said, pleased to be given something more to do. "I can also check if one of 'em's done any bird, I mean done time. I've got a contact in the prison service."

"Anything you can think of," Ambrose agreed. "But get me Mrs Vaudin's maiden name and place of birth as soon as you can. I'm on leave next week."

He set off for St George's Hall soon afterwards.

Winters was interviewing a heavily built man who was protesting vehemently about being delayed. Being careful not to interrupt, Ambrose sat on one of the hard, upright chairs that lined the Hall, and watched. He recognised the suspect: Kenneth Clarke, the lodger at the victim's home on Franklin Street. In his thirties and beginning to go bald, he had two fronds of lank hair slicked back across his head. A salesman at the lino shop on Finkle Street, he was normally bland and suave: 'a typical salesman,' Ambrose had thought when he went in with Mary a few months ago. Today the man was incoherent, one minute whining, the next aggressive. Winters and PC Vernon had to repeat their questions several times. Twice, Winters had to warn him he could be arrested for obstructing the police. Ambrose recognised the signs. They didn't yet have a confession, but there were grounds for taking him back to the Station. The confession would follow soon afterwards.

As he sat listening but not quite catching all the dialogue, Ambrose's mind returned to the Harvey case and the missing photographs. With a start, he realised he had been overlooking a significant detail. Miss Havering had mentioned three photos, but they had been concentrating on just two. She'd said she couldn't remember whether there was an inscription on the third picture, giving the impression it was the same as the others: of two girls with their German lovers. He'd assumed the same. But what if it had been of another girl entirely, another couple, even?

Sighing, Ambrose considered the possibility. If it was of another couple, somebody else entirely could have killed Robin Harvey, somebody he didn't know the first thing about. Instead of solving the case, he seemed to be making it more complicated.

It was a relief to return to a straightforward, thoroughly nasty murder with an obvious suspect and an understandable motive. As soon as DS Winters had formally arrested Clarke and arranged for him to be taken down to the Station, Ambrose crossed to the trestle table they were using as an Incident desk. "Sounds like good work," he remarked. "Fill me in."

Winters sighed, clearly drained by the morning's investigation. "Kenneth Clarke, the lodger," he replied. "Claims the girl had been giving him the come-hither for weeks. I doubt it, or if she did, I dunno what she saw in him. Says he met her as she was coming back from a friend's, and persuaded her to go a walk with him. They had an argument and she stormed off towards the allotments. That was the last he saw of her. Someone else must have attacked her. He went home."

"You don't believe him?" Ambrose asked ironically.

"No. His landlady, the victim's mother, says she didn't hear him come in that night. We can't find the clothes she thinks he was wearing that day. She also says she was getting worried at the way he kept looking at her daughter. She thought he followed her from the house a couple of times. She was going to ask him to leave."

"Pity she didn't," Ambrose remarked, sighing. "Though he may well have come back. Sounds like he was infatuated with the girl."

"The mother says her daughter never gave him any encouragement," Winters added, "but she would, wouldn't she? We still need to get some hard evidence: find the suspect's clothes and whether there's any blood on them, whether anyone saw them together that night, etc., but Clarke's story is contradictory and he has no alibi. He's a strong bloke, lifting all that lino I suppose. If he thought the victim was going to give him what he wanted and she refused, he could have swiped her one when she tried to run away. Doc Halstead says it looks like a single blow to the head killed her, though there were several other injuries post mortem, as if the killer had completely lost his rag. Clarke's known to have a bad temper. He's been in trouble at work. We have enough to hold him for a few hours." Getting up, Winters stretched his back. "I'm whacked," he admitted.

"See you back at the Station," Ambrose replied. "I'll take over the questioning if you like. Give you a break."

"Thanks, Guv," Winters replied with a weary smile.

'At least that's one case almost tied up,' Ambrose thought with relief as he drove back across the town. 'And I should be home on time.' Then he grimaced. He was tempting fate. Mary was busy making arrangements for their trip to Guernsey. She would have a lot to discuss with him. He didn't want to be late.

When he arrived back at the Station, the Desk Sergeant was still trying to get information out of Clarke so that he could fill in the right forms. Ambrose had a few moments before he needed to go to the interview room. Seeing WPC Meadows and PC Green sitting side by side at a desk, he smiled. It was good to have Meadows back, and Green was shaping up a lot better than he'd feared. He paused at the desk to see how they'd got on.

"Found anything about the Vaudins?" he asked Meadows.

"Plenty." She looked down at her notes. "Vaudin: Maiden name Mauger, born 3rd May 1923, daughter of Elizabeth and Eli Mauger of Brioc Farm. Married John Vaudin in Southwark, London, April 3rd, 1947. He was born in Jersey, about 1920. We're onto that at the moment. Sounds like they met over here after the War. Probably found they came from the same part of the world, got pally, one thing lead to another and they married here."

Ambrose nodded. "Sounds likely," he agreed. "When did they move to Jenners Park?"

PC Green answered him. "Mr Vaudin opened a bank account there in March 1950. Mrs Vaudin died October 12th last year, at Jenners Park Hospital."

"She had a history of heart problems," Meadows explained. "There are no surviving children. There's a suggestion one may have died in infancy, but we haven't chased that up yet at Somerset House. That's the next line of enquiry."

"Excellent," Ambrose said. He should be able to trace the Mauger family while he was in Guernsey. There might be tales of their daughter collaborating with the Germans, perhaps even memories that she had a particularly close friend, the 'Me' of the photos. Things were looking up.

"Spend another half hour on the case," he asked Meadows. "What does Mr Vaudin do for a living? Does his job bring him to Chalk Heath? Did they have friends here before Mrs Vaudin died? That sort of thing. Then pack it in. You've both got other things to do." He smiled as he left them. "You seem to make a good team."

Meadows laughed. "I've never heard him say that before," she admitted to Green afterwards. "I suppose we do. We seem to have shifted a lot of stuff quickly." She paused uncertainly. "I'm sorry I made a fool of myself yesterday."

"What over?" Green asked in surprise. "Oh, the flowers and that chap following you, you mean? I think I've sorted that."

"How?"

"Probably better if I don't say," Green replied cagily.

"Tell me who he is and I'll give him what for!" Meadows demanded.

Green laughed. "That's why I won't tell you who he is," he insisted. "We've already had one murder this week."

Meadows managed to laugh too. "I'm beginning to get my suspicions," she warned.

"I'd leave 'em at that," Green advised.

But Meadows refused to leave the mystery unsolved. "Was it the ginger-haired painter?" she asked.

"What makes you say that?"

Meadows flushed. "The colour of his hair I suppose. And the way he looked at me sometimes."

Green played with his pencil reflectively, working out his reply. "I don't think he meant any harm," he said at length. "He fell for you, sort of fixated on you. That's the word isn't it? He told me he was worried about you being out alone on your beat at night; a woman on her own going into some pretty unpleasant places, trying doors and all that. So he followed you to make sure no one attacked you. He thought he was protecting you."

Meadows snorted.

"He did save you when he saw the tile fall," Green pointed out.

Reluctantly Meadows nodded. "I suppose I should thank him for that," she admitted, "But I don't want to go near him, and I don't want him near me. He gives me the willies."

"Don't worry," Green advised. "I've had words with him. Fortunately the painting's all finished so he'll be on another job elsewhere. I don't think you'll see him again. "

In acute embarrassment, Meadows stared at the telephone in front of her. "Thanks," she said awkwardly. "You're not bad...for a Londoner."

"Would you Adam and Eve it," Green laughed back. "A compliment!"

Chapter Twenty Four

"At least the St George's case is pretty much sorted," Winters said, pushing his empty plate away. He glanced at his watch. "No wonder I was starving. It's nearly three o'clock."

Ambrose nodded, mopping egg yolk with a slice of bread. "That was good," he agreed. "At least if you're late, you get extra helpings. Last time I came in early, Doreen was rationing the sausages."

"Fran reckons I eat too much fried stuff," Winters replied ruefully. "But, like I said to her, how's a plate of salad going to keep you going in this climate? And where can you get it anyway? Doreen thinks salad is one lettuce leaf and half a tomato."

"You do her an injustice," Ambrose objected, smiling. "She gave me a slice of pickled cucumber last year." Finishing his meal, he drank his second cup of tea. "Fancy a drive up to Maple View?" he asked afterwards. "We can't do much more at St George's until tomorrow. It'll take Vernon and Higgins a while to find the missing clothes, if they can, and the house to house enquiries are still on-going. Let's see if we can crack a harder nut while we wait."

"I presume you mean the Fielding case," Winters said. "It's bugging you, isn't it? Got something new?"

"Perhaps," Ambrose replied cautiously. "I looked at Doc Halstead's report again this morning. He mentions a red fibre caught under the Major's toe nail, the big toe on his left foot."

Winters looked up with interest. "But the bath mat was brown when we found him. So Doc did find a trace of the missing bath mat?"

"That's my hope," Ambrose agreed. "It might be nothing, maybe a bit of wool from his sock. The Doc's report says he had a split toenail, but it looked like an old injury. It could have been catching on all his

173

socks. But if it is a bit of another bath mat, then it ties in with a theory I'd like to test. You game to act as guinea pig? Everyone else is busy and we deserve a breather."

"Sure," Winters agreed. "So long as I only have to *pretend* to crack my head open."

They returned to the Station to let the Desk Sergeant know where they were going, and for both of them to call in at their offices: Winters to collect the case file, and Ambrose to retrieve a large carrier bag from the top of his filing cabinet. Winters raised an eyebrow when he saw the bag but said nothing. He passed the file to Ambrose as they got into the car. "We've conducted more interviews since you last looked," he explained. "I'll bring you up to speed as I drive."

"Fine." Opening the file on his lap, Ambrose glanced at Winters' notes. "I gather you haven't got very far with the residents," he commented. "They keep themselves to themselves I suppose."

"Apart from Miss Huddlestone." Winters replied as he turned out of the car park. "She knows about everyone and their grandmother. Unfortunately she was having her hair permed that afternoon. If she'd been at the house, she might have had a peep and seen what happened. She'd certainly have spotted an outsider. As it is, none of the residents knew anything until the Ambulance turned up. The only useful information we got was from old Mr Roberts. He went to use the bathroom that afternoon, but it had the 'engaged' sign on it. So he went into the Ladies' instead."

"Could he remember the time?" Ambrose asked.

"Between three and four. But he's not exactly reliable. According to Mavis he's getting a bit confused."

"So the Major might have been lying there before four o'oclock," Ambrose remarked thoughtfully. "That's consistent with Meadows' theory. If the bath was filled well before the the Major was found, she wouldn't have heard the tap dripping. She wasn't home then."

"Unless when Roberts came, someone else was using the lav and the Major only went in afterwards," Winters pointed out. "We tried asking whether the other male residents had gone to the bathroom that afternoon, but no one could remember. All they'd say is that the Major always went in at four o'clock on the dot, every day, but no one actually saw him do it that day. A couple of them even refused to answer: it wasn't the sort of question one asks a gentleman!"

For a few moments both were silent. "What about Stephen Hendrickson, the chap who appeared just after Meadows came on the scene? He has to be in the frame," Ambrose pointed out. "He has easy access from the attic, and he's a lot younger and fitter than most of the guests. Any motive?"

"Not that we can find. Probably can't afford Maple View on his salary, but doesn't seem to be in debt. Took the place because it's quiet and he can sleep when he's on nights. He works as a ticket clerk at the station. He's only been there a few weeks since being posted to Chalk Heath. He'd like to help with our enquiry but doesn't know anything. You've met that sort of bloke before."

"I have indeed," Ambrose agreed. "He's probably telling the truth this time though."

They were passing Victoria Park. Both paused, unwilling to voice more awkward questions. "And the housekeeper?" Ambrose asked instead.

"She repeated pretty much what she told us on the day. She went down to Lucas' Hardware Store, to buy cleaning stuff and a new mop. She didn't see the Major after she returned, not until she tried the bathroom and found him. I got the impression she was still struggling to get over it. Natural I suppose."

"And Abigail McEwan?"

Winters checked his notes. "She said she didn't come up to Maple View until Mavis phoned her," he replied. "She was having tea and cakes with a couple of lady friends at Molly's Café that afternoon. She says she got there at three thirty and left for home about five to get ready for an evening do at the Town Hall. In the end, she was so upset by what happened she couldn't face it. Mac had to go on his own."

"What about the Hon Madge? Has she been officially questioned about either death?"

"Sort of," Winters replied awkwardly. "She got quite shirty, until I pointed out that she knew her way round Maple View, and where the key was hidden at Curiosity Corner, so she had to be on our list. After that she was a bit more co-operative, but only a bit. She doesn't have an alibi for the afternoon. She was alone at home working on the Prize Giving. Said she made some phone calls about arrangements for the dinner. We might be able to check those."

Winters turned into the car park at Maple View. As he did so, he had to brake sharply as a little red car pulled out of the drive in front of him. With an expression of alarm, followed by a slight nod of apology, the Honourable Marjorie Hodgkiss turned into the main road.

"Bloomin' 'eck!" Winters grumbled. "Talk of the Devil! She needs to slow down a bit."

"It's Thursday, isn't it?" Ambrose asked.

"That doesn't entitle her to drive like maniac," Winters responded, still annoyed.

Ambrose shook his head. "I meant it's Maple View Bridge Club day. She's probably been playing a mean game and suddenly realised she needed to be somewhere else." Frowning, he looked towards the car disappearing down the hill. "Is it my imagination or was her expression a bit odd?" he asked.

"She probably gave herself a fright," Winters acknowledged.

"Maybe that was it," Ambrose agreed. "But I thought she wasn't too pleased to see us."

Neither, it seemed, was Mavis the Housekeeper. She rushed to open the back door when Ambrose knocked. "What is it, Inspector?" she asked, almost pulling them both inside. "No more trouble I hope?" She glanced curiously at the carrier bag he was carrying. "Is that for Mrs McEwan? I'm afraid she isn't here."

"No, just some shopping," Ambrose replied vaguely. "Sorry. I didn't mean to alarm you. We've just popped up to have a look at things again." He nodded towards DS Winters. "My colleague and I want to refresh our memories."

"I hope the residents don't see you," Mavis said, her voice full of concern. "Some of them have only just got over the shock. Poor Mr Roberts has been quite strange this past week."

"We're just checking something for our report," Ambrose assured her. "We'll keep ourselves out of sight."

"You leave us to it," Winters said briskly. "We'll pop upstairs for a few minutes and let ourselves out."

"Oh I couldn't..." Mavis began to protest.

Ambrose was friendly but firm. "We'll be much less conspicuous if there's only the two of us and you're not following us around," he insisted.

Reluctanly Mavis returned to her rooms.

Treading as softly as they could, Winters and Ambrose went up the stairs. "You go into the bathroom and lock the door," Ambrose instructed, "if there's a lock on it by now. I want to pick something up on the way."

Softly he turned towards the Housekeeper's room. As he'd hoped, the door was unlocked. Going inside, he closed the door behind him.

It took him a few moments to find what he was looking for, then putting both flagons into the carrier bag and stuffing a couple of cloths around them, he headed to the Gentlemen's bathroom.

Winters heard his soft tap on the door and let him in. "Lock replaced," he commented quietly. "So, what's the experiment?"

Taking the flagons out of the bag, Ambrose passed one labelled 'Wood Polish' to him, together with a cloth. Then, bending down, he lifted the bath mat and put it to one side. "Now we polish where the mat was," he explained. "Careful. It'll make the tiles slippery."

Together they polished the floor. Then Ambrose took the last item out of his bag: a red bath mat he'd bought at the General Store on his way to work. Turning it over, he showed Winters the back. "No non-slip binding," he whispered. Then he laid the mat on the polished area. "You're lighter than me," he remarked. "Climb into the bath. Let's see what happens when you step out. Don't worry, I'm here to catch you."

It was a good job he was. With a wry smile, Winters took off his shoes and socks and stepped into the bath. Then he stepped out, onto the mat. At once it slipped from under him, carrying his feet forwards while pitching his body backwards. Urgently Ambrose grabbed his arm, preventing Winters from falling against the bath. For a few panic-stricken seconds Winters struggled to regain his footing, his feet slipping in different directions while Ambrose struggled to keep both of them upright. If they fell, at least one of them could be badly hurt.

Mercifully Ambrose could take Winters' weight. "Wooah!" he said, trying not to raise his voice. Gradually he helped Winters stand upright again. "Move to the right," he advised.

As soon as he was away from the polished area, Winters regained his balance.

Though they straightened themselves out quickly, the incident left them shaken. "Bloody Hell!" Winters said. Ruefully he rubbed an elbow. Then he felt the rim of the cast iron bath beside him. "You wouldn't half give your head a crack if you hit this," he remarked. "And the floor wouldn't do you much good either."

For a full moment both were silent. Then Winters managed a wry smile. "Do you think I can count this as a work related injury?" he asked, examining the bruise on his elbow.

"I reckon so," Ambrose replied. He was appalled at how nearly he'd caused a colleague a serious injury. "I'm sorry," he apologised. "I thought we'd just test if the floor was slippery enough for an old man to fall. I never dreamt you'd go flying. Are you okay?"

"Just about. Never mind an old man," Winters said softly, "without the non-slip fixing on the bath mat, anyone'll slip on those tiles if they've been polished. Wet feet'd make it worse too. I think we know how the Major was killed." His expression hardened. "Of all the cold, premeditated…" He couldn't finish the sentence.

"We have a particularly nasty killer," Ambrose agreed. "Poor Major Fielding. I doubt if he even knew he was in danger. It'll be hard to prove it wasn't an accident, though. You can predict the defence: 'The flagons were mixed up. The tapes came off the mat…' Unless we can prove our suspect had both opportunity and motive, we'll never win." He shook his head in disgust. Then he picked up the red mat and stuffed it back in the bag. "But they're not going to get away with it if I can help it," he added, his voice taking on a determined note.

"After nearly breaking my neck, I'm not keen on that either," Winters agreed.

"Let's get this polish off before anyone else falls," Ambrose said, pouring some of the cleaner onto the tiles, and rubbing hard. "There. That's safer. We'd better tell Mavis to give the place another clean. Pop down and tell her some tale. You're good at inventing stories. I'll replace the mat and put the stuff back in the Housekeeper's room."

"Isn't she going to wonder what we've been up to?" Winters asked..

"I imagine she'll guess," Ambrose admitted. "She realised the significance of the missing polish herself. That's why she made a point of telling Meadows. It'd be interesting to know if Mavis has any theories about where it went."

"If she has, she isn't saying."

"She may be too afraid to," Ambrose pointed out. "See you by the back door. Which ever of us is there first, tuck under the stairway where the residents can't see."

Within ten minutes, they were getting back into Winters' car. "What did you tell her?" Ambrose asked as he dumped the carrier bag at his feet.

"The truth," Winters answered. "I had to. She asked straight away if we were trying to find out how the Major fell. It seemed pointless pretending otherwise. I think she suspects one of the residents." He paused uncomfortably. "Possibly Pauline Meadows."

"What?" Ambrose asked in surprise.

"Looked at from her point of view, it's a possibility. She doesn't know Meadows like we do. She's bound to be suspicious of someone who's only recently moved in, and was at home when the Major fell.

Or at least, when we all thought he'd fallen. Meadows' rooms are near the Gents Bathroom, too."

"Stop it! You'll have me suspecting her next," Ambrose said, only half joking. "Lord! What a mess! When we get back down to the Station, let's have a quiet cuppa. We need to think about where we go from here."

Chapter Twenty Five

As soon as they'd settled in Ambrose's office, he took out a quarto pad from his drawer and began writing headings in pencil. It was a technique he'd often found helped clear his mind. "So," he began, "Let's bounce a few ideas around. We now know what happened and how it was done, but not who by, or why. We don't even know if the Major's death is connected with Robin Harvey's, though my gut feeling is that it is."

"Mine too," Winters agreed.

"We have a woman with a connection to both victims, who knew where the key to the shop was kept and who regularly went to Maple View for her Bridge Club," Ambrose continued, writing another heading. "So why haven't we brought her in for further questioning?"

"Because of who she is," Winters admitted. "She's not going to take kindly to it, and she has influential friends. If we can't prove we have excellent grounds for bringing her in, we won't just have egg on our faces, we'll be out of our jobs."

"Ok." Once again Ambrose scribbled a note on the pad. "So what grounds do we have? As you say, basically that she knew the dead men and how to get into their homes. Not good enough. This is a small town. Anybody who's anybody knows each other. We need motive."

"Agreed. So was it all about the Poetry Competition or those missing photos?"

"Could be either," Ambrose mused, "or indeed it could be something completely different. We can't establish that Madge knew about the photos, even if stealing them was the killer's motive. And if it was, what has that to do with the Major?"

"Perhaps he knew about them or had another set?" Winters replied. He shook his head at his own suggestion. "I can't see how the photos can be relevant to both cases," he admitted. "Of course we're only assuming that Mrs Vaudin was one of the two women shown on the photos."

Ambrose looked up. "That's an idea. Maybe Mrs Vaudin was the photographer." He wrote another note, then stared ahead of him reflectively. "In that case, who are the two women with the Germans? Madge and her sister? Maybe I'll find the missing piece of the puzzle when I'm over there. I mentioned that Mary and I are spending a few days in Guernsey, didn't I? "

Winters nodded. "You might be lucky," he replied dubiously. "And if you're not, at least you'll get a nice break. I gather it's pretty over there."

"I need a better idea of what to ask," Ambrose admitted, sighing. He came to a decision. "I'll have to see what I can find out from the Hon Madge. Informally that is. She can bite my head off, but if I say I want to chat to her about the competition she might agree to meet me. I can try slipping in the odd question."

"Rather you than me!" Winters laughed.

Ambrose looked at his watch. "We have a meeting of the Friends of the Theatre tonight. I wonder if she'd come a bit early for a chat?"

To his surprise when he rang her, Miss Hodgkiss was quite amenable to the idea. She wanted to ask him a favour and had been hoping to see him.

"Oh Lord! I bet she wants me to give out the prizes," Ambrose guessed as he put the phone down. "Oh well, the show must go on, as they say. The poets who won aren't to blame for their judges keeling over. Or *are* they?" He shook his head in mock despair.

The Hon Madge was waiting for him in the theatre bar. Smiling broadly, she was at her most persuasive. "I knew you would help," she said triumphantly when he agreed. "I'm so grateful. With all that's been happening, I was late contacting Mr Llewellyn. He was the gentleman Mr Harvey recommended. And of course, by the time I got round to it, he was fully booked."

'Not much of a compliment to me,' Ambrose thought wryly: he was clearly second best. He let Miss Hodgkiss talk on about the prize giving, and the arrangements she'd had to make on her own. "I was determined not to cancel," she insisted. "Having to postpone was bad enough. But it just wouldn't have been right to go ahead so soon after the Major's death."

"I'll be on leave next week," Ambrose said casually. "What's the new date?"

"Three weeks from Saturday. You'll be back in time, I hope?"

"Yes. I'm only away for a few days. We're taking Mary's aunt to Guernsey." Ambrose paused, choosing his words carefully. "You know the island quite well I believe. I think you said your family have a place in St Peter Port. Is it nice?"

"Very," Miss Hodgkiss replied. She opened her handbag, as if looking for something. Ambrose had the impression she wanted to change the subject.

He pretended not to notice. "I imagine it's taken a while to recover after the War. They were occupied by the Germans weren't they?"

"Like a lot of places," Miss Hodgkiss replied tersely.

"But the Channel Islands were the only part of the UK to fall," Ambrose commented. "That must have been very difficult."

"You have no idea."

"Were you there, then?" Ambrose asked, his interest increasing.

"Some of the time. Now if you'll excuse me, I have important business to see to."

Ambrose tried a personal appeal. "Please stay a moment," he implored. "You might be able to help me. We believe some photos may have disappeared from Mr Harvey's shop. They were of a couple of German Officers with their lady friends. Would you know anything about them?"

"Are you implying I took them?" The Hon Madge's voice rose in anger. The couple at the next table looked curiously towards her.

"Of course not," Ambrose replied soothingly. "I just wondered whether he'd ever shown them to you. He might have thought you'd be interested."

"What interest would I have in such photos?" The Hon Madge's voice was quieter now, almost a snarl. "Are you suggesting I knew German Officers? Because if you are, you could not be more insulting!" She looked towards the table near her, clearly recognising fellow committee members, and turned her face away. "This conversation is at an end!" she said more quietly.

Ambrose was becoming embarassed himself. "I didn't mean to give offence," he apologised. "I'm just hoping you can cast some light on Mr Harvey's death."

"Then interview me properly, under caution, or whatever you call it, and I'll have a solicitor present."

"We may have to do that," Ambrose warned. "But it'd be much easier if you tell me now. Did Mr Harvey show you the photographs?"

"No he did not!" Miss Hodgkiss retorted. "And if you think I might have been one of the girls on them, you're very much mistaken!"

Two women at a table on the other side were also looking across. Miss Hodgkiss' face was going red, though she did her best to remain dignified. Getting up, she reached for her handbag. Then she paused, her voice dropping to a whisper.

"If you're hoping to trace photos of a couple of Germans and their Jerry Bags, you're completely mad. No one would have taken photos like that. They have to be forgeries. Do you think we were swanning around with our box brownies taking holiday snaps, and getting them developed at the local pharmacy? Even the Germans wouldn't have dared. They'd have been sent back home for consorting with the locals." She snorted in derision. "You weren't there. You have no idea!"

Then she walked firmly and briskly towards the exit.

Chapter Twenty Six

Monday 11ᵗʰ April

"You OK?" Ambrose asked in concern. His wife was looking very pale.

"That old taxi was a bit much after the boat," Mary admitted. "I was all right until we started swinging round corners. And the roads are so narrow! I was sure we were going to hit a wall." She managed a smile. "I never thought we'd get Aunty's wheelchair in. You must have been uncomfortable, too, cramped at the back."

"I've had pleasanter rides," Ambrose admitted ruefully. "Still we're here. It was worth the trip just to see your Aunt's face when she saw Mr Blondel waiting for us."

"Yes." Sitting on an old cane chair in the window, Mary looked out. "It's beautiful, isn't it? I thought St Peter Port looked old-fashioned, like Chalk Heath ten years ago, but that view from the harbour! Even though I was feeling sick, it took my breath away." She sighed, beginning to feel better. "Just look at that sea! It's as blue as a baby's eyes. You never get that colour in Margate!" She paused, settling back into the chair. In the distance they could hear her Aunt's voice, talking happily to their hosts.

"They've got a lot of catching up to do," Mary commented, smiling. "She's a game old stick isn't she? I didn't think she'd make it up that gang plank, but she hauled herself up without a murmur. I hope I'm as active at her age."

"You're a chip off the same block," Ambrose assured her, tousling her hair. "Your Gran must have been the sort that drove wagons across prairies. I wish I'd known her."

184

Smiling, Mary let out a sigh of relief. "That's better," she said. "I'm getting off the boat now. Funny how the motion stays with you. I'll change before tea. I feel scruffy after so much travelling. You must be tired too, pushing that wheelchair all over the place. Fortunately Aunty's not heavy."

There was a burst of laughter from downstairs. "They seem genuinely pleased to see her," Ambrose remarked. "It's good of them to put us up too."

"Aunty said we're doing them a favour. They want to develop their Bed and Breakfast business and we're testing this new extension for them. It looks like it used to be a barn." Glancing round, Mary indicated the heavy beams across the ceiling. "You'd better mind your head," she warned. Then she took in the hand basin, set into a new vanity unit, and looked towards the brightly patterned curtains. "They've done it up nicely, haven't they?" Getting up, she gave Ambrose an unexpected kiss. "And nicer still to be here, just the two of us!" she added. "Even if you are working."

For a few moments they were quiet, glad of the time together. "Tell you what," Ambrose said. "I'd rather work here. My office doesn't have half as good a view."

They stood side by side at the window, looking out. One way they could see green fields and cows. In the other direction, sand and jagged rocks marked the edge of a tranquil bay. "Do you have to spoil things by asking questions?" Mary whispered. "It seems just a little *ungrateful.*" Then she shook her head at her own foolishness. "I know. That's why we came," she admitted. "This is all just a bonus."

"I'll be tactful," Ambrose promised.

A gong sounded downstairs. Hurriedly they got ready for tea.

The guests' dining room was also the farm kitchen, with a long wooden table and benches in the window. They all sat together, with Joan's wheelchair folded against the wall near the door, and Joan herself seated on an upright chair at the head of the table. For the first quarter of an hour, conversation gave way to the mound of sandwiches and fruit bread Janet Blondel had prepared. "Gâche" she called it, pleased when Mary asked for the recipe.

Ambrose thanked the couple for letting them stay at such short notice.

"It's a pleasure to have you," Mrs Blondel insisted. "The season hasn't begun yet and it's good to air the new rooms. Seeing Joan again is lovely." She turned towards Mary's aunt. "We had some good times together before the War, didn't we? Joan's family came every year," she added by way of explanation. "From when she and your uncle were first married." There was a pause, as if Mrs Blondel were recalling the deaths of Joan's daughter and husband, and didn't know how to continue.

Joan herself filled the space. "Annie and Ted both loved coming here," she said, turning towards Mary. "Annie used to herd the cows like a natural and Ted would muck out the barn, when I couldn't even get him to wash up at home. In those days we took working holidays. We couldn't afford layabout ones. Every year we had two wonderful weeks and went home healthier but fatter!" She laughed. "Those were good years, before the world went mad again." Glancing at the photos on the mantlepiece, she added, "How's your son?"

Mrs Blondel smiled, "Well, thank you," she replied. "It took him a while to settle back here, like a lot of the children. After five years in Stockport, this place seemed very quiet. But he's happily married now."

"Stockport?" Ambrose asked in surprise.

"A lot of the children were evacuated there," Mr Blondel explained. "It was very different to here."

"I can imagine," Ambrose replied drily.

"We were so sorry to hear about Annie," Mr Blondel added, turning back to Aunt Joan. "And then to lose Ted too. That must have been very hard."

Joan shook her head. "It's no use regretting your losses," she said firmly. "I'm very lucky to have Mary and Paul to help me." She smiled her thanks. "Moving near them was the best thing I've ever done. I couldn't have gone on coping on my own in a London flat. But enough about me. Unless I'm mistaken, Paul is here on business as well as to give me a break. Can you tell us what it's about? Nothing serious I hope?"

Ambrose smiled. He and Mary hadn't said a word about his ulterior motive in coming, but Joan was so astute she had guessed. "It's mainly a holiday," he said to their hosts. "Mary and I haven't been away together for a long time. Our son's old enough to stay with one of his school friends now, and it seemed a good opportunity to visit your lovely island, while helping Aunt Joan. It's fortunate that it also gives me chance to do a bit of research."

"What into?" Mr Blondel asked.

"A bit of background," Ambrose replied vaguely. "We have a case that has Guernsey connections. I thought I might trace the families over here."

"Ask my wife," Mr Blondel laughed. "She knows everybody."

'We're in luck!' Ambrose thought, but he turned casually towards his hostess. "I wonder if you've come across a family by the name of Mauger," he asked.

Mrs Blondel thought for a moment. "Oh yes," she said. "The Maugers. They owned Brioc Farm near St Peter Port. One son and a daughter: Jim and Adelaide. Jim went to England to join the forces as soon as War broke out. He never came back. We all assumed he was killed, sadly. Adelaide left the island after the Occupation ended. I think she married."

"And the parents?" Ambrose asked.

"Eli and Beth never seemed to get over being left on their own. They sold up about ten years ago. There's a nice young couple there now. Don't know much about farming I gather but they're willing to learn."

Ambrose wondered how to proceed. "Did Adelaide have any special friends?" he asked. "She died recently and we'd like to get in touch with them."

"Not that I can recall," Mrs Blondel replied.

There was a guardedness in her manner, as if she did know of friends but was unwilling to name them. "Did she leave the island under a bit of a cloud?" Ambrose suggested. "We've been given that impression."

"I couldn't say. I didn't know them well."

Again there was a slight frostiness, that sense he was treading on dangerous ground. He let the conversation drift back to memories of the island before the War, and how fast things were changing on the mainland. Life was looking up, what with the Health Service and Grammar Schools, and young people having the chance of a decent job. If only Russia and America would stop being so stupid. As Mr Blondel said, they were like two schoolboys in the playground, each boasting that their stick was the biggest. The trouble was, boasting could lead to blows.

"I don't think Russia will actually invade the West," Mary said, more confidently than she felt. "It's just bluster."

"Speaking as someone who's experienced invasion," Mr Blondel said quietly, "I assure you it can happen when you least expect it."

"Goodness! How did we get onto such miserable things?" Joan asked. "I'm going to have another piece of your excellent fruit cake. Do you know, they eat it with cheese in Yorkshire? I was so surprised when I was staying in the Dales. The waitress handed me a huge slab of Wensleydale to go with my Christmas cake. I didn't know whether I was meant to eat it or keep it for the mice in my room."

Everyone laughed and the atmosphere lightened. Ambrose tried a different approach. "An acquaintance of ours comes to St Peter Port regularly," he said. "Her family have a holiday home there. She's quite a character. I wonder if you've met her? The Honourable Marjorie Hodgkiss."

"Oh yes," Mr Blondel replied, smiling. "As you say, quite a character. Her family own Star Cottage, just on the outskirts of St Peter Port. My wife used to clean for them when they were over. Didn't you, Love? She cleaned for several English visitors, before she married me and started cleaning here."

"And I carried on doing for others too," his wife reminded him. "We needed the money. I used to wobble down the lanes on my bike, with a bag of cloths and brushes dangling on either side of the handlebars. I came off once. Ended up in a hedge with a toilet brush in my face."

Once again there was laughter. Ambrose waited, then tried again. "You knew the Hodgkiss family?"

"Oh yes. The parents were a bit uppity; never let you forget they were a class above, but they were nice enough once you got to know them. And even the gentry can have their sad stories."

"Oh?" Ambrose asked, trying not to sound too interested.

"Miss Marjorie and her brother got stuck over here when the Germans invaded. They were very unlucky."

"I gather they had a bad time," Ambrose bluffed. "I never knew how they came to be here."

Mrs Blondel poured another cup of tea as she answered. "They'd come over to rescue things from the cottage. They were both very good sailors; used to sail across from Portsmouth regularly. Everyone knew we were vulnerable, but we were supposed to be demilitarised and safe. So Marjorie and Charles dashed across to empty the cottage. I arranged to meet them to help them pack. On the way, their boat developed engine trouble. They were moored for days, trying to get a part. Just as they were about to leave, the Germans arrived. There was no way they could get out after that, so they had no choice but to go back to the cottage."

"How awful!" Mary said.

"Oh, they weren't the only English who got trapped. At first I don't think they were treated any worse than the rest of us, but Charles was arrested and disappeared the same night. Presumably he was doing something forbidden: hiding a radio perhaps, distributing an underground newsletter, that sort of thing. Who knows? We all assumed he was sent to a concentration camp in Europe, but even now people don't talk about such things." Staring into her tea cup, Mrs Blondel fell silent, her mouth taking on a hard line.

"And Miss Marjorie?" Mary prompted gently.

"It must have been very hard. I mean, she'd grown up with money and people waiting on her. Now she she had to get by like the rest of us. She survived, bartering things like we all did, growing what she could in the garden. She fitted in well actually and made lots of local friends, staying with them sometimes. I suppose that helped when she no longer had Charles as company. Then she disappeared too. It was the same time as the authorites were interning men born in England, so I thought they must have taken her too. But no one knows for sure why she suddenly wasn't there any more."

There was a long silence. "I was glad to see Marjorie when she and her sister came back," Mrs Blondel said suddenly. "At first I thought she'd changed a lot, but after a while she was her old self. But I'm surprised you know her," Mrs Blondel remarked. "From what Joan's said in her letters, Chalk Heath doesn't sound the sort of place you'd expect a woman like her to live. You find it a bit boring, don't you, Joan?"

"I did at first," Aunt Joan admitted. "But there's lots going on once you get to know the place. I help two days a week at the local school, hearing the children read, and go to events at the library. There's the theatre too. People are very good and give me lifts, and when they can't I have Jimmy. He's my tame taxi driver. He couldn't be more helpful. He even changed a light bulb for me last week!"

"I'll bet you sweet-talked him into doing it," Mary commented drily.

"I may have fluttered my eyelashes a bit."

Their hosts laughed. Ambrose smiled too but his mind was whirring.

Mary touched his foot under the table, reminding him that he was with others. "Would you like us to help with the washing up?" she asked Mrs Blondel.

"Of course not! You're our guests. Why don't you sit outside for a bit? The yard's a real suntrap and there's still a bit of afternoon left."

So they sat outside watching the sun set over the byre roof, all three of them quietly enjoying the peace. After half an hour or so, though, the sun dropped and the shadows grew cooler. "It's much warmer here isn't it?" Joan remarked, "But I suppose we'd better go inside soon. Is your room comfortable?"

"Very," Mary assured her.

"Have you found out anything useful, Paul?"

In surprise, Ambrose nodded. "A good deal," he admitted.

"I'll be spending tomorrow afternoon with some neighbours we used to know," Joan continued. "While you're at the library. I'll see if they know anything about the Mauger family; I got the impression Janet was avoiding saying something."

Ambrose glanced at her in surprise. "There's not a lot you miss, is there?" he commented. "Thank you. I can rely on you to be tactful I'm sure."

Chapter Twenty Seven

Tuesday 12th April

Mr Blondel offered to drop them off a short walk from the Priaulx Library. He had to go to St Martin to pick up some new tools, and insisted it was no trouble to go out of his way. "It'll be better than you getting the bus," he said. "It's quite a walk to the stop." Mary wasn't sure a ride in his old truck was any better, but she thanked him and climbed into the front seat. At least this time Ambrose wouldn't be sharing the back with a wheelchair.

Mr Blondel had been longer getting ready than they'd hoped (something to do with a sick cow), and they were later than planned. When they got to St Peter Port, he apologised for not taking them all the way to the library, but he was running late and wasn't overfond of that part of town. "The German Naval Signals HQ was that way," he explained, indicating the road to their left. "And the Field Kommandant took over a hotel down there." He nodded in the other direction. "Straight down there," he directed as he stopped on a corner and pointed to the road opposite.

Waving their thanks, they set off at a rapid pace with Mrs Blondel's directions to guide them.

"Walk uphill slightly, cross two junctions," Mary read, "then go down Candie Road. It gets quite steep. The library's on your left. If you see a tower like a pepperpot on your right, you've gone too far." She smiled as she read on. "The library's in a big house, set in its own grounds, near some public gardens."

Pausing, Mary looked at a window box ablaze with flowers. "Geraniums!" she said in delight. "You wouldn't dare put them out this early at home. It must be much warmer here." With interest she glanced at the houses as they passed. "It feels very French doesn't it? At least how I imagine France to look like. That's somewhere I'd love to go, though I think I'd rather see if we can afford to fly. I don't fancy the ferry. Not after yesterday!"

"Would you be any better flying?" Ambrose asked.

Mary laughed. "I don't know until I try. At least it'd be over quicker." She paused, her tone changing. "I can't get over what Janet Blondel told us about the Hon Madge," she admitted. "Did it surprise you?"

"Yes and no," Ambrose admitted. "Pauline Meadows told me she thought the woman had some sadness that she never talked about." He paused, recalling the photo on the welsh dresser Meadows had described. Maybe it was the missing brother, not a lover. But why had Madge disappeared so suddenly? He sighed. He'd stayed up late talking to Aunt Joan and Mr and Mrs Blondel. His felt tired, but not only from lack of sleep.

"You seem worried," Mary commented.

"I am. This case is beginning to get to me. Every time I think we're on to something, it proves to be a blind alley, or worse."

"Worse?"

"We seem to be heading into some dark places."

For several moments they were silent. As they walked Ambrose considered how much to say to Mary. He was in danger of telling her too much and breaking confidentiality. "Can you recall when Miss Hodgkiss came to Chalk Heath?" he asked finally.

"She seems to have always been there," Mary admitted, "but I think it was soon after your transfer. I remember saying she was just what the town needed, someone with a bit of 'go'. Nowadays, I often wish her 'go' would give us a rest." Sighing, she shook her head. "Madge never actually says much about herself, does she? She talks a lot but it's all about what she's doing or what's needed from others, not about herself."

Ambrose didn't interrupt. He'd found before that it paid to let Mary follow her thoughts.

"I was also thinking about what Mrs Blondel said about Chalk Heath," she continued. "If you passed through on the train, you'd say it was the sort of place where nothing happens. Perhaps that's what Marjorie Hodgkiss wanted, somewhere she could vanish. Only she's incapable of vanishing. Within months she was back to her old self, needing to do things and to be someone. Do you get what I mean?"

"I do."

They were approaching a tall, gabled house, set in its own grounds beyond a pair of imposing stone gateposts. With its gracious bay windows and chimneys, it recalled times when women in elegant dresses strolled about its gardens. "I think this must be it," Mary remarked. She paused. "I presume you'll want to talk to the librarian while I make myself scarce. I suppose I could walk around the public gardens. That'll be them, where the big trees are."

Ambrose shook his head. "You don't need to go," he said. "In fact you could be a real help. I've arranged for papers from the late 40s to be brought out. Could you make a start on them while I talk to Miss Ozanne?"

"What am I looking for?"

"Any name or face you recognise."

"Ah," Mary said softly. "Someone with Chalk Heath connections perhaps?"

"That sort of thing."

They'd arrived at the library entrance. Miss Ozanne welcomed them at the door, having clearly been looking out for them. A small woman in an unexpectedly bright jacket, she introduced herself. "So pleased to meet you, Inspector," she began. "I'm Theresa Ozanne. I'm a volunteer at the library. Do come through."

A scent of furniture polish and old leather binding greeted them as she led the way, past mellow wooden panelling and shelves lined with books. "Nice," Mary whispered. As they walked, the librarian continued talking, as if she was used to charging for her time and considered the simple act of walking unproductive. "Thank you for letting me know you were running late," she continued. "I've put the newspapers and other ephemera on the desk outside my office. Where do you want to start? If it's all right with you, I'd like to talk about the photographs first. I'm absolutely fascinated by them, have been ever since Mr Harvey wrote to me."

"It's very good of you to see us," Ambrose replied. "Perhaps my wife can start on the papers while you and I have a chat in your office?"

"Of course." Glancing towards Mary, the librarian indicated a stack of ledgers and document boxes laid out on the table. "Nineteen forty-five to nineteen fifty," she explained. "Some of the papers are catalogued, but it's an on-going task and there are still gaps in our collection. I'm afraid you'll have to go through most of them page by page. If you know what you're looking for, you should be able to skim through quite quickly. Don't hesitate to call if you need help." She hesitated. "I can rely on you to be careful I'm sure. Some of the pages are quite flimsy. It was difficult to get good quality paper so soon after the Liberation."

Reassuring the librarian she would be careful, Mary took the muslin gloves passed to her and, settling at the table, began to unpack the first box.

Miss Ozanne seemed satisfied. "This way," she told Ambrose briskly. "As I explained, I'm a volunteer here. I help to catalogue and preserve the library's collection, but I also offer my services as a genealogical researcher. They kindly let me use this room at the back. You'll have to excuse the clutter. I'm working on a family tree at the moment. It's a beauty, so many interesting offshoots. If I'm not careful, I get carried away looking for second cousins twice removed. I imagine it's the same with some of your cases? Lots of leads that take you off at a tangent?"

"Oh yes," Ambrose agreed ruefully. "I know exactly what you mean."

They settled in Miss Ozanne's office. It was indeed littered with papers and notes, but all were carefully named and ordered. "Now tell me about the photographs," she invited.

"I was hoping you would tell me."

Miss Ozanne frowned in bewilderment. "I assumed you'd be bringing them," she replied.

"They've gone missing."

"Oh dear! They sounded so interesting."

Ambrose chose his words carefully. "Did Mr Harvey's secretary tell you he'd died?" he asked.

"Yes. Such a tragic accident!" Miss Ozanne looked at him sharply. "Though given that you've travelled so far to speak to me, I suspect you're not sure it *was* an accident?"

"There are some inconsistencies," Ambrose agreed.

"Like the photos going missing?"

"Exactly."

Miss Ozanne might be very helpful. Ambrose decided to be frank with her. "It seems likely that someone broke into the shop to retrieve them," he continued, "and Mr Harvey died as a result. This is therefore a murder investigation, although it's quite possible the death was a tragic accident. I didn't want to explain on the telephone. I'd be grateful if you'd tell me everything Mr Harvey said about the pictures. It may throw some light on the case. You were negotiating to buy them I believe."

"That's correct." Miss Ozanne's manner became more serious and businesslike. Ambrose suspected she'd had to deal with police enquiries before.

"He had an eye for valuable material," she carried on. "We bought some letters from him last year. When he wrote about the photographs I immediately expressed interest on behalf of the library. Material from the Occupation period is so rare."

"You didn't assume they were forgeries?"

"They could be," the librarian admitted. "That's why I wanted to see them first. However, they could belong to an important group of images we are keen to collect." She got up, and crossing to a filing cabinet, retrieved a small folder. Taking three pictures from it, she laid them in front of Ambrose.

They appeared to be enlargements from poor quality originals. A fold marked one, and another had blemishes like water marks across the centre. Ambrose recognised St Peter Port Harbour. A German supply ship was being offloaded. The second image showed two poorly dressed workers carrying a heavy load down Candie Road, near the library. He found the third harder to identify. It looked like a large concrete bunker.

"Fortifications," Miss Ozanne explained. "There are several more photos like these in our collection. We believe others may have survived."

"Who took them?" Ambrose asked. "Surely it would have been dangerous?"

"Total madness. The photographer was a young man called David Tostevin. We don't know a lot about him, other than that he was a keen amateur who had a darkroom in the cellar of his parents' house, and a lot of photographic materials stored in it. He decided to record the Occupation, so that after the islands were liberated individuals could be brought to account. It was difficult to photograph the Germans, particularly senior officers, so he mainly took shots of ordinary people to show their conditions. Of course he was found out and accused of spying. His camera was confiscated along with the material in his cellar. He himself was interned in a camp on the

Continent. So far we haven't traced which. Sadly he never came back." Lapsing into silence, Miss Ozanne stared ahead of her.

"But many of his photos survived?" Ambrose prompted.

"Yes. He hid them, or entrusted them to friends. Quite a few have surfaced recently. It seems that after the Liberation his friends gave some of them to the people they portrayed. Obviously we're eager to acquire them. It sounded like Mr Harvey might be holding three of these."

"Do have any idea what the photos were of?"

"I can show you Mr Harvey's original letter, and the notes I took during our phone call." Miss Ozanne reached for a file she'd placed on top of the cabinet and passed it to Ambrose.

He read both the letter and the notes several times. The first two photographs were described almost exactly as Miss Havering had remembered. The only new information concerned the third photo. It had been labelled, 'Pigs being confiscated at Brioc Farm.'

"Any ideas about the third photograph?" Ambrose commented.

"Well," Miss Ozanne paused uncertainly. "Brioc Farm was quite near here actually, although it is no longer a working farm. I looked it up after Mr Harvey wrote. At first the German occupiers paid for food and went to the shops, just like everyone else. But when food started to become scare, they ordered farmers to rear livestock for them. I assumed the third photo showed Germans taking pigs from Brioc Farm for their own supplies. There were also suggestions of a black market in food. Certainly some people seemed to have more food than others." She stopped suddenly, as if unsure of whether to continue.

Ambrose quickly thanked her, to avoid an embarrassing silence. When he suggested going back through to Mary, the librarian gratefully agreed.

Mary looked up as they approached her table. "Finished already?" she asked.

Ambrose nodded. "Seen anything interesting?" he said, as he sat down next to his wife.

"I've been reading lots of fascinating articles about life here during the War," Mary replied. "I'm currently reading about the Langlois family, although I don't think it's relevant." She pronounced the name 'long-lwoi', remembering her school girl French.

Behind them the librarian stifled a laugh. They'd forgtten she was there. They both looked at her, puzzled.

"I'm afraid a lot of our names aren't pronounced as you'd expect," Miss Ozanne explained. "It often confuses our visitors. So Langlois is pronounced 'long-lay'. And then there's Ferbrache, which is 'Fairbrush'. Or the name Ogier." She wrote it down for Ambrose. "We say 'o-shjer' here but in Jersey they say 'o-shjay'."

The librarian looked as if she could continue this conversation for a while.

Ambrose stood abruptly. He had an odd feeling in the pit of his stomach. "Do you know anything about the Ferbrache family?" he asked, trying to sound casual. "Were they well off?"

The librarian shook her head. "I looked the farm up in the trade directories once," she replied. "It hardly got a mention. It certainly can't have been very large. It was also very isolated. It's about as far as you can get from St Peter Port without falling into the sea, near Pleinmont."

Puzzled, Ambrose persisted. "Do you know anything about the family? Was there a young woman in her twenties?"

"I wouldn't have thought so. It seems to have been owned by an elderly man. The same name occurs in the directories right back into the thirties. The place was sold to a Jaques Duquemin ten years ago, presumably after old Mr Ferbrache died."

"I can see if I can look into it further," the librarian continued, "and let you know, but I'm afraid I'm very busy today. I'm so sorry." Her voice was full of apology, even a little nervous.

"No, don't worry," Ambrose assured her, remembering Aunt Joan's promise to ask around. "I won't take up any more of your time. Thank you for your help."

"Useful?" Mary asked softly as he sat back down beside her.

"Possibly, but not what I expected."

Mary knew him too well to ask more. Returning to a ledger of bound newspapers, she continued skimming pages. Ambrose picked up another volume and started reading.

They'd been working for another hour when Mary suddenly stopped. An article had caught her eye. In surprise she let out her breath.

"Did you say something?" Ambrose whispered.

"Look at this." Carefully Mary pushed the ledger towards him, indicating a small item towards the foot of the page. "I don't think you were looking for this, but it's absolutely fascinating."

The headline read: '*Scandal over fate of local Jewish girl*'.

"*Mystery still surrounds the fate of a local Jewish girl, Andrea Goodman, who was working at Brioc Farm during the War. She had managed to keep her Jewish origins secret from the occupying forces, but suddenly disappeared one evening. Rumour has it she was denounced by another girl who was a regular visitor to the farm, but nothing was ever proved. There was suspicion Miss Goodman had been silenced when she discovered an illicit affair between the other girl and a German officer. The suspected denouncer herself disappeared from public view shortly afterwards, but whether she was interned or left to have the German's child is a matter of much dispute. The new owners of Brioc Farm are planning a short memorial service in memory of Miss Goodman, who is assumed to have died in a concentration camp after being deported.*"

"Gosh," Mary said softly. "I had no idea that kind of thing happened here."

"Neither did I," Ambrose replied sadly.

He stopped suddenly, a thought forming. Mary glanced at his expression, then looked away. She knew better than to disturb him.

"Pass me a sheet of paper if you would," Ambrose asked.

Methodically he copied the article out and then took both his copy and the original newspaper to Miss Ozanne. "Can you verify that I've copied this correctly?" he asked.

Puzzled, the librarian read both through and then wrote at the bottom of Ambrose's page, "I verify that this is an accurate copy." She added the date and source of the newspaper item.

"Thank you," Ambrose said afterwards. "I'd be grateful if you could follow this item up, and let me have any further information you can find. Here's my address." He passed her a handwritten note with the Chalk Heath Police Station details. "Is it likely that someone *did* betray Miss Goodman like this?" he asked.

"It's possible," Miss Ozanne replied grimly. "The Germans encouraged people to inform on others. Sometimes people did it out of sheer spite, others because they wanted to curry favour. There were even reports of lists appearing mysteriously in public places, with the names of all those suspected of having hidden a wireless radio. Deported people were often never seen again, so one can only imagine what happened to them."

Miss Ozanne shrugged sadly and carried on. "If a local girl was having a German officer's baby, she certainly wouldn't want that to become public knowledge. But would she actually denounce someone, either in revenge or to try to keep her secret? I don't know. I do know that no one would accuse someone of betrayal like that without good reason. And the betrayer would *never* be forgiven."

"Would it be worse than sleeping with the enemy or having an illegitimate child?" Ambrose asked.

"Definitely. There are several families with blond children who don't look like their fathers, and no one asks any questions. But to betray someone! If that rumour got around, whether it was true or not, the woman would pretty well have to leave the islands."

Ambrose was very quiet as he and Mary walked towards the bus stop. He was still thoughtful when they sat at the table for the evening meal. He only half listened to a discussion about the peculiar position of the Channel Islands; not really part of the United Kindom, but belonging to the Crown itself. As soon as he could, without seeming rude, he turned to Joan. "How did your day go?" he asked. "Did you enjoy chatting with the neighbours?"

Joan laughed. "We talked till we needed a third cup of tea," she replied. "I'm ashamed of the number of scones I ate. I shall go back a stone heavier." Pausing, she glanced at Ambrose. "I caught up on old acquaintances," she added enigmatically.

Ambrose understood. He waited until Mrs Blondel went out into the yard. Her husband had already left to check the animals were safely bedded down. "Did you find anything out about the Mauger family?" he asked Joan.

"Only that the daughter got too close to a German Officer and there was a lot of talk. She left the island soon after the Liberation and got a job in London."

"Did she have a particular friend she went about with a lot? Someone there was gossip about?"

Joan looked at him keenly. "I gathered one of her friends got pregnant during the Occupation, and wouldn't name the father," she replied. "She seems to have disappeared from sight before the birth, though, so no one knows where she went or whether she had the baby."

"Thank you," Ambrose replied, "You've been very helpful."

Joan smiled slyly. "I'm glad my little holiday has been useful to you," she commented.

Chapter Twenty Eight

Monday 18th April

"Would you do me a favour?" PC Green asked softly.

"Depends what it is," Meadows replied.

"Come and look at something before we go on the beat."

"I've seen loads of etchings," Meadows said, smiling. "You'll have to think of a better chat-up line than that."

To her amusement, Green went red to the roots of his hair. He lowered his voice till it was not much more than a whisper. "I think I know where the two Botany Bays are. The runaways," he added. "But no one'll listen. They reckon I've got a bee in my bonnet, that they'll have left Chalk Heath long ago. But I don't reckon they have."

In surprise, Meadows considered his earnest expression. "So where haven't we checked?" she asked, finishing her tea.

Green stirred his cup nervously. "That's the trouble." He glanced warily towards the table where Vernon and Higgins were sitting. "It *has* been checked. If I say the boys could be there, it'll sound like I'm criticising, that I'm saying the place wasn't checked properly."

"And that won't go down well," Meadows agreed. "So where do you think they are?"

"In the bombed-out place. I think the boys could be upstairs."

"How can they be?" Meadows shook her head in disbelief. "There aren't any stairs."

"Not at the front, but there's a side door. It leads to a hallway and a flight of stairs. They're still intact."

Meadows' disbelief turned to interest. "You've been inside, haven't you?" she asked.

Green nodded. "Only into the hallway. I didn't go up on my own. If the boys are there, I couldn't arrest them both. I'd probably scare them off."

"Very sensible," Meadows commented. "But why are you so sure they're there?"

"I could smell oranges."

Meadows raised an eyebrow. "We've had a report of fruit being nicked from Bensons."

"I heard that at the desk. That's why I think the boys are there. His shop would be handy for a couple of tea leaves."

"Ok," Meadows agreed. "I'll call there with you on my way out. But we ought to let the desk know. I'll say you've seen suspicious activity there."

An hour later they were standing opposite Curiosity Corner. Remembering the morning she and the DS found Mr Harvey's body, Meadows shuddered. The scene had left a deep impression: her first fatality, and a man she had liked too. Turning back, she considered the bomb site beside her. To the left, it looked unreal, as if a child had opened the side of a doll's house, to reveal hearths and wallpaper and doors suspended in mid air. There was even a patch of bedroom carpet where some of the boards remained. Willowherb and thistle were shooting among the rubble.

"Are you sure the stairs lead somewhere?" she asked softly. "There isn't much upstairs left."

"The building's like an 'L' shape," Green pointed out. "This is the long part and it was only hit at the far end. The side door I found must lead into the short bit. If you can get in there, you might be able to climb up to what's left of the long side. See what I mean?" He picked up a stick and drew a rough diagram in the dust.

"If you say so," Meadows replied dubiously. All the same, she followed Green round to the right, and up an alley that led off the main road. Though full of bricks and weed it was passable. Scrambling as quietly as they could, they reached the side door and stood listening. Beyond them were the remains of a garden, an old apple tree coming into bud. There was no sound from the building. A line of windows above them suggested the upper floors on that side had indeed survived the blast, but all were in darkness. Meadows was about to whisper that Green must be mistaken when she noticed a bramble ahead of her. It had been bent back, away from the path. Carefully she pushed at the door. It opened inwards.

In the gloom she could just make out a flight of stairs. The atmosphere smelt of damp and decay. Behind the dampness there was the faint aroma of orange. Softly she stepped back out.

"Stay here," she whispered. "Don't under any circumstance go in alone. I'm going to the phone box on the corner to call for help. We don't know who's in there. It may not be boys. And those stairs don't look safe."

It took her less than five minutes to run round to the phone box and call the station. Higgins took the call. Steadying her breath, Meadows explained the situation. "Whoever's in there's been in a while, judging by the smell," she said. "They may not like us disturbing them. We need an extra person in case they do a runner."

Fortunately PC Vernon was available, though not pleased to be sent out while he was doing his expenses. "Don't let that young idiot go in until I get there," he said. "And don't you either. I'll come straight over."

To Meadows' relief as she returned up the alley, she saw Green leaning against the wall, out of view of the door. "Vernon's on his way," she whispered. She guessed he would have preferred someone else, but he said nothing.

It took PC Vernon less than quarter of an hour to reach them, but it seemed much longer. "You wait outside," he said to Meadows. "It's probably just an old tramp but he might get rough. Leave him to us."

A year ago, Meadows would have protested at being treated like 'the little woman' but she had learnt to say nothing. Besides, she could be a useful back-stop if one of the boys tried to run outside, provided she remembered not to catch him with her bad arm. As the men went up the stairs she waited, listening intently. The steps creaked several times.

Immediately there was a soft sound above them, as if someone was moving as quietly as they could, across a landing, towards the front of the building. Evidently it was possible to get across the top floor, as Green had suggested.

The soft footsteps turned to louder running, two sets and then four as if Green and Vernon were chasing the boys. "Stop!" she heard Vernon order. "Don't go any further. You'll fall!"

Longing to go in and help, Meadows waited in the shadows. Suddenly feet were running down the stairs towards her. Leaning back into the darkness, she braced herself, hoping her injured shoulder wouldn't let her down. The steps came faster and nearer. Still she waited until she could hear the boy panting. Then she strode forward and shot her leg out, tripping him. Before he could regain his balance, she had grabbed him tight, pulling one arm behind his back. "Got you!" she said victoriously. "Hold still."

Beginning to cry, the boy stopped struggling. Meadows suspected he was so tired and hungry he was almost grateful to be captured. "It's all right," she said. "I'm not going to hurt you. Just take you back to the Police Station for a meal and a wash, before your teachers fetch you home."

"It's not home!" the boy wailed. "I want my Mum!"

"The sooner you do your time, the sooner you'll see her," Meadows said, hoping she was right. 'Don't get sentimental!' she told herself but she held the boy more gently.

There was the sound of footsteps coming down the stairs. In the light from the street Meadows could see Vernon appearing, with the second boy held close beside him. "You caught the little rascal!" he said when he saw Meadows. "Well done." Green was following closely behind.

Fortunately Vernon had driven down and parked just around the corner. Frog-marching the two boys, they led them towards the car. Opening the back door, Vernon and Green pushed the lads firmly inside. "You'll have to walk back," Vernon said to PC Green. "Come in the car with me, Meadows. You'll be needed to help book them in."

"We were both about to go on the beat," Meadows said uncertainly.

"Someone'll have to cover," Vernon insisted. "You've got to deal with these two." He paused, including PC Green. "It's your collar. You deserve the credit. The Guvner'll have words about the lads not being found before, but at least you've got them."

In the lamp light Meadows saw Green's face flush with pleasure, and she smiled at him. 'Let bygones be bygones,' her smile said, and his nod agreed.

Back at the Station they went through the arrest formalities, Meadows showing Green the process. Then he took the two boys to the Gents' toilets to get them washed. One of the civilian typists lived nearby and she rushed home to fetch some her son's hand-me-down clothes. "I was going to give them to my sister's boys," she said. "If the school sends them back she can still have them. But these two need them now."

As the boys devoured a plate of sandwiches from the Copper Kettle, Meadows tried to get them to talk to her. It took a lot of patience. Gradually she got the younger of the two to tell her what they'd been doing. He revealed he was called Teddy, and his companion was Ron, though he wouldn't admit their surnames. "We was going to Lunnon," he said. "Me Mum lives there. Only we couldn't get on a train."

The older boy grunted and looked up. "He was too scaredy-cat," he said through a mouthful of bread. "I got on one of them long wagons but he wouldn't follow me. So I had to jump off again. We give up after that."

Meadows nodded. Despite the older boy's carefree manner he'd clearly taken care of the younger one. "Did you sleep in the old building each night?" she asked.

"Yep. Stayed there most of the day too." The boy laughed. "Your rozzers came looking for us one day. Stomped about making a lot of noise and never found us. We was upstairs. Saw them coming a mile off."

Glancing at PC Green, Meadows winced. Then an idea came to her. "Could you see out the front?" she asked. "I mean over the street towards the shop on the corner?"

"The funny shop you mean? Sells books and stuff?"

"Yes."

"Sure," the boy replied, affecting an accent he'd heard in the movies. "We sat in the window watching people and they never even knew we was there!"

Meadows looked away, trying not to betray too much interest. She was tempted to ask him more but she might make him clam up, or refuse to repeat what he told her. The DI needed to question the boys, not her. "Would you like some ice cream?" she asked instead.

"You bet! Ain't had ice cream in months."

"I'll buy you some ice cream if you tell my boss all the things you saw," she promised. "I'll just go and fetch him"

But to Meadows' disappointment, Higgins looked up as she headed for DI Ambrose's office. "He's not to be disturbed," he called. "Doing a case review with the DS. You'll have to wait."

"I have something important for him," Meadows said.

"It's more than my life's worth," Higgins insisted. "You could put a note under his door in quarter of an hour or so."

Sighing, Meadows turned away.

Ambrose heard their voices but ignored them. He and Winters were at last beginning to get somewhere.

"Say that last bit again," Winters prompted, annoyed by the noise from outside the door.

"I came across a newspaper report that troubled me. A young Jewish girl was denounced to the Germans, was deported and never seen again. Presumed dead. The report said she'd been living at Brioc Farm and another girl had denounced her."

"How does that fit in to Chalk Heath?" Winters asked, bemused.

"Remember the information we got about Mrs Vaudin, née Mauger? She lived at Brioc Farm in Guernsey."

"Of course!" Winters exclaimed. "So do we know who denounced the poor Jewish girl? Was it Mrs Vaudin herself?"

"Probably not," Ambrose replied. "There was supposition it was another girl who visited Brioc Farm regularly, and was having a fling with a German officer. Perhaps the Jewish girl was denounced to stop her telling everyone else about the affair? The suspect disappeared shortly afterwards, maybe to have the officer's baby in secret."

"Oh Lor!" Winters said softly. "That'd be a secret worth killing for."

"We may have the motive at last," Ambrose agreed.

"So the photos *were* of Mrs Vaudin and her friend, consorting with the enemy?"

"Precisely, and the friend is presumably the one who reported the Jewish girl to the Germans."

"And had the German officer's baby."

They were both silent, realising the enormity of what they were saying.

"We have to follow this through, regardless of who it is," Ambrose said at last. "Supposing Robin Harvey showed her the photos, knowing her Guernsey connection. Maybe he told her the Priaulx Library wanted them for their collection. She'd want to get hold of them before he could send them back to Guernsey."

"So she hid in the shop and looked for them after Robin Harvey had gone upstairs," Winters continued.

"Then she fled when he came down, knocking into the bookcase, or making him knock into it. It could have been a genuine accident."

"But surely she would have heard his cries for help?" Winters asked. "Or at least the crash?"

"Perhaps she didn't," Ambrose said, wanting to give their suspect the benefit of the doubt. "Perhaps she was already out of the shop by the time it fell?"

"But what about the Major?" Winters asked.

Sighing, Ambrose shook his head. "There's no way that was an accident," he admitted. "She set everything up so he'd fall, and even gave herself an alibi. Somehow she tricked him into having his bath early. Perhaps she told him the locksmith was coming at four. The trouble is, we don't have a motive yet. Unless he saw the photos and recognised her, then told her he had."

"But why would Robin Harvey show him the photos?"

"Why indeed?"

They had come to a halt and sat in silence again. There was a faint rustle at the door and a sheet of paper slid under it. They could tell it was WPC Meadows.

"Persistant blighter isn't she?" Ambrose remarked, shaking his head in amusement. "Let's take five minutes off." Leaning down, he picked up the note.

"Found the two runaways," he read aloud. "They've been hiding in the derelict building opposite Curiosity Corner. Could have seen who entered the shop the night Robin H died. Might have gone in themselves. Promised them ice cream if they'll talk to you."

Immediately Ambrose got up. "Now this sounds promising! Come with me, Sam," he said. "You're better with kids than I am."

It took Winters several moments to get the boys talking, despite Meadows' promise of ice-cream. Once he played on the older one's vanity, however, he began to get through to him. "You'll have a lot to tell the others when you're back," he commented. "Running rings round the rozzers; nicking food and getting away with it. I'll bet none of them have managed to stay out so long without being picked up. And right in the centre of town too."

Ron sat up straighter, his voice becoming more confident. "They wouldn't dare!" he said proudly.

"But you did," Winters remarked. "You weren't afraid to take milk off steps under people's noses, or fruit from the greengrocer's. Did you get money too? I'll bet the funny old shop opposite was easy pickings."

The boy shuffled uneasily. Winters tried surprise tactics. "You went right in and took what you could, and then ran when the bookcase fell," he said.

"Bookcase?" Ron asked, looking genuinely mystified. "What'd we want with a bookcase? We got a few bob left on the counter, and a couple of books to read, only they was dead boring and we chucked them. That's all."

Ambrose joined in, startling the boy further. "You must've seen the ambulance," he said. "And you were in the shop the night before, weren't you?"

"No," the boy insisted, recognising the change in tone. "We never went in, well only once and that was ages after the ambulance." He turned to his companion. "Tell him, Teddy. We don't know nothing about no bookcase." He paused, an expression of cunning coming to his pinched, young face. "But we know who did go in, don't we?" He whispered something to Teddy.

"Oh her!" the younger boy replied. "The one in pink."

"Go on," Ambrose prompted.

"There was this woman," the older boy continued, sensing that he was getting nearer to his ice cream. "She parked round the corner. Then she walked to the shop and went in. Only she never come out, not for ages. We kept looking for her 'cos Teddy said her trousers were pink and I told him they was red. Then when she did come out she was running and it was dark and we couldn't tell what colour they was. If this bookcase thingy was nicked it'll be her what took it."

Winters spoke carefully and steadily. "Did you see what she looked like?" he asked. "Was she tall or short?"

"Dunno. The old guy'd know."

"Old guy?" Ambrose asked casually.

"Yeah. The bloke in the funny straw hat with one of them sticks, the sort you see at the flicks."

"You mean a cane?" Winters suggested. "Like Fred Astaire has when he dances?"

"Yeah. Looked like he'd been in the army. My old Gramp walks like that, only his stick ain't nothing like so fancy. This old guy was real posh. Ask him who the woman was what he talked to."

The boy was obviously telling the truth. Ambrose nodded to WPC Meadows. "I reckon you can buy those ice creams," he said. Then he turned to Winters. "I think we need a little chat," he said calmly.

Once they were back in his office, he shook his head in despair. "What did you make of that?"

"You mean who was the old guy?" Winters asked, though he knew the answer.

"Major Fielding. So now at least we know why he died. He saw the attacker coming out of Curiosity Corner and had to be silenced. But how on earth do we prove it? No judge would accept the evidence of two kids. Particularly not *those* two kids. What use is it solving a crime if you can't get a conviction?"

"Should we tell Mac what we know?" Winters asked. "Or keep quiet?"

They both looked at each other in silence.

Ambrose stood up slowly, with purpose.

"We need more proof," he declared. "Sam, I need you to get a marriage and two birth certificates for me. Under no circumstances tell anyone what you are doing."

Winters felt he was being a little slow. "Did you say *two* birth certificates?"

Nodding, Ambrose wrote the details on a piece of paper.

"Get me those and then I'll go and speak to Mac," Ambrose said.

Winters drew his breath in surprise. "Rather you than me," he said grimly. "Do you think we'll be able to get enough evidence to prove it to a judge?"

"Perhaps not," Ambrose admitted, "although it does rather depend on who the judge is."

Mystified, Winters watched Ambrose leave the room.

Chapter Twenty Nine

Wednesday 20th April

Ambrose paused outside Mac's office, feeling like a school boy sent to the Headmaster for detention. He couldn't remember the last time he'd felt this nervous. He hadn't slept the night before, tossing and turning, keeping poor Mary awake too. He kept trying to work out what to say, the words rattling around his head until they became all jumbled. In the end he'd given up and fallen asleep, only for his usual nightmare to startle him awake at 5 in the morning. He felt jaded and tired.

Plucking up courage to knock on the door, he entered slowly when Mac called him in.

"Trouble?" Mac asked, seeing the look on Ambrose's face. "Sit before you fall down, man!"

Ambrose accepted the chair gratefully.

Swallowing hard, he launched into his prepared speech.

"We think we've worked out who did it, but we can't prove it."

Mac looked confused. "Who did what?" he demanded. "You've caught the runaways and solved the murder of that poor girl found in the allotments. Not a bad week, I'd say. I was even going to compliment you on how well you've settled PC Green in. He's shaping up nicely, don't you think?"

Before Ambrose could reply, Mac carried on. "Not to mention, of course, our local heroine WPC Meadows. I've put her forward for a commendation, although don't go telling her in case it goes to her head. Besides, I haven't heard yet whether it will be awarded, though with Marjorie putting her weight behind it, I'm sure it's just a formality."

"There are the other cases," Ambrose tried again.

"Good god man, not the accidents? I thought you'd given those up. You caught the poor deranged soul who was sending the packages. Surely those cases are closed now?"

"No," Ambrose replied, shaking his head.

Mac put down his pipe and stared at Ambrose. "You're treating Robin Harvey and the Major's deaths as murders?" he asked. "What about the falling church roof? Was that an attempt to kill the Honourable Marjorie? This is beginning to sound improbable."

"Ironically, no, I think that *was* just an accident," Ambrose admitted. "Although the murderer had a stroke of luck there. It put us on to the wrong line of enquiry. We focussed on the poetry competition, because that was the only thing that linked Mr Harvey, the Major and Marjorie Hodgkiss."

Sucking on his pipe again, Mac considered Ambrose carefully. "All right. Supposing the deaths weren't accidental. If you take the church roof incident out of it, what are you left with? What *does* connect the owner of Curiosity Corner and a retired Major? That's worth killing them for?"

"I think I know the answer to that," Ambrose said sadly. "The only question is whether I can prove it."

"Well run it past me then," Mac replied. "If I think we have enough evidence to convict, I'll speak to the boss myself."

Ambrose was surprised. He'd expected Mac to resist longer, need more persuasion. He mentally tore up half his prepared speech: it was no longer needed. Taking a deep breath, he started. "We know that something was taken from Curiosity Corner, the night Robin Harvey died: some photos from the War in Guernsey. They showed two Germans and their local lovers. One of the girls looked like she was pregnant."

Mac cut straight to the point. "You think Harvey heard someone downstairs looking for the photos, disturbed the intruder and got killed as a result?"

"Precisely. That explains why the lights were off and Robin Harvey had taken a torch down with him. He was trying to catch the intruder in the act. Except it backfired terribly. The intruder may not have realised Mr Harvey had collided with the bookcase, or that it had fallen on him."

"You'd have thought Harvey's calls would have been audible, wouldn't you?"

Ambrose nodded grimly. "Probably, although we'll never know for sure. Even if we ask the intruder, she may not tell us the truth."

"She?" Mac asked quickly. "You think the intruder was one of the girls on the photos, not the Germans?"

"I'm pretty sure we'd have noticed anyone around here who looks like a retired German officer," Ambrose pointed out. "Plus, why would he care if someone found out he'd been consorting with a Guernsey girl, or even got her pregnant? He could have been disciplined or even court martialed at the time, but not now. No, it has to be someone who has something to lose *now*. Someone who thought they'd put the War behind them, who's got a position of authority now."

"So a woman who was in Guernsey during the War, who is now wealthy or of high 'standing' in society? Was there any blackmail involved?"

"I did think about that. But there's no evidence the owner of the photos, who died recently, had received any money. She was born in Guernsey but left just after the Liberation. I think she was one of the girls from the photo, but not the one who was pregnant."

"I see," Mac replied. "So you think the other girl, the one who was 'in the family way' as my wife would say, is the one who tried to get the photos back? But surely that means Robin Harvey's death is still just a tragic accident? We'd struggle to prove the intruder pushed the bookcase on purpose, or that she knew what had happened. She may well have left the shop long before Robin Harvey blundered into the bookcase. And you could say it was his own fault for not making sure his furniture was secure."

"I'm just pointing out what the defence would say," Mac added quickly, seeing Ambrose's face. "But where does the Major come into it? You're not telling me he was involved in the War in Guernsey are you?"

"No," Ambrose admitted, "but we've got eye witnesses who saw the intruder leaving Curiosity Corner just around the time Robin Harvey was falling under a book case. And those witnesses say she stopped to talk to someone who sounds remarkably like the Major."

"Reliable witnesses?"

"Not in the slightest," Ambrose sighed. "It was the two runaways. They were hiding in the abandoned building opposite, and saw a lady run out, then speak to the Major."

"Good god, man," Mac replied. "So, wrong place, wrong time for the Major. But that means it was cold blooded murder to get him out of the way, to stop him talking?" Mac screwed his face up. "That changes everything."

"It does indeed," Ambrose replied. "At first I thought it would take quite a bit of planning to make the Major's death also look like an accident. But then I realised it was actually horribly simple. A change of bath mat, to one without anti-slip tape on the bottom, and a quick polish of the floor with the wrong tin was all it needed. It made the floor like ice. The Major went flying when he stepped out of the bath."

"Cracked his head and bled to death," Mac finished grimly.

"Meadows spotted the inconsistency, although she didn't realise it at first. The Major had been lying on the floor for at least an hour by the time the Housekeeper found him."

"How do you know that?"

"The tap had stopped dripping. It keeps going for nearly an hour after being used. Someone had also put the towel over him, to keep his modesty."

"You're telling me that the culprit went into the bathroom to check the Major had fallen, covered him up, then did nothing to help him as he died?"

"It looks that way. Plus they'd have had to swap the bath mat back to the one with the non-slip tape."

"That is cold and calculating."

They sat in silence for a moment.

"So the only question is who are we talking about," Mac said finally. "Although I think I know where you're leading to with all this."

Ambrose was surprised. He hadn't expected Mac to work it out, or to take it this calmly.

"But if you're going to accuse the Honourable Marjorie of cold-blooded murder, you need far more proof than you have," Mac pointed out.

Ambrose swallowed hard.

"I did think at first it was Marjorie Hodgkiss," he admitted. "And that she'd had the child adopted, or it had died. But there are two reasons I know it can't have been her. First, she wouldn't have needed the Major's death to appear to be later than it actually was, as she had no alibi and didn't pretend she had one. Second, she never, ever wears trousers. We also believe she was interned on the Continent for the last years of the War. We can probably confirm it if we make enquiries. She's unlikely to be the girl who had the baby."

Mac stared at him. There was a long silence.

Ambrose started again. "There is someone else who we know was in Guernsey during the War," he said quietly. "Who we know has a child."

He pushed a piece of paper across the table towards Mac, who didn't move.

Eventually Mac put his hand out to pull the document towards him. It was a birth certificate:

"Abigail Ferbrache, born St Quentin, Bailiwick of Guernsey, 1920. Parents John and Marianne Ferbrache."'

"So what?" Mac demanded. "I know my wife was born in Guernsey. She married a local chap who died in the War. I met her when she came over here with her son Brian. They came for a new start."

"Except there's no marriage certificate for an Abigail Ferbrache at any time until she married you," Ambrose replied, so quietly Mac strained to hear. "And there's no record of Brian's birth, not in Guernsey or here in the UK. The certificate she has must be a forgery."

His words hung between them like a cloud.

"Not a widow?" Mac let out his breath in surprise. He paused to catch his thoughts. "And you're telling me Brian was the son of a Nazi officer? I brought the boy up as if he were my own!" He stopped, struggling to keep his voice down.

Ambrose nodded. "Judging by her looks now, she was a stunner when you met her, Sir. I can see how you fell for her. I think she went off to her grandfather's farm to have the child. It was isolated enough for people not to know she'd given birth. Then after the Liberation she came over here with forged papers, as you say for a new start."

"She was running a dress shop in Jenners Park when I met her," Mac said, thinking out loud. He was struggling to retain his composure, his mouth going slack and his voice husky. "But where did the money come from? How did she buy the shop if she'd had to leave Guernsey under a cloud? I always thought her husband was wealthy."

Ambrose replied as gently as he could. "Maybe the money came from the officer in the photo, or his parents," he suggested. "If he was well-born they might have wanted to hush his affair up. He shouldn't have been fraternising with a local girl in the first place. Supposing she contacted him and asked for help setting herself up in England? He may even have given her an allowance for the boy's maintenance. We shouldn't assume that just because the man was in the Occupying Force, he wasn't honourable. The caption on the photos suggests they were genuinely in love."

There was another silence.

"I think she tricked the Major into having his bath early," Ambrose continued quietly. "She may have told him the locksmith was due that afternoon to fix the lock. That way she could set herself up with the alibi at Molly's Café for four o'clock."

Again, there was silence. Finally Ambrose broke it.

"There's one more thing," he added. He passed over the copy of the newspaper article he'd copied back at the Priaulx Library. "I think a young lady called Andrea Goodman was your wife's first victim," he said simply. "It looks like she was willing to do anything to keep her secret, even then."

There was nothing else to say. Ambrose stood quietly and left Mac alone with the newspaper report and the tears running down his cheeks.

Epilogue

They sat on the bench close together, away from the workers eating sandwiches or glancing at the newspaper in their lunch break. Mary had just collected the photographs of Guernsey from the developers. "Don't we look well?" she teased. "It's amazing what a holiday can do."

"Mmm," Ambrose agreed, his mind elsewhere.

"This is a nice one of you," Mary chattered on. "You looked handsome in that new sweater." She smiled at him, pleased by the memory. "And doesn't Joan look happy? I'll have this one enlarged for her."

"Yes," Ambrose agreed, though he barely looked at the picture.

Mary paused. "What is it, Love?" she asked. "You're not paying the least attention, are you? Has something gone wrong?"

Staring ahead of him, Ambrose nodded. His mouth was set in a tight line, an expression Mary recognised. "Why are you so angry?" she persisted. "Or is it something you can't tell me?"

For a minute Ambrose didn't reply, still staring ahead of himself. Then he drew in his breath. "It's not something I should share," he replied carefully.

"But you need to tell someone," Mary suggested. "Or you feel like you'll burst."

Smiling at her choice of phrase Ambrose nodded. Then he sighed and stared ahead again.

"Come on, Love. Talk to me at least, or we'll be having sleepless nights again. That doesn't do me any good either."

Accepting the sense of what she was saying, Ambrose nodded. "I don't think I've ever been so angry in my life," he admitted. His voice shook slightly.

"Are they shutting Chalk Heath?"

"No, that's not it. They're obviously preparing for us working with Jenners Park, but there's nothing been said about closing."

"That's a relief!" Mary admitted. "We're only just getting the house as we want it. So what is it then? You know you can trust me. I learnt how to keep things to myself in the War. It's become a habit by now."

Turning towards her, Ambrose came to a decision. He owed her an explanation. "No names," he said, and glanced towards the people on the other benches. He couldn't afford to take chances.

For another moment they sat in silence while he worked out how to talk without revealing too much. Finally, he decided he could only plunge straight in. "She's got away with it," he said bitterly. "No arrest, no charges. Nothing. Just bundled away. After all the work Sam and I put in! Not to mention your work too. Both cases closed. Accidental deaths…" He couldn't go on, aware that his voice would rise if he did.

"Whose decision?" Mary asked softly.

"Mac's of course. He presented me with the files, all signed off. 'Good work,' he said, 'But without a confession there's too little evidence for a conviction, and you're not going to get her to admit anything.' Oh, he had all the arguments. Made me sound vindictive for wanting to continue." He mimicked Mac's tone. "'Much better handled my way, Ambrose: too many lives will be ruined if it goes to court. And you won't get a result anyway old boy'. That's what he said."

He couldn't trust himself to continue so lapsed into silence.

"I heard she'd been diagnosed with TB," Mary said carefully. "The ladies at Molly's Café said her doctor had found a shadow on her lung, and admitted her to a sanatorium at once. Somewhere on the Isle of Wight. She'll get better treatment there apparently."

Ambrose sighed in relief. He hadn't needed to give names. "That's what's being put about," he agreed. "It's actually a mental home. Private I think."

"Ah!" Mary said, her tone suggesting understanding. "That is a better solution, you know."

"Why? When justice isn't being done?"

"But it is!" Mary insisted. "She'll be as effectively imprisoned as in any jail, and I doubt if there's time off for good behaviour or probation. Mac will see to that. If you did things your way a lot of lives would be ruined, as he says, and you mightn't prove your case in the end. Then what?"

In surprise Ambrose turned towards her. "You usually take my side," he said coldly.

"I am," Mary insisted. "You've got the result you wanted. She'll be punished, and Robin Harvey and the Major will have justice. What good will a scandal do? Or the hurt a trial will cause, especially if it might fail? Just imagine how a woman like her will feel, being shut away from the world, and with people who are, well, mentally sick, unpleasant perhaps, maybe even dangerous. She will loathe it. And she must have been sick in her mind herself to some extent. I mean, normal people don't kill, not in peace time, even to protect those they love."

Mechanically turning the photos over one by one, Ambrose considered her advice. "I've always played things straight," he said. "By the book."

"I know you have. And this isn't your decision. Are you going to challenge your boss? What will happen?"

"I don't know."

"I do. With Mac being so respected you won't even be listened to. At the least, you'll have to apply for a transfer. I'll stick by you if you do decide to make it a matter of principle, but I don't think it's worth it. Not when you've got the result you want, even if it is by another way." Gently taking the photos from him, Mary put them back in the envelope. "What does Sam say? Does he know?"

"He's flaming mad as well, but he says he daren't rock the boat, with the mortgage and the children at school and Fran only just settled and..."

"Precisely," Mary interrupted. "He can't afford to damage his career. Nor can you really, not when you're doing so well. And think about the effect on poor Brian's career if it came out that he's the illegitimate son of a German occupier? He's also a victim in this, in a way. But that's beside the point. I know you. You have to feel things are right. Just tell me what you decide. I need some warning if we're going to have to move."

Glancing at his watch, Ambrose sighed. "I'll have to get back soon," he said. "Don't worry, Love. You're right, as usual. It probably is best if I let things go. Mac's announced he's retiring soon, and there are a lot of changes coming." He managed to smile. "Some of them are quite nice."

"Oh?"

"I've been asked to form my own Serious Crime team across the two divisions, in readiness for any amalgamation. I get to pick six officers to work under me. We'll be focussing on the bigger cases, so it'll be interesting, and challenging."

In delight Mary clapped her hands. "Who are you going to choose? Sam, presumably?"

"Of course. And WPC Meadows: she's shown real aptitude for detective work. And PC Green I think. They work well together. That leaves three for me to choose from Jenners Park. I've got a few ideas. I just need to sound people out."

Mary smiled. The old enthusiasm was returning to his voice. "You'll make a good team," she said. "And I'm glad we don't have to move. Besides, there's a certain irony here, don't you think?"

"What irony?"

"She fled one island and looks like ending her days on another, even smaller. From Guernsey to the Isle of Wight."

Other novels, novellas and short story collections available from Stairwell Books

Carol's Christmas	N.E. David
Feria	N.E. David
A Day at the Races	N.E. David
Running With Butterflies	John Walford
Foul Play	P J Quinn
Poison Pen	P J Quinn
Wine Dark, Sea Blue	A.L. Michael
Skydive	Andrew Brown
Close Disharmony	P J Quinn
When the Crow Cries	Maxine Ridge
The Geology of Desire	Clint Wastling
Homelands	Shaunna Harper
Border 7	Pauline Kirk
Tales from a Prairie Journal	Rita Jerram
Here in the Cull Valley	John Wheatcroft
How to be a Man	Alan Smith
A Multitude of Things	David Clegg
Know Thyself	Lance Clarke
Thinking of You Always	Lewis Hill
Rapeseed	Alwyn Marriage
A Shadow in My Life	Rita Jerram
Tyrants Rex	Clint Wastling
Abernathy	Claire Patel-Campbell
The Martyrdoms at Clifford's Tower 1190 and 1537	John Rayne-Davis
The Go-to Guy	Neal Hardin
Return of the Mantra	Susie Williamson

For further information please contact rose@stairwellbooks.com

www.stairwellbooks.co.uk
@stairwellbooks